The Baron in the Trees

BOOKS BY ITALO CALVINO

The Baron in the Trees

The Castle of Crossed Destinies

The Cloven Viscount

Collection of Sand

The Complete Cosmicomics

Difficult Loves

Fantastic Tales

Hermit in Paris

If on a winter's night a traveler

Into the War

Invisible Cities

Italian Folktales

Marcovaldo

Mr. Palomar

The Nonexistent Knight

Numbers in the Dark

The Road to San Giovanni

Six Memos for the Next Millennium

Under the Jaguar Sun

The Uses of Literature

The Watcher and Other Stories

Why Read the Classics?

ITALO CALVINO

The Baron in the Trees

Translated from the Italian by ANN GOLDSTEIN

An Imprint of HarperCollins*Publishers*
Boston New York

First Mariner Books edition 2017

Mariner Books
An Imprint of HarperCollins Publishers, registered in the United States of America and/or other jurisdictions.

www.marinerbooks.com

First published in Italy as *Il barone rampante,* by Giulio Einaudi Editore, S.p.A., Torino, 1957

Library of Congress Cataloging-in-Publication Data is available.
ISBN 978-0-544-95911-8 (paperback) | 978-0-544-95914-9 (ebook)

Printed in the United States of America
23 24 25 26 27 LBC 11 10 9 8 7

The Baron in the Trees

I

It was the fifteenth of June in 1767 when Cosimo Piovasco di Rondò, my brother, sat among us for the last time. I remember as if it were today. We were in the dining room of our villa in Ombrosa, the windows framing the thick branches of the great holm oak in the park. It was midday, and our family, following the old custom, sat down to dinner at that hour, even though among the nobility it was now the fashion, inspired by the late-rising court of France, to dine in the middle of the afternoon. The wind was blowing in from the sea, I remember, and the leaves were stirring. Cosimo said, "I told you I don't want it, and I don't!" and he pushed away the plate of snails. Never had such grave disobedience been seen.

At the head of the table was the Baron Arminio Piovasco di Rondò, our father, wearing his wig long over his ears in the style of Louis XIV, out of fashion in this as in so many of his habits. Between me and my brother sat the Abbé Fauchelafleur, our family's almoner and the tutor of us boys. Across from us was the Generalessa Corradina di Rondò, our mother, and our sister, Battista, the house nun. At the other end of the table, opposite our father, sat, dressed in the Turkish style, the Cavalier Avvocato Enea Silvio Carrega, the administrator and hydraulic engineer of our estates, and, as the illegitimate brother of our father, our natural uncle.

Several months earlier, when Cosimo turned twelve and I eight, we had been admitted to our parents' table, or, rather, I had benefited prematurely from my brother's promotion, so that I wouldn't be left to eat alone. I say benefited only as a manner of speaking: in reality for both Cosimo and me the happy times were over, and we felt regret for the meals in our little room, the two of us alone with the Abbé Fauchelafleur. The abbé was a withered, wrinkled old man, who had a reputation as a Jansenist and had in fact fled the Dauphiné, his native land, to avoid a trial by the Inquisition. But the strict character that was usually praised by everyone, the inward severity that he imposed on himself and others, constantly yielded to a fundamental inclination to apathy and indifference, as if his long meditations, eyes staring into emptiness, had led only to a great boredom and lethargy, and in even the least effort he saw the sign of a destiny that it was useless to oppose. Our meals in the company of the abbé began after long prayers, with orderly, decorous, silent movements of spoons, and woe to you if you raised your eyes from the plate or made even the slightest sucking sound as you sipped the broth. But by the end of the soup the abbé was tired, bored; he gazed into space and clicked his tongue at every swallow of wine, as if only the most superficial and transient sensations could reach him. By the main course we had already started eating with our fingers, and we finished our meal throwing pear cores at each other while the abbé every so often let out a lazy *"Ooo bien! . . . Ooo alors!"*

Now, instead, as we dined with the family, childhood's sad chapter of daily grievances took shape. Our father and our mother were always right in front of us; we had to use knives and forks for the chicken, and sit up straight, and keep elbows off the table—endless!—and then there was our odious sister Battista. A succession of scoldings, spiteful acts, punishments, obstinacies began, until the day Cosimo refused the snails and decided to separate his lot from ours.

I became aware of this accumulation of family resentments only later; I was just eight then, everything seemed to me a game, the battle of us children against the adults was the battle that all children fight. I didn't understand that my brother's determination concealed something deeper.

Our father, the baron, was a dull man certainly, although not a bad one: dull because his life was dominated by thoughts that were out of step, as often happens in eras of transition. In many people the unrest of the age instills a need to become restless as well, but in the wrong direction, on the wrong track; so our father, despite what was brewing at the time, laid claim to the title of Duke of Ombrosa and thought only of genealogies and successions and rivalries and alliances with potentates near and far.

Thus at our house we always lived as if at the dress rehearsal of an invitation to court, I don't know whether the Empress of Austria's or King Louis's, or maybe that of the mountain nobles of Turin. A turkey was served, and our father watched to see that we carved it and picked off the meat according to all the royal rules, while the abbé barely tasted it, in order not to be caught out, he who had to support our father's reprimands. As for the Cavalier Avvocato Carrega, then, we had discovered the deceitful depths of his heart: into the folds of his Turkish robes entire thighs vanished, which he could take bites of later as he liked, hiding in the vineyard; and we would have sworn (although his movements were so swift that we never managed to catch him in the act) that he came to the table with a pocketful of bones already picked, to leave on his plate in place of the turkey quarters that had vanished whole. Our mother, the *generalessa,* didn't count, because she had brusque military manners even when she helped herself at the table—*"So, Noch ein wenig! Gut!"* —and no one objected; but with us she insisted, if not on etiquette, on discipline, and backed up the baron with her parade-ground orders—*"Sitz' ruhig!* And wipe your nose!" The only one who was at her ease was Battista, the house nun, who stripped the flesh off fowl with a minute persistence, fiber by fiber, using some sharp knives that only she had, something like a surgeon's lancets. The baron, who should have held her up as an example, didn't dare to look at her, because with those mad eyes under the wings of her starched cap, the teeth clenched in that yellow mouselike face, she frightened even him. So you can see how the table was the place where all the antagonisms emerged, the incompatibilities among us, along with all our follies and hypocrisies, and how it was at the table, precisely, that Cosimo's rebellion was determined. That's why I'm describing all this at length, since there will be no more elaborately laid tables in my brother's life, you can be sure.

It was also the only place where we encountered the adults. For the rest of the day our mother withdrew into her rooms to make lace and embroidery and filet, because in truth the *generalessa* was able to attend only to this traditional women's work, and only here could she vent her warrior passion. The lace and embroidery usually represented geographic maps, and having laid them out on pillows or tapestries, our mother dotted them with pins and little flags, marking the battlefields of the Wars of Succession, which she knew thoroughly. Or she embroidered cannons, with the various trajectories taking off from the gun, and the firing brackets, and the angles of projection, because she was an expert in ballistics, and further had at her disposal the entire library of her father the general, with treatises on the military art and shooting tables, and atlases. Our mother was a Von Kurtewitz: Konradine, the daughter of General Konrad von Kurtewitz, who, commanding the troops of Maria Theresa of Austria, had occupied our lands twenty years earlier. She was motherless, and the general brought her along to the camp; nothing adventurous—they traveled well equipped, lodged in the best castles, with a host of servants, and she spent the days making pillow lace. The stories told, that she, too, went into battle, on horseback, are all legends; she had always been a small woman with rosy skin and a turned-up nose, as we remember her, but that paternal military passion had stayed with her, maybe in protest against her husband.

Our father was among the few nobles in our area who had allied themselves with the empire in that war: he had welcomed General von Kurtewitz into his domain with open arms, had put his men at the general's disposition, and, to better demonstrate his dedication to the imperial cause, had married Konradine, all in the eternal hope for the dukedom, and that went badly for him, too, as usual, because the Austrians soon moved out and the Genoese burdened him with taxes. But he had gained a fine spouse, the *generalessa,* as she was called after her father died on the expedition to Provence, and Maria Theresa sent her a gold choker on a damask pillow—a spouse with whom he almost always agreed, even if she, reared in military camps, dreamed only of armies and battles and reproached him for being nothing but an unsuccessful schemer.

But in essence they had both remained in the era of the Wars of Succession, she with artillery in her head, he with genealogical trees; she who dreamed for us children a rank in an army, it didn't matter which, he who saw us instead married to some grand duchess elector of the empire . . . Despite all this, they were excellent parents, but so distracted that the two of us were left to grow up almost on our own. Was it a bad thing or good? Who can say? Cosimo's life was so far out of the ordinary, mine so orderly and modest, and yet our childhood was spent together, both of us indifferent to the adults' obsessions, as we sought pathways different from those trodden by other people.

We climbed the trees (these first innocent games are now charged in my memory with the light of initiation, of premonition; but who would have thought of it then?), we followed the streams, jumping from rock to rock, we explored caves on the seashore, we slid down the marble banisters of the staircases in the villa. One of Cosimo's most serious reasons for clashing with our parents had its origin in one of these slides, because he was punished—unjustly, he thought—and from then on harbored a rancor against the family (or society? or the world in general?) that was later expressed in his decision of June fifteenth.

We had already been warned against sliding down the marble banister, to tell the truth, not out of fear that we would break a leg or an arm, because our parents never worried about that, and that's why—I think—we never broke anything, but because as we got bigger and heavier, we might knock down the statues of our ancestors that our father had had placed on the bottom pilasters of the banisters on every flight of stairs. In fact, Cosimo had already caused a great-great-grandfather bishop to tumble, miter and all; he was punished, and from then on he learned to brake a moment before reaching the bottom of the stairs and jump down, a hairsbreadth from crashing into the statue. I, too, learned, because I followed him in everything, except that I, always more modest and prudent, jumped off halfway down the staircase, or slid down bit by bit, braking constantly. One day he went down the banister like an arrow, and who was coming up the stairs! The Abbé Fauchelafleur, strolling with his breviary open before him but with his gaze fixed on nothing, like a hen. If only he had been half asleep as usual! No, it was one of those moments that came even to him, of extreme attention, of alarm at all things. He sees Cosimo, he thinks, "Banister, statue, now he'll bang into it, now they'll scold me, too" (because for every one of our pranks he, too, was scolded, as not knowing how to monitor us), and he flings himself on the banister to stop my brother. Cosimo collides with the abbé, sweeps him down the banister (he was a tiny old man, all skin and bones), can't brake, crashes into the statue of our ancestor Cacciaguerra Piovasco, a Crusader in the Holy Land, and they all collapse at the foot of the stairs, the Crusader in fragments (he was of plaster), the abbé, and him. There were endless reprimands, whippings, extra exercises, confinement with bread and cold soup. And Cosimo, who felt innocent because the fault was not his but the abbé's, came out with that fierce invective: "I don't care a bit about your ancestors, Father, sir!" The announcement of his vocation as a rebel.

Our sister did the same, in essence. Even though the isolation in which she lived had been imposed by our father after the affair of the young Marquis della Mela, she had always been a rebellious and solitary soul. How that business of the young marquis had happened we never knew. How had the son of a family hostile to us sneaked into the house? And why? To seduce, in fact to assault, our sister, it was said, in the long fight between the families that ensued. In fact, we could never imagine that freckled simpleton as a seducer, and still less of our sister, who was certainly stronger than him, and famous for arm wrestling even with the stable boys. And then, why was it he who cried out? And how in the world did the servants, hurrying, along with our father, find him with his pants in shreds, ripped as if by the claws of a female tiger? The Della Melas would never admit that their son had made an attempt on Battista's honor and agree to marriage. So our sister ended up buried at home, in a nun's habit, without having taken the vows even of a tertiary, given her dubious vocation.

Her unhappy soul revealed itself above all in the kitchen. She was a really skilled cook, because she had both diligence and imagination, prime talents of every cook, but when she put her hands to something you never knew what surprises might arrive at the table: once she had prepared some crostini, very refined, in fact, with pâté of mouse liver, and she told us only when we had eaten them and found them good; not to mention the locusts' legs, the hard, serrated back ones, set like a mosaic on a cake, and the pig tails roasted as if they were ring cakes, and the time she cooked a whole porcupine, with all its spines, who knows why, surely just to shock us when she raised the cover of the dish, because while she always ate whatever type of thing she prepared, not even she wanted to taste this, despite its being a young porcupine, pink and certainly tender. In fact, much of this horrible cooking was attempted only for show rather than for the pleasure of making us taste, along with her, foods with ghastly flavors. These dishes of Battista's were products of the finest animal or vegetable filigree work: heads of cauliflower with rabbit ears set on a collar of rabbit skin, or the head of a pig from whose mouth a red lobster emerged, as if the pig were expelling the tongue, and the lobster held the pig's tongue in its claws as if it had torn it out. Then the snails: she had managed to decapitate I don't know how many snails and had stuck each of the heads—those very soft little horses' heads—on a cream puff, I think with a toothpick, and when they came to the table they looked like a flock of tiny swans. And even more shocking than the sight of those delicacies was the thought of the zealous persistence that Battista certainly had put into preparing them, and the image of her slender hands as they dismembered those small animal bodies.

The way the snails excited the macabre imagination of our sister drove us, my brother and me, to a rebellion, made up of solidarity with the poor tortured beasts, disgust for the taste of the cooked snails, and impatience with everything and everyone, and so it's not surprising if, starting there, Cosimo developed his act and what followed from it.

We had made a plan. When the *cavalier avvocato* brought home a basketful of edible snails, they were put in a barrel in the cellar so that they would fast, eating only bran, and would be purged. If you shifted the wooden cover of this barrel a kind of inferno appeared, where the snails were moving up the staves at a slow pace that was a premonition of their death agony, among bits of bran, stripes of clotted opaque slime, and colored snail excrement, memory of the good times of open air and grasses. Some of the snails were outside their shells, heads extended and horns spread, some huddled up in themselves, with only distrustful antennae sticking out; others were in small groups like neighbors, others asleep and closed up, others dead, with the shell upturned. To save them from encountering that sinister cook and to save us from her banquets, we made a hole in the bottom of the barrel and from there, using crushed blades of grass and honey, marked out a route, as hidden as possible behind casks and tools in the cellar, to draw the snails along the pathway of flight, up to a window that opened onto an untended and scrubby flower bed.

The next day, when we went down to the cellar to check the effects of our plan and in the light of a candle inspected the walls and the passageways—"One here! And another here!" "And see where this one got to!"—already a line of snails was moving at small intervals from the barrel to the window along the floor and the walls, following our track. "Quick, snails! Hurry up, escape!" we couldn't keep ourselves from saying to them, seeing the creatures going so slowly, and not without detouring in idle circles on the cellar's rough walls, attracted by occasional deposits and molds and encrustations. But the cellar was dark, cluttered, uneven; we hoped that no one would discover them, that they would all have time to escape.

Instead, that restless soul our sister Battista used to spend the night hunting mice throughout the house, holding a candlestick and with a gun under her arm. That night she passed through the cellar, and the light of the candle illumined a straggler snail on the ceiling, with its trail of silver slime. A gunshot echoed. We all started in our beds, but immediately our heads sank back into the pillows, accustomed as we were to the house nun's nighttime hunting. But with the snail destroyed and a piece of plaster knocked down by that unreasonable shot, Battista began shouting in her shrill voice, "Help! They're all escaping! Help!" The servants, half dressed, hurried to her aid, along with our father, armed with a saber, and the abbé without his wig, while the *cavalier avvocato,* before he could understand a thing and fearing trouble, fled into the fields and went to sleep in a hayloft.

In the light of the torches they all began to chase the snails through the cellar. No one really cared, but by now they were awake and, out of the usual egotism, didn't want to admit that they had been disturbed for nothing. They discovered the hole in the barrel and immediately knew it was us. Our father seized us in bed, with the coachman's whip. We ended up with purple stripes on our backs, our buttocks, and our legs, locked in the dirty storeroom that served as our prison.

They kept us there for three days, on bread, water, salad, pork rind, and cold minestrone (which, fortunately, we liked). Then the first meal with the family, as if nothing had happened, everything in order, that midday on June fifteenth —and what had our sister Battista, superintendent of the kitchen, prepared? Snail soup and snails for the main course. Cosimo wouldn't touch even a shell. "Eat or we'll lock you in the storeroom again!" I gave in and began to swallow the mollusks. (It was a bit of cowardice on my part, and made my brother feel even more alone, so that in his leaving us there was also a protest against me, who had disappointed him; but I was only eight, and then what's the point of comparing my force of will, or rather, what I could have had as a child, with the superhuman obstinacy that marked the life of my brother?)

"And so?" our father said to Cosimo.

"No, and no!" said Cosimo, and pushed away the plate.

"Away from this table!"

But Cosimo had already turned his back on us and was leaving the room.

"Where are you going?"

Through the glass door we saw him in the hall, picking up his three-cornered hat and his small sword.

"I know!" He ran into the garden.

Shortly afterward, through the windows, we saw him climbing up the holm oak. He was dressed and coiffed with great propriety, as our father wanted him to come to the table, though he was only twelve: hair powdered and ponytail tied with a ribbon, three-cornered hat, lace tie, green tailcoat, tight mauve trousers, sword, and long white leather gaiters that came to midthigh, the only concession to a way of dressing more suited to our country life. (I, being only eight, was exempted from the powder in my hair, except on gala occasions, and from the sword, which, however, I would have liked to carry.) So he climbed up into the gnarled tree, arms and legs moving through the branches with the assurance and speed gained from the long practice we'd done together.

I've already said that we spent hours and hours in the trees, and not for utilitarian reasons, like many boys, who climb up just to look for fruit or birds' nests, but for the pleasure of overcoming difficult protuberances and forks, and getting as high as possible, and finding beautiful places to stop and look at the world below, to make jokes and shout at those who passed under us. So I found it natural that Cosimo's first thought at that unjust anger against him was to climb the holm oak, a tree familiar to us, which, spreading its branches at the height of the dining-room windows, imposed his contemptuous and insulted behavior on the sight of the whole family.

"*Vorsicht! Vorsicht!* Now he'll fall, poor thing!" exclaimed our mother anxiously, who would have happily seen us charging under cannon fire but meanwhile was in agony at every one of our games.

Cosimo climbed up to the fork of a large branch where he could sit comfortably, and there he sat, legs dangling, arms crossed, with his hands in his armpits, his head pulled down between his shoulders, the hat low on his forehead.

Our father leaned out the window. "When you're tired of sitting there you'll change your mind!" he shouted.

"I'll never change my mind," said my brother from the branch.

"I'll show you, as soon as you come down!"

"I'm never coming down again!" And he kept his word.

2

Cosimo was in the oak. The branches were waving, high bridges over the earth. A light wind was blowing; it was sunny. The sun shone among the leaves, and to see Cosimo we had to shield our eyes with our hands. Cosimo looked at the world from the tree: everything was different seen from up there, and that was already an entertainment. The avenue had a completely different prospect, as did the flower beds, the hydrangeas, the camellias, the small iron table where one could have coffee in the garden. Farther on, the foliage thinned out and the vegetable garden sloped down in small terraced fields supported by stone walls; the low hill was dark with olive groves, and behind, the built-up area of Ombrosa raised its roofs of faded brick and slate, and ships' flags peeked out from the port below. In the background the sea extended, high on the horizon, and a slow sailboat passed by.

Now the baron and the *generalessa,* after their coffee, came out into the garden. They looked at a rosebush, made a show of paying no attention to Cosimo. They gave each other their arm, but right away they separated, in order to discuss and gesticulate. I went under the oak, as if playing on my own but in reality trying to get Cosimo's attention; he was still angry at me, though, and stayed up there looking into the distance. I stopped and crouched behind a bench so that I could continue to observe him without being seen.

My brother was like a sentinel. He looked at everything, and everything was as if nothing. A woman with a basket passed through the lemon groves. A mule driver went up the slope, holding on to the tail of the mule. They didn't see each other; the woman, at the sound of the iron-shod hooves, turned and leaned out toward the street, but wasn't in time. Then she began to sing, but the mule driver was already rounding the turn; he strained his ears, cracked the whip, and to the mule said, "Aah!" And it all ended there. Cosimo saw this and that.

The Abbé Fauchelafleur came along the avenue with his open breviary. Cosimo grabbed something from the branch and dropped it on his head; I couldn't figure out what it was, maybe a little spider, or a splinter of bark; he missed. With his sword Cosimo began to poke around in a hole in the trunk. An angry wasp emerged; he chased it away, waving his hat, and followed its flight with his gaze as far as a pumpkin plant, where it alighted. Swift as always, the *cavalier avvocato* came out of the house, descended the garden steps, and vanished amid the rows of vines; to see where he was going, Cosimo climbed up another branch. There, amid the foliage, he heard a flutter, and a blackbird rose in flight. Cosimo was disappointed, because he had been up there all that time and hadn't noticed it. He sat staring into the sun to see if there were others. No, there were none.

The oak was near an elm; the two crowns almost touched. A branch of the elm passed about eighteen inches above a branch of the other tree; it was easy for my brother to take the step and thus get to the top of the elm, which we had never explored, because its boughs were high and couldn't be reached from the ground. Always looking for where a branch passed beside the branches of another tree, he crossed from the elm to a carob tree, and then to a mulberry. So I saw Cosimo advance from one branch to the next, walking suspended over the garden.

Several branches of the big mulberry extended to the boundary wall of our villa and hung over it, into the garden of the D'Ondarivas. Although we were neighbors, we knew nothing about the Marquises d'Ondariva and Nobles d'Ombrosa: since they had enjoyed for many generations certain feudal rights to which our father laid claim, a mutual resentment divided the two families, and a high wall, like the keep of a fortress, divided our villas—I don't know if our father or the marquis had had it built. One should add to that the jealousy with which the D'Ondarivas guarded their garden, which was populated, so it was said, by plant species never seen before. In fact, the father of the current marquis, a disciple of Linnaeus, had urged all the family's vast networks of relatives at the courts of France and England to have the most precious botanical rarities of the colonies sent to him, and for years ships had unloaded at Ombrosa sacks of seeds, bundles of cuttings, bushes in pots, and even whole trees, with enormous clumps of earth wrapped around the roots, until in that garden had grown—it was said—a mixture of forests of the Indies and the Americas, if not actually New Holland.

All we could see of it was the dark leaves of a tree newly imported from the American colonies peeking over the edge of the wall: a magnolia, whose black branches sprouted a fleshy white flower. From our mulberry Cosimo was on the top of the wall; he took a few steps, balancing, and then, holding on with his hands, dropped onto the other side, where the leaves and flowers of the magnolia were. From there he disappeared from my view; and what I will now recount, like many of the events in this story of his life, he reported to me later, or it was I who gleaned the stories from scattered testimonies and deductions.

Cosimo was in the magnolia. Although its branches were close together, this tree was easily accessible to a boy like my brother, expert in all species of trees; and the branches stood up to his weight, although they weren't very large and were of soft wood that the tips of Cosimo's shoes scraped, opening white wounds in the black bark; it wrapped the boy in a fresh scent of leaves as the wind stirred them, turning them to a green that was now opaque, now bright.

But it was the whole garden that gave off a perfume, and although it was so irregularly dense that Cosimo still couldn't see it all, he was exploring it with his sense of smell, and he tried to distinguish its various scents, which had been known to him ever since, carried by the wind, they reached our garden and seemed to us one with the secret of that villa. Then he looked at the foliage and saw new leaves, some as big and shiny as if a film of water were running over them, some tiny and composite, and trunks that were all smooth or all scaly.

There was a great silence. Only a flight of tiny warblers rose above him, crying. And he heard a faint voice singing: "Oh là là là! The *ba-lan-çoire . . .*" Cosimo looked down. Hanging from a branch of a big tree nearby was a swing, with a girl of about ten sitting on it.

She was a fair-haired girl, with her hair arranged in a tall style that was a little odd for a child, and a blue dress that was also too adult; the skirt, lifted by the swing, was dripping with lace. The girl was gazing with eyes half closed and nose in the air, as if she were used to playing the lady, and she was taking bites of an apple, bending her head each time toward the hand that had at the same time to hold the apple and hold on to the rope of the swing, and every time the swing was at the lowest point of its arc she gave herself a push, hitting the ground with the tips of her shoes, and from her lips blew out the bits of chewed apple skin, and sang, "Oh là là là! The *ba-lan-çoire . . .*" like a girl who now no longer cares about the swing, or about the song, or (but maybe a little more) about the apple, and already has other thoughts in her head.

From the top of the magnolia, Cosimo dropped to the lowest branches, and now he was standing with his feet planted each in one fork and his elbows resting on a branch in front of him as if it were a windowsill. The flights of the swing carried the girl right under his nose.

She wasn't paying attention and didn't notice him. Suddenly she saw him there, standing in the tree, in three-cornered hat and gaiters. "Oh!" she said.

The apple fell out of her hand and rolled to the foot of the magnolia. Cosimo unsheathed his sword, lowered himself down from the bottom branch, touched the apple with the tip of the sword, pierced it, and offered it to the girl, who in the meantime had swung to and fro and was back again. "Take it—it's not dirty, just a little bruised on one side."

The fair-haired girl had already regretted her display of amazement at the unknown boy who had appeared in the magnolia and had recovered her haughty, nose-in-the-air expression. "Are you a thief?" she said.

"A thief?" said Cosimo, offended; then he thought about it. On the spot he liked the idea. "Yes," he said, lowering the hat over his forehead. "Do you have something against it?"

"What have you come to steal?"

Cosimo looked at the apple he had skewered on the tip of the sword, and it occurred to him that he was hungry, that he had touched scarcely any food at the table. "This apple," he said, and began to peel it with the blade of the sword, which, in spite of family prohibitions, he kept very sharp.

"Then you're a fruit thief," said the girl.

My brother thought of the gangs of poor boys from Ombrosa who climbed over walls and hedges and ransacked the orchards, a kind of boy he had been taught to despise and to flee, and for the first time he thought of how free and enviable that life must be. There: maybe he could become like them, and from now on live like that. "Yes," he said. He had cut the apple in slices and began to eat it.

The fair-haired girl burst into a laugh that lasted the whole back-and-forth of the swing, up and down. "Come on! I know the boys who steal fruit! They're all my friends! And they go barefoot, in shirtsleeves, uncombed, not in gaiters and a wig!"

My brother turned as red as the skin of the apple. Being made fun of not only for the powder, which he didn't like in the least, but also for the gaiters, which he liked enormously, and being judged of an aspect inferior to that of a fruit thief, that type he had until a moment before despised, and above all to discover that that damsel who was acting like the mistress of the garden of the D'Ondarivas was a friend of the fruit thieves but not his friend—all these things together filled him with contempt, shame, and jealousy.

"Oh là là là . . . In gaiters and wig!" sang the girl on the swing.

A vengeful pride possessed him. "I'm not one of those thieves you know!" he cried. "I'm not a thief at all! I just said that so as not to scare you, because if you knew who I really am, you'd die of fear. I'm a bandit! A ferocious bandit!"

The girl continued to fly up under his nose; one would have said she wanted to touch him with the tips of her shoes. "Come on! Where's your gun? Bandits all have a gun! Or a harquebus. I've seen them! They've stopped our carriage five times on our trips from the castle to here!"

"But not the chief! I'm the chief! The chief of the bandits doesn't have a gun! He has only a sword!" And he held out his sword.

The girl shrugged her shoulders. "The chief of the bandits," she explained, "is called Gian dei Brughi and he always comes and brings us presents at Christmas and Easter."

"Ah!" exclaimed Cosimo di Rondò, hit by a wave of family partisanship. "Then my father is right when he says that the Marquis d'Ondariva is the protector of all the lawlessness and smuggling around here!"

The girl passed close to the ground, but instead of pushing off she braked with a rapid kick and jumped down. The empty swing flew into the air on its ropes. "Get down from there immediately! How dare you enter our property!" she said, pointing a finger at the boy.

"I haven't entered and I won't come down," said Cosimo, equally heated. "I've never set foot on your property and I wouldn't for all the gold in the world."

Then the girl very calmly picked up a fan that was lying on a wicker chair and, although it wasn't very hot, fanned herself as she walked back and forth. "Now," she said tranquilly, "I'll call the servants and have you captured and beaten. That'll teach you to sneak onto our land!" She kept changing her tone, this girl, and each time my brother was thrown off.

"Where I am isn't land and isn't yours!" proclaimed Cosimo, and already he was tempted to add, "And after all, I am the Duke of Ombrosa and the lord of all the land!" But he restrained himself, because he didn't like repeating the things that his father always said, now that he had run away from the table in an argument with him. He didn't like it and it didn't seem right to him, also because those claims about the dukedom had always seemed like obsessions to him; what did it have to do with the matter that he, too, Cosimo, should begin to boast that he was the duke? But he didn't want to contradict himself and continued the conversation as it occurred to him. "Here it's not yours," he repeated, "because yours is the ground and if I put a foot there then I would be sneaking in. But not up here, no, and I go anywhere I like."

"Yes, then it's yours, up there . . ."

"Of course! My personal territory, everything up here," and he made a vague gesture toward the branches, the leaves against the sun, the sky. "All the branches of the trees are my territory. Tell them to come and get me, if they can!"

Now, after all that bluster, he expected that she would somehow or other make fun of him. Instead she appeared unexpectedly interested. "Ah yes? And how far does that territory of yours reach?"

"As far as you can go if you move through the trees—this way, that way, beyond the wall, into the olive grove, up the hill, to the other side of the hill, into the woods, into the bishop's lands . . ."

"Even as far as France?"

"As far as Poland and Saxony," said Cosimo, whose knowledge of geography was limited to the names mentioned by our mother when she talked about the Wars of Succession. "But I'm not an egotist like you. I invite you into my territory." Now they had begun to use the familiar *tu,* but it was she who had started it.

"And who does the swing belong to?" she said, and sat down in it, with the open fan in her hand.

"The swing is yours," Cosimo confirmed, "but since it's tied to this branch it's my dependent. So if you sit there touching the ground with your feet, you're in yours, but if you rise into the air you're in mine."

She gave herself a push and flew up, her hands clutching the ropes. From the magnolia Cosimo jumped onto the big branch that held the swing, grabbed hold of the ropes, and began making it swing himself. The swing went higher and higher.

"Are you scared?"

"No. What's your name?"

"Cosimo. And you?"

"Violante, but I'm called Viola."

"I'm also called Mino, because Cosimo is an old person's name."

"I don't like it."

"Cosimo?"

"No, Mino."

"Ah . . . You can call me Cosimo."

"Not a chance! Listen, you, we have to have clear agreements."

"What do you mean?" he said, upset every time.

"I mean, I can come up into your territory and I'm a sacred guest, all right? I come and go as I like. You, on the other hand, are sacred and inviolable as long as you're in the trees, in your territory, but as soon as you touch the ground in my garden you become my slave and are in chains."

"No, I'm not going to go down into your garden, or mine either. For me it's all enemy territory. You'll come up with me, and your friends who steal fruit can come, maybe also my brother Biagio, though he's a little bit of a chicken, and we'll have an army in the trees, and we'll make the land and its inhabitants do as we say."

"No, no, none of that. Let me explain to you how things are. You are the lord of the trees, all right? But if you once touch the ground with your foot you lose your whole kingdom and remain the lowest of the slaves. You understand? Even if a branch breaks and you fall, it's all lost!"

"I've never fallen out of a tree in my life!"

"Sure, but if you fall, if you fall you turn into ashes and the wind blows you away."

"All nonsense. I'm not going down to the ground, because I don't want to."

"Oh, how boring you are."

"No, no, let's play. For example, could I go on the swing?"

"If you can sit on the swing without touching the ground, yes."

Next to Viola's swing there was another one, hanging on the same branch but pulled up by a knot in the ropes so that they wouldn't bump into each other. Cosimo, holding on to one of the ropes, let himself down from the branch—an exercise he was very good at because our mother made us do a lot of gym practice—got to the knot, untied it, stood on the swing, and, to give himself a push, shifted the weight of his body by bending his knees and thrusting forward. So he pushed himself higher and higher. The two swings were going in opposite directions and now they reached the same height and, midway through their flights, passed close by each other.

"But if you try sitting down and giving yourself a push with your feet, you'll go higher," Viola hinted.

Cosimo sneered.

"Come down and give me a push—be good," she said, smiling at him kindly.

"No, it's said that I must not get down at any cost . . ." and Cosimo began not to understand again.

"Be nice."

"No."

"Oh, oh! You were about to fall. If you'd set foot on the ground you would've lost everything!" Viola got off the swing and began to push Cosimo's swing gently. "Ooh!" She had all of a sudden grabbed the seat of the swing where my brother had planted his feet and turned it upside down. Luckily Cosimo was holding tight to the ropes. Otherwise he would have fallen to the ground like a lead weight.

"Traitor!" he cried, and climbed up, gripping the two ropes, but the ascent was much harder than the descent, especially because the fair-haired girl was in one of her malicious moods and from below was pulling the ropes in all directions.

Finally he reached the big branch and climbed onto it.

With his lace tie he dried the sweat on his face. "Ha-ha! You didn't succeed!"

"Almost!"

"But I thought you were my friend!"

"You thought!" and she started fanning herself again.

"Violante!" a sharp female voice broke in just then. "Who are you talking to?"

On the white steps that led to the villa a woman had appeared: tall and thin, in a very wide skirt, she was peering through a lorgnette. Cosimo withdrew among the leaves timidly.

"With a boy, *ma tante,*" said the girl, "who was born in the top of a tree and because of a spell can't set foot on the ground."

Cosimo blushed, wondering if the girl was talking like that to make fun of him in front of the aunt, or to make fun of the aunt in front of him, or only to continue the game, or because she didn't care a bit about him or the aunt or the game. He saw that he was being examined by the lorgnette of the lady, who approached the tree as if to contemplate a strange parrot.

"Uh, mais c'est un des Piovasques, ce jeune homme, je crois. Viens, Violante."

Cosimo flared up with humiliation: that she had recognized him with that natural air, not even asking why he was there, and had immediately summoned the girl, firmly but not harshly, and Viola, who, obedient, without even turning, followed her aunt's summons—all appeared to imply that he was a person of no account, who scarcely existed. So that extraordinary afternoon sank into a cloud of shame.

But look, the girl makes a sign to her aunt, the aunt lowers her head, the child says something in her ear. The aunt points her lorgnette toward Cosimo again. "Well, sir," she says to him, "would you like to take a cup of chocolate? That way we, too, will become acquainted," and she gives a sidelong glance at Viola, "since you're already a friend of the family."

Cosimo gazed at aunt and niece with round eyes. His heart was pounding. Here he had been invited by the Ondariva family of Ombrosa, the proudest family in the area, and the humiliation of a moment before was transformed into revenge and he took revenge on his father, being welcomed by the adversaries who had always looked down on him, and Viola had interceded for him, and he was now officially accepted as a friend of Viola's and would play with her in that garden that was different from all other gardens. All this Cosimo felt, but at the same time an opposite feeling, if also confused, a feeling made up of shyness, pride, solitude, willfulness; and in this clash of feelings my brother grabbed the branch above him, climbed up, moved into the leafiest part, crossed into another tree, and disappeared.

3

It was an afternoon that would never end. Every so often there was a thud, a rustling, as there often is in a garden, and we ran out hoping that it was him, that he had decided to come down. But no: I saw the crown of the magnolia with its white flower quiver, and Cosimo appeared on the other side of the wall and climbed over it.

I went to meet him in the mulberry. He seemed annoyed to see me; he was still angry. He sat on a branch of the mulberry above me and began nicking it with his sword, as if he didn't want to speak to me.

"It's easy to climb in the mulberry," I said, just to say something. "We never went up it before."

He went on scratching at the branch with the blade, then he said bitterly, "So did you like the snails?"

I held out a basket. "I brought you two dried figs, Mino, and some cake."

"Did *they* send you?" he said, still irritated, but he was already salivating as he looked at the basket.

"No. If you only knew, I had to escape secretly from the abbé!" I said quickly. "They wanted to keep me doing lessons all evening so that I wouldn't be in touch with you, but the old man fell asleep! Mama is worried that you might fall and wants to look for you, but ever since Papa couldn't see you in the oak he's been saying that you came down and are hiding somewhere, reflecting on your bad behavior, and there's no need to be afraid."

"I never got down!" said my brother.

"Were you in the D'Ondarivas' garden?"

"Yes, but I went from tree to tree, without ever touching the ground!"

"Why?" I asked; it was the first time I'd heard him pronounce that rule of his, but he had spoken of it as of something already settled between us, as if he were eager to reassure me that he hadn't broken it, so I no longer dared to insist on my demand an explanation.

"You know," he said, instead of answering, "it would take days to explore the whole of that place, the D'Ondarivas'! With trees from the forests of America—if only you could see!" Then he remembered that he was fighting with me and that he should therefore get no pleasure from telling me about his discoveries. He broke off abruptly. "Anyway, I'm not taking you there. You can go out with Battista from now on, or with the *cavalier avvocato*!"

"No, Mino, take me there!" I said. "You mustn't be angry with me because of the snails—they were disgusting, but I couldn't bear to hear them yelling anymore!"

Cosimo was gobbling up the cake. "I'll test you," he said. "You have to prove to me that you're on my side, not theirs."

"Tell me everything you want me to do."

"You have to get me some ropes, long and strong, because to make certain crossings I'll have to tie myself; then a pulley, and hooks, nails, the large kind . . ."

"What do you want to make? A crane?"

"We'll have to bring up a lot of stuff, we'll see later: planks, reeds . . ."

"You want to build a cabin in a tree! Where?"

"If necessary. We'll choose the place. Meanwhile my address is there in that hollow oak. I'll lower the basket with the rope and you can put everything I need in it."

"But why? You're talking as if you were going to stay hidden indefinitely . . . Don't you think they'll forgive you?"

His face flushed. "What do I care if they forgive me? Anyway, I'm not hiding—I'm not afraid of anyone! And you, are you afraid to help me?"

Not that I hadn't understood that my brother was refusing to come down for now, but I pretended not to understand in order to force him to declare himself, to say, "Yes, I wish to remain in the trees until teatime, or until sunset, or until dinnertime, or until it's dark"—something that, in other words, would mark a limit, a proportion to his act of protest. But he said nothing of the sort, and I felt a little afraid of that.

They called, from below. It was our father shouting: "Cosimo! Cosimo!" And then, convinced that Cosimo wouldn't answer him: "Biagio! Biagio!" he called me.

"I'm going to see what they want. Then I'll come and tell you," I said quickly. That urgency to inform my brother, I admit, was combined with an urgency to slip away from there, out of fear of being caught plotting with him at the top of the mulberry and having to share with him the punishment that was surely waiting. But Cosimo didn't seem to read in my face that shadow of cowardice; he let me go, not without having displayed with a shrug his indifference to what our father might have to say.

When I returned he was still there; he had found a good place to sit, on a pollarded limb, his chin resting on his knees and his arms around his calves.

"Mino! Mino!" I said, climbing up, breathless. "They've forgiven you! They're waiting for us! Tea is on the table, and Papa and Mama are already sitting down and they've put slices of cake on our plates. Because there's a chocolate cream cake, but not made by Battista, you know! Battista must be locked in her room, livid with fury! They patted me on the head and told me, 'Go to poor Mino and tell him we'll make peace and not talk about it again!' Hurry up, let's go!"

Cosimo was biting a leaf. He didn't move. "Say," he said, "try to get a blanket, without letting them see, and bring it to me. It must be cold here at night."

"But you won't spend the night in the trees!"

He didn't answer, his chin on his knees; he was chewing a leaf and looking around. I followed his gaze, which ended right on the wall of the D'Ondarivas' garden, just where the white magnolia flower peeked out and, farther on, a kite was wheeling.

So it was evening. The servants went back and forth, setting the table; in the dining room the candelabra were already lighted. Cosimo must have seen everything from the tree, and Baron Arminio, turning to the shadows outside the window, cried, "If you want to stay up there, you'll die of hunger!"

That night for the first time we sat at dinner without Cosimo. He was astride a high branch of the oak, sideways, so that we could see only his dangling legs. We could see, I mean, if we went to the windowsill and peered into the shadows, because the room was lighted and outside it was dark.

Even the *cavalier avvocato* felt obliged to look out and say something, but as usual he managed not to express an opinion on the matter. He said, "Ooooh . . . Strong tree . . . Lasts a hundred years . . ." Then some Turkish words, maybe the name of the oak; in short, as if he were speaking of the tree and not of my brother.

Our sister Battista, on the other hand, betrayed a kind of envy toward Cosimo, as if, used to keeping the family in suspense because of her strange behavior, she had now found someone who surpassed her; and she continued to bite her nails (to bite them she didn't raise a finger to her mouth but lowered it, with her hand upside down, her elbow lifted).

The *generalessa* thought of certain soldiers on sentry duty in the trees in an encampment in Slavonia or Pomerania, I no longer remember which, and of how, sighting the enemy, they succeeded in preventing an ambush. This memory suddenly brought her back from the helplessness of maternal fear to her preferred military atmosphere, and as if she had finally managed to understand her son's behavior, she became calmer and almost proud. No one paid any attention to her except the Abbé Fauchelafleur, who nodded gravely at the warrior story and the parallel my mother drew from it, because he would seize on any subject provided he could see what was happening as natural and clear his mind of responsibilities and worries.

After dinner we used to go to bed early, and we didn't change our schedule that night either. By now our parents had decided not to give Cosimo the satisfaction of paying attention to him, expecting that tiredness, discomfort, and the cold of the night would dislodge him. Each went to his room, and on the façade of the house the lighted candles opened eyes of gold within the window frames. What nostalgia, what a memory of warmth that house, so well known and so near, must have brought my brother, who was spending the night out in the open! I looked out the window of our room and made out his shadow curled up in a hollow of the oak, between branch and trunk, wrapped in the blanket and —I think—with the rope tied several times around him so he wouldn't fall.

The moon rose late and shone over the branches. In their nests the titmice slept, curled up like him. In the night, outside, the silence of the park was traversed by countless rustlings and distant sounds, and the wind passed through. At times a far-off roar arrived: the sea. From the window I strained my ears to that irregular breath and tried to imagine how it would sound, without the familiar womb of the house, to someone who was just a few yards away but completely entrusted to it, with only the night around him, the only friendly object to which he could cling the trunk of a tree with its rough bark traveled by tiny endless tunnels in which the larvae slept.

I went to bed, but I didn't want to blow out the candle. Maybe that light in the window of his room would keep him company. We shared a room, with two child's beds. I looked at his, untouched, and the darkness outside the window where he was, and I turned over between the sheets, experiencing, perhaps for the first time, the joy of being undressed, barefoot, in a warm white bed, and as if at the same time sensing his discomfort, tied up in the rough blanket, his legs laced into their gaiters, unable to turn, the bones aching. It's a feeling that since that night has never left me—the consciousness of how fortunate it is to have a bed, clean sheets, a soft mattress! In that feeling my thoughts, for so many hours directed toward the person who was the object of all our anxieties, closed over me, and so I fell asleep.

4

I don't know if it's true that, as you read in books, in olden days a monkey that left Rome jumping from tree to tree could reach Spain without touching the ground. In my time, the only place where the trees were so dense was the shoreline of the gulf of Ombrosa, from one end to the other, and its valley, up to the mountain ridges; and for that reason our district was renowned everywhere.

These places are no longer recognizable. First the French came, cutting down woods as if they were fields that are reaped every year and grow back. They didn't grow back. It seemed a thing of the war, of Napoleon, of the times; but it didn't stop. The hills are bare, so that to look at them, for us who knew them before, is disturbing.

At that time, wherever we went, we always had leaves and branches between us and the sky. The only place where the vegetation was lower was the lemon groves, but in their midst rose twisted fig trees, which, higher up, obstructed the whole sky over the gardens with the cupolas of their dense foliage, and if not figs it was brown-leaved cherries, or the more tender quinces, peach, almond, and young pears, fruitful plums, and then service trees or carobs, when it wasn't a mulberry or an ancient walnut. Where the gardens ended the olive grove began, silver-gray, a cloud with fraying edges. In the background was the town, stacked between the harbor below and the fortress above; and there, too, treetops sprouted everywhere amid the roofs: holm oaks, plane trees, even oaks, and a less interested and prouder vegetation that erupted—an orderly eruption—in the area where the nobles had built their villas and surrounded their parks with railings.

Above the olives the woods began. The pines must once have reigned over all the region, because they still infiltrated the slopes, in slivers and clumps, down to the shore of the sea, as did the larches. The oaks were denser and thicker than they seem today, because they were the first and most prized victims of the ax. Higher up, the pines gave way to chestnuts, the woods went up the mountain, and no limits could be seen. This was the universe of sap in which we lived, we the inhabitants of Ombrosa, almost without noticing it.

The first to fix his thoughts on this was Cosimo. He understood that since the trees were so thick, he could travel many miles, going from branch to branch, without ever having to get down. At times a stretch of bare earth obliged him to make lengthy detours, but he soon learned all the necessary routes, and he measured distances not according to our estimates but always having in mind the circuitous path he had to follow along the branches. And where he couldn't reach the nearest branch even with a leap, he began to use some contrivances, but I'll talk about that later; now we are still in the dawn when, waking, he found himself at the top of a holm oak, amid the din of the starlings, soaked with cold dew, stiff, his bones aching, pins and needles in his legs and arms, and happily he began to explore the new world.

He reached the last tree in the parks, a plane. The valley sloped down under a sky of rings of clouds and smoke rising from slate roofs, farmhouses hidden behind the shore like piles of rocks, a sky of leaves lifted into the air by fig and cherry trees, while shorter plum and peach trees spread sturdy branches. Everything could be seen, even the grass, blade by blade, but not the color of the earth, which was covered by the lazy leaves of pumpkin or by the clumps of lettuces or cabbages in the nurseries. And so it was on either side of the deep funnel-shaped valley opening like a *V* to the sea.

And through this countryside ran a kind of wave, not visible or even audible, except occasionally, but what could be heard was enough to spread its restlessness: a sudden explosion of sharp cries, and then a pelting, thudding sound, and maybe even the crack of a broken branch, and more cries, but different, of raging voices, converging in the place from which the first sharp cries had come. Then nothing, a sensation of emptiness, or of something passing, something that was to be expected not there but somewhere else entirely, and in fact that mixture of voices and sounds resumed, and the places where it originated, whether on this side of the valley or the other, were wherever the small serrated leaves of the cherry trees stirred in the wind. So Cosimo, with the part of his mind that was gliding absent-mindedly—another part of him, instead, knew and understood everything ahead of time—formulated this thought: "The cherries are speaking."

Cosimo headed toward the nearest cherry tree, or rather a row of tall cherry trees, of a beautiful leafy green, and loaded with black cherries, but my brother didn't yet have the eye to immediately distinguish amid the branches what was there and what wasn't. He stayed where he was: first he heard the noise and then he didn't. He was on the lowest branches, and he felt on himself all the cherries that were above; he wouldn't have been able to explain how, but they seemed to converge on him. In other words, it seemed a tree with eyes rather than cherries.

Cosimo looked up and an overripe cherry fell on his forehead with a *chak!* He half closed his eyelids to look up against the sky (where the sun was getting brighter) and saw that there and in the neighboring trees a crowd of boys were perched.

Seeing themselves seen, they were no longer silent, and in sharp but muffled voices said something like "Look at him there, that's quite the dandy!" And each one, parting the leaves in front of him, descended from the branch where he was to the lower one, toward the boy in the three-cornered hat. Their heads were bare or hooded in sacks or they wore fringed straw hats; their shirts and pants were ragged; those who weren't barefoot had cloth wrappings on their feet, and some had taken off their clogs in order to climb and tied them around their neck. It was the big gang of fruit thieves, whom

Cosimo and I—obedient, in this, to the family injunctions — had always kept away from. That morning, however, my brother didn't seem to be looking for anything else, although it wasn't clear even to him what he expected.

He sat still, waiting, as they descended, pointing at him and, in that harsh undertone of theirs, hurling remarks like "What's it this guy here's looking for?" and spitting cherry pits at him or throwing cherries that were rotten or pecked by blackbirds, twirling them on their stems with the move of a slinger.

"Oooh!" they went suddenly. They had seen the small sword that hung at his back. "See what he's got?" And laughter. "The butt-slapper!"

Then they turned silent and suffocated their laughter, because something was about to happen that would drive them wild with delight: two of the little rascals, very quietly, had climbed up to a branch just above Cosimo and were dropping a sack over his head (one of those dirty sacks they used to put their booty in; when they were empty, they wore them on their heads like hoods draping over their shoulders). In a moment my brother would have found himself in a sack without even knowing how he got there, and they could tie him up like a salami and give him a beating.

Cosimo scented the danger, or maybe he scented nothing: he felt mocked because of the sword and wanted to unsheathe it as a point of honor. He brandished it high, the blade grazed the sack, he saw it, and with a low lunge ripped it out of the thieves' hands and tossed it away.

It was a good move. The others let out "Oh!"s of disappointment and admiration and hurled insults in dialect at the two who had let the sack be carried away: *Cuiasse! Belinùi!*

Cosimo didn't have time to be pleased by his success. An opposing fury broke loose from the ground: they barked, they threw stones, they shouted, "This time you won't escape, you little bastard thieves!" And the tines of a big pitchfork were raised. The thieves in the branches huddled together, pulling up legs and elbows. All that uproar around Cosimo had sounded the alarm to the farmers, who had been on the lookout.

The attack had been prepared in force. Tired of having their fruit stolen just as it ripened, a number of the small landowners and tenant farmers of the valley had banded together; because of the thieves' tactic of descending on an orchard all together, ransacking it, and fleeing to a completely different place, and so on again, a similar tactic had to be employed against them: that is, to lie in wait together on a farm where sooner or later they would come, and catch them in the act. Now the dogs, unleashed, were barking, standing on their hind legs at the foot of the cherry trees, their mouths bristling with teeth, while the pitchforks were hoisted up in the air. Three or four of the thieves jumped to the ground just in time to get their backs pricked by the tines of the pitchforks and the bottoms of their pants bitten by the dogs, and they ran away, screaming and knocking down the rows of vines. So no one dared to descend: the boys sat stunned on the branches, they and Cosimo. Already the farmers were leaning ladders against the cherry trees and were climbing up, preceded by the pointed teeth of the pitchforks.

It took a few minutes for Cosimo to realize that it made no sense for him to be scared because that band of vagabonds was scared, just as that idea that they were so smart and he wasn't made no sense. The fact that they sat there like fools was already proof: what were they waiting for to escape to the surrounding trees? My brother had arrived that way and could leave that way; he pulled the hat down on his head, looked for the branch that had served as a bridge, moved from the last cherry tree in the row to a carob, swinging from the carob dropped to a plum, and so on. The boys, seeing him move through the branches as if he were in the square, realized that they had to follow him immediately, otherwise who knows what they would have suffered before finding their way, and they trailed him silently, on all fours, along that circuitous route. Meanwhile, by climbing into a fig, he crossed over the hedge bordering the field and dropped onto a peach, its branches so delicate that the boys had to pass through it one at a time. The peach served only to let them get hold of the twisted trunk of an olive that was sticking up over a wall; from the olive you could get, with a leap, to an oak that stretched a strong arm over the stream, and so cross over to the trees on the other side.

The men with the pitchforks, who thought that now they had the fruit thieves in hand, saw them escape through the air like birds. They followed, running with the barking dogs, but they had to go around the hedge, then the wall, then in that part of the stream there were no bridges and they wasted time finding a ford, and the scamps had run far away.

The fruit thieves ran like men, feet on the ground. Only my brother remained in the branches. "Where did that acrobat in the gaiters get to?" they asked one another, no longer seeing him in front of them. They looked up: there he was, climbing in the olive trees. "Hey, you, get down, they won't catch us now!" He didn't come down; he jumped through the foliage, from one olive tree he moved to another and disappeared from view amid the dense silvery leaves.

The band of little vagabonds, with the sacks on their heads and poles in hand, now attacked some cherry trees deep in the valley. They worked methodically, stripping branch after branch, when who should they see, perched, legs crossed, at the top of the tallest tree, plucking cherries by the stems with two fingers and putting them in the three-cornered hat that rested on his knees? The boy in the gaiters! "Hey, where do you come from?" they asked, arrogant. But they were startled, because it seemed as if he'd flown there.

My brother was picking out the cherries from the hat one by one and bringing them to his mouth as if they were candied. Then he spit out the pits with a puff of his lips, careful not to stain his waistcoat.

"That ice cream eater," said one, "what's he want from

us? Why's he getting in our way? Why don't he eat the cherries in his own orchard?" But they were a little intimidated, because they had understood that in the trees he was much more skillful than the rest of them.

"Every so often among these ice cream eaters," said another, "a smart one is born by mistake—look at the Sinforosa."

At that mysterious name, Cosimo pricked up his ears and, he didn't know why, blushed.

"The Sinforosa has betrayed us!" said another.

"But she's smart, even if she's an ice cream eater herself, and if she'd still been here blowing the horn this morning they wouldn't have caught us."

"So even an ice cream eater can come with us, of course, if he wants to be one of us!"

(Cosimo understood that "ice cream eater" meant an inhabitant of the villas, or a noble, or anyway a person of high rank.)

"Hey you," one said to him, "plain dealing: if you want to be with us, you make our raids with us and teach us all your moves."

"And let us into your father's orchard!" said another. "Once they shot me with salt!"

Cosimo was listening to them, but as if absorbed in his own thoughts. Then he said, "But tell me, who is the Sinforosa?"

Then all those ragged brats amid the leaves burst out

laughing and laughing, so that some practically tumbled out of the cherry tree, and some fell backward, holding on to the branch by their legs, and some hung by their hands, guffawing and shouting.

With that noise, of course, they had the pursuers on their heels again. In fact the team of men and dogs must have been right on the spot, because a loud barking broke out, and there they all were with the pitchforks. Except this time, with the experience of the immediate setback, they had first occupied the nearby trees, climbing up on ladders, and from there, with pitchforks and rakes, surrounded the thieves. With the men spread out up in the trees, the dogs, on the ground, didn't understand right away which way to head, and scattered, barking, with their muzzles raised. Thus the thieves could quickly jump to the ground and run away, each in a different direction, in the midst of the disoriented dogs, and if some were bitten in the calf or hit by a stick or a stone, most cleared the field safely.

Cosimo remained in the tree. "Get down!" the others shouted at him as they ran to safety. "What are you doing? Are you asleep? Get down while the way is clear!" But with his knees gripping the branch, he unsheathed his sword. From the nearby trees, the farmers stuck out the pitchforks, with poles tied to their tops so they would reach him, and Cosimo, whirling his sword around, kept them off, until they planted a pitchfork right against his chest, pinning him to the trunk.

"Stop!" cried a voice. "It's the young Baron of Piovasco! What are you doing, sir, up there? How in the world did you get mixed up with that rabble?"

Cosimo recognized Giuà della Vasca, a tenant farmer of our father's.

The pitchforks retreated. Many of the team took off their hats. My brother, too, raised the tricorne with two fingers and bowed.

"Hey, you down there, tie up the dogs!" they shouted. "Let him come down! You can come down, sir, but be careful, the tree is tall! Wait, we'll put up a ladder for you! Then I'll take you home!"

"No, thank you, thank you," said my brother. "Don't trouble yourself, I know the way, I know my own way!"

He disappeared behind the trunk and reappeared on another branch, made another circuit of the trunk and reappeared on a higher branch, then disappeared behind the trunk again, and they saw only his feet on a higher branch, because the foliage above him was thick, and the feet jumped, and nothing more could be seen.

"Where did he go?" the men said to one another, and they didn't know where to look, up or down.

"There he is!" He was at the top of another, distant tree, and he disappeared again.

"There he is!" He was at the top of yet another, swayed as if borne by the wind, and jumped.

"He's fallen! No! He's there!" Only the hat and ponytail could be seen above the peak of green.

"What sort of master do you have?" they asked Giuà della Vasca. "Is he a man or a wild animal? Or the devil in person?"

Giuà della Vasca was speechless. He crossed himself.

They could hear Cosimo's song, a kind of syllabic cry.

"O the Sin-fo-ro-saaa . . . !"

5

The Sinforosa: gradually, from the conversations of the little thieves, Cosimo learned many things about this character. They called by that name a girl from the villas who rode around on a white pony and had befriended the ragamuffins; for a while she had protected and also, bossy as she was, commanded them. On the white pony she cantered along roads and paths, and when she saw ripe fruit in unguarded orchards she alerted them, accompanying their assaults on horseback like an officer. Slung around her neck was a hunting horn; while they stripped almond or pear trees, she cruised up and down the slopes on her pony, overlooking the countryside, and when she saw suspicious movements among the landlords or farmers who might discover the thieves and fall on them, she blew the horn. At that sound the rascals jumped out of the trees and ran away; thus, as long as the girl was with them, they'd never been taken by surprise.

What happened next was more difficult to understand: that "betrayal" of Sinforosa's to their detriment seemed partly that she had lured them into her villa to eat fruit and then let the servants beat them; partly it seemed that she had become fond of one of them, a certain Bel-Loré, who was still teased because of it, and of another at the same time, a certain Ugasso, and had set one against the other, and that that beating by the servants had been not because of stolen fruit but because of an expedition by the two jealous favorites, who had finally allied against her; or they spoke also of some cakes she had promised many times and had finally given them, but they were flavored with castor oil, so the boys had had upset stomachs for a week. Some episodes like these or of this type or all these episodes together had caused a rupture between Sinforosa and the gang, and they now spoke of her with bitterness, yet at the same time with regret.

Cosimo listened to these things, all ears, as if the details were being reassembled into an image he knew, and at last he decided to ask, "Which villa does this Sinforosa live in?"

"Come on, you mean you don't know her? You're neighbors! The Sinforosa of the villa d'Ondariva!"

Cosimo certainly didn't need that confirmation to be sure that the friend of the vagabonds was Viola, the girl of the swing. It was—I think—precisely because she had told him she knew all the fruit thieves in the area that he had immediately set out in search of the gang. Also, from that moment on, the mania that propelled him, if still indefinite, became more acute. Now he would have liked to lead the band to ransack the trees of the villa d'Ondariva, now put himself at her service against them, maybe first inciting them to harass her so that he could defend her, now perform feats of daring that she would hear of indirectly; and in the midst of these intentions he followed the band more and more sluggishly, and when they descended from the trees he remained alone, and a veil of melancholy passed over his face, as clouds pass over the sun.

Suddenly he jumped up and swift as a cat climbed up through the branches and hurried over orchards and gardens, humming between his teeth something or other, a nervous humming, almost mute, his eyes staring ahead as if they saw nothing, and he kept his balance by instinct, just like a cat.

We saw him thus obsessed pass through the branches in our garden several times. "He's there! He's there!" we burst out shouting, because still, whatever we tried to do, he was always in our thoughts, and we counted the hours, the days that he was in the trees, and our father said, "He's mad! He's possessed!" And he argued with the Abbé Fauchelafleur: "He has to be exorcised! What are you waiting for, you, I'm talking to you, Abbé, why are you standing there idly! My son has a devil in his body, do you understand, *sacré nom de Dieu!*"

Suddenly the abbé seemed to shake himself, the word *devil* seeming to reawaken in his mind a precise chain of thoughts, and he began a very complicated theological discourse on how the presence of the devil should be correctly understood, and we couldn't tell if he intended to contradict my father or was speaking like that in general; in other words, he did not express an opinion on the fact of whether a relationship between the devil and my brother should be considered possible or be ruled out a priori.

The baron became impatient, the abbé lost the thread, I was already bored. As for our mother, however, maternal anxiety, a fluid sentiment that dominated everything, had been consolidated, as every feeling of hers tended to do after a while, into practical decisions and a search for the right tools, just as the concerns of a general ought to be resolved. She had dug out a long field telescope, on a tripod; she applied her eye to it, and so she spent the hours on the terrace of the villa, constantly adjusting the lens to focus on the boy in the midst of the foliage, even when we would have sworn he was out of range.

"Do you still see him?" our father asked from the garden, as he paced back and forth under the trees; he could never distinguish Cosimo, except when he was right over his head. The *generalessa* nodded, and at the same time signaled us to be quiet, not to disturb her, as if she were following the movements of troops on a rise. It was clear that at times she didn't see him at all, but she had got the idea, who knows why, that he would reemerge in that particular place and not somewhere else, and she kept the telescope trained on it. Every so often she had to admit to herself that she was wrong, and then she removed her eye from the lens and began to examine a survey map that she kept open on her knees, one hand firmly on her mouth in a thoughtful attitude and the other following the hieroglyphics of the map, until she determined the point that her son must have reached and, having calculated the angle, aimed the telescope at some treetop in that sea of leaves, slowly focused the lens, and from the anxious smile that appeared on her lips we understood that she had seen him, that he really was there!

Then she picked up some small colored flags she had next to the stool, and she waved one and then another with decisive, rhythmic movements, like messages in a conventional language. (I felt some vexation, because I wasn't aware that our mother had those flags and knew how to handle them, and certainly it would have been nice if she had taught us to play with the flags, especially earlier, when we were both younger; but our mother never did anything as a game, and there was no hope for it now.)

I have to say that with all her battle equipment, she remained a mother just the same, with her heart in her throat and a handkerchief crumpled in her hand, but one would have said that being the *generalessa* calmed her, or that experiencing that apprehension in the guise of a *generalessa* rather than simply as a mother kept her from being tortured by it, because she was a delicate woman, whose only defense was that military style inherited from the Von Kurtewitzes.

She was there waving one of her flags and looking through the telescope when suddenly her whole face brightened and she laughed. We understood that Cosimo had answered her. How, I don't know—maybe by flourishing his hat or waving the tip of a branch. Certainly from then on our mother changed; her earlier apprehension disappeared, and even if her fate as a mother was different from that of others, with a son so strange, lost to the usual life of the affections, she finally accepted Cosimo's strangeness before the rest of us, as if she were satisfied now by the greetings that from then on he sent her every so often, unpredictably—by that exchange of silent messages.

The curious thing was that our mother had no illusion that Cosimo, having sent her a greeting, had decided to put an end to his flight and return to us. Our father, on the other hand, lived perpetually in that state of mind, and the tiniest bit of news that concerned Cosimo caused him to muse: "Ah yes? Did you see him? Will he come back?" But our mother, the most distant from him, perhaps, seemed the only one who could accept him as he was, maybe because she didn't try to find an explanation.

But let's go back to that day. Behind our mother, even Battista, who almost never appeared, peeped out for a moment and with a gentle expression offered a plate with some kind of milk-soaked bread and held up a spoon: "Cosimo . . . Want some?" She got a slap from her father and went back into the house. Who knows what monstrous mush she had prepared. Our brother had disappeared.

I was yearning to follow him, especially now that I knew he shared in the enterprises of that raggedy gang of boys, and it seemed to me that he had opened the gates of a new kingdom, to look at not with fearful distrust but with comradely enthusiasm. I went back and forth between the terrace and a high-up attic from which I could roam over the treetops, and from there, more by sound than by sight, I followed the band's explosive bursts through the gardens, I saw the tips of the cherry trees waving, and every so often a hand sticking out that touched and tore off, a head uncombed or hooded in a sack, and among the voices I heard Cosimo's, too, and I wondered, "How did he get down there? Just a short time ago he was here in the park! Is he already faster than a squirrel?"

They were in the red plum trees above the Big Pond, I remember, when they heard the horn. I heard it, too, but paid no attention, not knowing what it was. But they! My brother told me that they fell silent, and in their surprise at hearing the horn again they seemed not to remember that it was a signal of alarm but only wondered if they had heard correctly, if it was again Sinforosa who was riding the roads on her pony to warn them of dangers. Suddenly they rushed out of the orchard, but they didn't flee to flee, they fled to find her, to join her.

Only Cosimo stayed, his face as red as a flame. But as soon as he saw the boys running and realized that they were going to her, he began to leap through the branches, at risk of breaking his neck with every step.

Viola was at a bend in a road that sloped uphill, not moving, one hand holding the reins and resting on the horse's mane, the other brandishing a whip. She looked the boys up and down and brought the tip of the whip to her mouth and bit it. Her dress was blue; the horn was gilded, hanging on a chain around her neck. The boys had stopped all together and they, too, were biting, plums or fingers, or scars they had on their hands or arms, or the edges of the sacks. And gradually, with their biting mouths, as if compelled to vanquish an uneasiness, not driven by a real feeling, and if anything eager to be contradicted, they began to speak, almost without voice, sounding in cadence as if they were trying to sing: "What have you . . . come to do . . . Sinforosa . . . now you're back . . . you're not . . . our friend anymore . . . ah, ah, ah . . . ah, coward . . ."

A rustling in the branches, and lo and behold, amid the leaves of a tall fig Cosimo, panting, stuck out his head. She, looking up, with that whip in her mouth, saw him and them, all flattened in the same gaze. Cosimo didn't resist; with his tongue still out he blurted, "You know, since then I've never come down from the trees!"

Undertakings based on an inner tenacity have to be mute and obscure; one has only to declare or glory in them and it all appears silly, without meaning, even petty. So as soon as my brother uttered those words he wished never to have said them; nothing mattered to him anymore, and he even felt the wish to get down and put an end to it. All the more when Viola slowly took the whip out of her mouth and said, in a kindly tone, "Oh yes? Very clever!"

A roar of laughter began rising from the mouths of those lice-ridden boys, even before they opened and burst into side-splitting howls, and Cosimo up in the fig tree had such a paroxysm of rage that the fig's traitorous wood couldn't bear up, and a branch broke under his feet. Cosimo dropped like a stone.

He fell with arms wide; he couldn't hold on. It was the

only time, to tell the truth, during his sojourn in the trees of this land that he didn't have the will or the instinct to keep his grip. Except that the tip of his coattail caught on a low branch: Cosimo, four handbreadths from the ground, found himself hanging in the air, head down.

The blood rushed to his head as if driven by the same force as the blush of shame. And his first thought as, upside down, he opened his eyes wide and saw the howling boys heads up, who were now seized by a general desire to turn somersaults, so that one by one they all reappeared right side up, as if holding on to an earth inverted over an abyss, and the fair-haired girl flying on the rearing horse—his thought was only that this was the first time he had spoken about being in the trees and it would also be the last.

With one of his darts he grabbed hold of the branch and pulled himself back up so that he straddled it. Viola, having calmed the horse, now seemed to have paid no attention to anything that had happened. Cosimo immediately forgot his confusion. The girl brought the horn to her lips and raised the dark note of alarm. At that sound the rascals (in whose bodies—Cosimo commented later—Viola's presence instilled a dazed excitement, like that of rabbits in the moonlight) took flight. They fled, as if instinctively, even though they knew she had done it in fun, and they, too, in fun, imitating the sound of the horn, ran down the hill behind her, galloping on the short-legged pony.

And they went down so blindly, at breakneck speed, that

sometimes they couldn't find her in front of them. She had swerved, raced off the road, and left them there. To go where? She galloped through the olive groves that descended to a smooth slope of fields and, seeking the tree in which Cosimo was just then scrambling, galloped around him and took off again. Then here she was again, at the foot of another olive tree, while my brother was hanging among the leaves. And so on, following routes as twisted as the branches of the olives, they descended together through the valley.

When the thieves became aware of the intrigue of those two between branch and saddle, they began to whistle all together, a malicious, derisive whistle. And, raising high this whistle, they went down toward Porta Capperi.

The girl and my brother were alone, chasing each other in the olive grove, but with disappointment Cosimo noticed that now that the gang was gone, Viola's joy in the game was fading, as if she were ready to give in to boredom. And he began to suspect that she had done it all just to make the others angry, but at the same time he also hoped that now she was doing it purposely to make him angry; what was certain was that she always needed to make someone angry to make herself more valuable. (All these feelings were but dimly perceived by the boy Cosimo; in reality he was climbing up and down the rough bark without understanding anything, like a fool, I imagine.)

As she rounds a hillock a tiny violent hail of pebbles rises. The girl shelters her head behind the horse's neck and escapes; my brother, clearly exposed to view in the crook of a branch, remains under fire. But the pebbles reach him too obliquely to do harm, except for a few that hit his forehead or ears. Those wild boys whistle and laugh, they cry, "Sin-fo-ro-sa is a gross one," and run away.

Now the ragamuffins have reached Porta Capperi, where green cascades of capers decorate the walls. From the hovels roundabout, mothers are shouting. But these are kids whose mothers are not shouting at them to come home, they're shouting because they've come home—why do they return for dinner instead of looking for food elsewhere? Around Porta Capperi, the poorest people of Ombrosa were crowded into wooden huts and sheds, broken-down coaches, tents, so poor that they were kept outside the city gates and far from the countryside, people who had swarmed out of distant lands and cities, driven by famine and by the poverty that was increasing in every state. It was sunset, and disheveled women with infants at their breast were fanning smoky stoves, beggars stretched out in the open air unbandaging their wounds, and others played dice, uttering hoarse cries. The boys of the fruit gang now mingled with the smoke of food frying, and with those quarrels; they were slapped back-handed by their mothers; they scuffled, rolling in the dust. And already their rags had taken on the color of all the other rags, and their birdlike joy, stuck in that human coagulation, weakened into a heavy dullness. So that at the appearance of the fair-haired girl galloping and Cosimo in the trees, they scarcely raised timid eyes; they retreated, sought to vanish in the dust and smoke from the stoves, as if between them a wall had suddenly arisen.

For those two, all this was a moment, a roll of the eyes. Now Viola had left behind the smoke from the hovels that mingled with the evening shadows and the cries of women and children and was racing through the pines along the beach.

There was the sea. It could be heard rolling over the rocks. The air was dark. A more jangly roll: it was the pony, striking sparks against the pebbles as it galloped. From a low twisted pine, my brother watched the clear shadow of the fair-haired girl crossing the beach. A cresting wave rose from the black sea, grew higher as it turned over, and now advanced all white and broke, and the shadow of the horse carrying the girl had grazed it at full speed, and a white spray of salt water bathed Cosimo's face where he sat in the pine tree.

6

Cosimo's first days in the trees had no goals or plans but were dominated only by the desire to know and possess that kingdom of his. He would have liked to explore it immediately to its farthest boundaries, study all the possibilities it offered, discover it tree by tree and branch by branch. I say "he would have liked," but in fact we saw him constantly turning up again above our heads, with that busy and very rapid quality of wild animals, who, though they are seen crouching motionless, always seem to be on the point of taking off.

Why did he return to our park? To see him vaulting from a plane tree to an oak within the range of our mother's telescope, one would have said that the force that drove him, his dominant passion, was still that fight with us, the wish to make us worry or rage. (I say "we" because I still couldn't understand what he thought of me: when he needed something it seemed that his alliance with me could never be doubted; at other times he crossed over my head as if he didn't even see me.)

But he was only passing through here. It was the magnolia

wall that drew him, it was there that we saw him disappear at all hours, even when the fair-haired girl had certainly not yet risen or when the host of governesses or aunts had surely made her retire. In the garden of the D'Ondarivas branches extended like the trunks of extraordinary animals, and from the ground rose star-shaped serrated leaves with the green skin of reptiles, and delicate yellow bamboos swayed with the sound of paper. Cosimo, in his yearning to enjoy fully that different green and the different light that shone through it, and the different silence, hung head down from the highest tree, and the upside-down garden became a forest, a forest not of the earth, a new world.

Then Viola appeared. Cosimo saw her suddenly on the swing that flew off, or in the saddle on the pony, or he heard the dark note of the hunting horn sounding from the end of the garden.

The Marquises d'Ondariva had given no thought to the child's excursions. As long as she was on foot, she had all the aunts following; as soon as she got in the saddle she was free as the air, because the aunts didn't ride and couldn't see where she went. And then her friendship with those vagabonds was an idea too inconceivable to surface in their minds. But they were immediately aware of that little baron who was sneaking around up in the trees, and were on the alert, although with an air of superiority and contempt.

For our father, on the other hand, bitterness at Cosimo's disobedience blended with his aversion for the D'Ondarivas, as if he wished to blame them, as if they were the ones who drew his son into their garden, and hosted him, and encouraged him in that rebellious game. All of a sudden he decided to initiate a hunt to capture Cosimo, and not on our lands but only while he was in the garden of the D'Ondarivas. As if to underline that aggressive intention toward our neighbors, he wouldn't lead the hunt, presenting himself in person at the D'Ondarivas' and asking them to give back his son—which, however unjustified, would have been a relationship on a dignified level, between noblemen—but sent a troop of servants under the command of Cavalier Avvocato Enea Silvio Carrega.

These servants came to the gates of the D'Ondarivas armed with ladders and ropes. The *cavalier avvocato,* in his long robe and fez, amid many apologies, asked, mumbling, if they would let them enter. At first the D'Ondarivas' servants thought they had come to prune some of our trees that were sticking out into theirs; then, at the half words that the *cavaliere* was offering—"We capt . . . we capt . . ."—they looked up into the branches, made short sideways runs, and asked, "But what has escaped—a parrot?"

"The son, the firstborn, the scion," said the *cavalier avvocato* hurriedly, and, having had a ladder set up against a horse chestnut, began to climb himself. Cosimo could be seen sitting among the branches, swinging his legs as if nothing were happening. Viola, also as if nothing were happening, went up and down the paths playing with a hoop. The servants handed the *cavalier avvocato* some ropes that were to be maneuvered in some way or other to capture my brother. But, before the *cavaliere* was halfway up the ladder, Cosimo was already at the top of another tree. The *cavaliere* had the ladder moved, and so on, four or five times. Every time, he ruined a flower bed, and Cosimo with two leaps had moved on to the next tree. Viola was suddenly surrounded by aunts and vice aunts, led into the house, and locked in so that she would not witness that commotion. Cosimo broke off a branch and, brandishing it with both hands, cleaved the air, making it whistle.

"But can't you go into your own spacious park to continue this hunt, dear sirs?" said the Marquis d'Ondariva, appearing solemnly on the steps of the villa in dressing gown and skullcap, which made him oddly similar to the *cavalier avvocato.* "I mean you, the entire Piovasco di Rondò family!" And he made a broad circular gesture that embraced the baron in the tree, the natural uncle, the servants, and, beyond the wall, all that we had under the sun.

At that point Enea Silvio Carrega changed his tone. He trotted up to the marquis and, mumbling, as if nothing were going on, began to talk to him about the water games in the pool in front of them and how he had had the idea of a much higher and more dramatic jet, which could also be used, by changing a washer, to water the lawns. This was new evidence of how unpredictable and untrustworthy the character of our natural uncle was: he had been sent there by the baron with a precise duty, and with a firm polemical intention regarding the neighbors; what did it have to do with starting a friendly chat with the marquis, as if he wished to ingratiate himself? Especially since the *cavalier avvocato* demonstrated these qualities as a conversationalist only when it was convenient for him and just when one was trusting in his bashful nature. And the thing was that the marquis listened to him and asked questions and led him around to examine all the pools and the fountains, the two of them dressed alike, in those long robes, nearly the same height, so that they could be mistaken one for the other, and behind them came the great troop of our servants and theirs, some with ladders on their backs, who no longer knew what to do.

Meanwhile Cosimo jumped undisturbed in the trees near the windows of the villa, trying to discover behind the curtains the room where they had locked Viola. He found her, finally, and threw a berry against the window.

The window opened; the face of the fair-haired girl appeared, and she said, "It's your fault I'm shut up here," closed it again, drew the curtain.

Cosimo was suddenly desperate.

When my brother was in the grip of his furies, there was really reason to be anxious. We saw him run (if the word *run* makes sense removed from the surface of the earth and transported to a world of irregular supports at different heights, with a void in between), and at any moment it seemed that he might miss his footing and fall. It never happened. He leaped, he moved rapidly along a slanting branch, hung from it, and suddenly rose to a higher branch, and with four or five of these precarious zigzags had disappeared.

Where did he go? That time he ran and ran, from the oaks to the olives to the beeches, and reached the woods. He stopped, out of breath. A meadow spread out beneath him. A low wind made a wave through the dense tufts of grass, in changing shades of green. A fine down from the spheres of those flowers called dandelions was flying around. In the middle there was an isolated pine, unreachable, with oblong pinecones. Tree creepers, swift speckled brown birds, perched on the thick-needled branches, in sideways positions, some upside down, tail up and beak below, and pecked at caterpillars and pine nuts.

That need to enter an element difficult to possess which had driven my brother to make his the ways of the trees was now working in him again, unsatisfied, and communicated to him the desire for a more detailed penetration, a relationship that would bind him to every leaf and scale and feather and flutter. It was the love that man the hunter has for what is alive but doesn't know how to express except by aiming the gun; Cosimo couldn't yet recognize it and tried to let it out by intensifying his exploration.

The wood was thick, impassable. Cosimo had to make a path with strokes of the sword, and little by little he forgot his rage, completely in the grip of the problems that he was gradually confronting and of a fear (which he didn't want to recognize but was there) of getting too far away from familiar places. So as he made his way through the deep forest, he came to a point where he saw two staring yellow eyes amid the leaves, right in front of him. Cosimo stuck out his sword, pushing aside a bough and letting it return slowly to its place. He drew a sigh of relief, he laughed at the fear he had felt; he had seen whose yellow eyes they were—they were a cat's.

The image of the cat, barely glimpsed by shifting the branch, remained clear in his mind, and after a moment Cosimo was again trembling with fear. Because that cat, in every way just like a cat, was a terrible, frightening cat, the mere sight of which might cause you to scream. Hard to say what was so frightening: it was a kind of tabby, larger than all tabbies, but that meant nothing. What was terrible was its whiskers, as straight as a hedgehog's spines; its breath, which could be seen almost better than heard, exhaled from a double row of teeth as sharp as hooks; its ears, which, more than pointed, were two flames of tension, provided with a falsely soft down; its fur, which, standing straight up and swelling around the neck, contracted into a yellow collar, and whose stripes, starting from there, quivered over the sides as if caressing themselves; its tail, unmoving, in a position so unnatural as to seem unsustainable. To all this, which Cosimo had seen in an instant behind the branch that he immediately let return to its normal place, was added what he hadn't had time to see but imagined: the extravagant tuft of fur around the paws that masked the stabbing power of the nails, ready to be launched against him; and what he still saw: the yellow irises that stared at him between the leaves, rolling around the black pupil; and what he heard: the increasingly deep and intense murmur. From all this he understood that he was facing the fiercest wild cat in the forest.

All the chirping and fluttering had gone silent. The wild cat leaped, but not at the boy—it was an almost vertical leap that astonished Cosimo more than it frightened him. The fear came afterward, when he saw the feline on a branch just above his head. It was there, contracted; he saw the belly with its long, almost white fur, the paws tensed with the nails in the wood, while it arched its back and went *fff* . . . and certainly was preparing to pounce. Cosimo, with a perfect yet not even thought-out movement, got to a lower branch. *Fff* . . . *fff* . . . went the wild cat, and at each of those *fff* sounds it made a leap, one here, one there, and landed on the branch above Cosimo. My brother repeated his move but found himself straddling the lowest branch of that beech. The jump to the ground below was fairly far, but not so far that it wasn't preferable to jump down rather than wait for what the beast would do, as soon as it had stopped emitting that torturous sound somewhere between a breath and a meow.

Cosimo raised one leg, as if he were about to jump down, but as two instincts clashed—the natural one of getting to safety and the obstinate one of not descending, at the cost of his life—at the same time he tightened his thighs and knees around the branch. To the cat it seemed that this was the moment to attack, while the boy was hesitating; it flew at him in a jumbled mass of fur, bristling claws, and breath; Cosimo didn't know what else to do except close his eyes and hold out his sword, a foolish move that the cat easily avoided, and it landed on his head, sure of carrying him down in its claws. One claw got Cosimo on the cheek, but instead of falling, locked as he was to the branch with his knees, he lay face up on the branch. The complete opposite of what the cat expected, and it found itself catapulted sideways and falling. It wanted to stop itself, plant its claws in the branch, and in that darting move it spun around in the air: a second, all Cosimo needed, in a sudden victorious assault, to thrust the sword into the stomach of the meowing animal and run him through.

He was safe, bloodstained, with the wild beast impaled on the sword as if on a spit and one cheek torn by a triple claw from below the eye to the chin. He was shouting with pain and victory and didn't understand a thing; he held tight to the branch, to the sword, to the corpse of the cat, in the desperate moment of he who has won for the first time and now knows what torture it is to win, and knows that he is now committed to continue the life he has chosen and will not be granted the escape of failure.

So I saw him arriving through the trees, all bloody down to his waistcoat, his ponytail undone under the shapeless tricorne, and holding by the tail that dead wild cat that now seemed merely like a cat.

I ran to the *generalessa* on the terrace. "Lady Mother," I cried, "he's wounded!"

"*Was?* Wounded how?" And she was already pointing the telescope.

"Wounded like a wound!" I said, and the *generalessa* seemed to find my definition pertinent, because following him with the telescope as he jumped more quickly than ever, she said, *"Das stimmt."*

She immediately got busy preparing gauze and bandages and salves as if she were to resupply the casualty station of a battalion, and gave everything to me to take up to him; the hope that, having to be treated, he might decide to return home didn't even surface. I ran into the park with the package of bandages and prepared to wait for him on the last mulberry near the wall of the D'Ondarivas, because he had already vanished into the magnolia.

He appeared triumphant in the garden of the D'Ondarivas with the dead beast in his hand. And what did he see in front of the villa? A carriage ready to depart, with servants loading bags onto the roof, and, in the midst of a swarm of dark and very severe governesses and aunts, Viola dressed for traveling and embracing the marquis and the marquise.

"Viola!" he cried, and held up the cat by the tail. "Where are you going?"

All the people around the carriage looked into the branches and, seeing him, scratched, bleeding, with that look of a madman, the dead beast in his hand, shivered with horror. *"De nouveau ici! Et arrangé de quelle façon!"* and as if seized by a fury the aunts pushed the child toward the carriage.

Viola turned, with her nose up, and with an expression of contempt, a bored and condescending disdain toward her relatives, which might also, however, be directed at Cosimo, uttered (certainly answering his question), "They're sending me to school," and turned to get into the carriage. She hadn't deigned to look at him, either at him or at his prey.

She had already closed the window, the coachman was on the box, and Cosimo, who still couldn't admit that departure, tried to attract her attention, to make her understand that he dedicated that gory victory to her, but he didn't know how to explain except to shout at her, "I vanquished a cat!"

The whip cracked, the carriage left amid the waving of the aunts' handkerchiefs, and from the window was heard a "Bravo!" from Viola, whether of enthusiasm or of derision one couldn't have said.

That was their farewell. And in Cosimo the tension, the pain of the scratches, the disappointment of not winning glory from his deed, the despair of that sudden separation —all became tangled and erupted in a fierce lament, of cries and screams and torn branches.

"Hors d'ici! Hors d'ici! Polisson sauvage! Hors de notre jardin!" the aunts railed at him, and all the servants of the D'Ondarivas rushed with long poles or stones to chase him out.

Cosimo, sobbing and shouting, hurled the dead cat in the face of those who were below him. The servants grabbed the beast by the tail and threw it on a manure heap.

When I found out that our neighbor had gone, I hoped for a while that Cosimo would come down. I don't know why; I connected with her, or partly with her, my brother's decision to stay in the trees.

Instead, he didn't even talk about it. I climbed up to take him bandages, and he dressed the scratches on his face and arms himself. Then he wanted a fishing line with a hook. Sinking it from the height of an olive tree that extended over the D'Ondarivas' manure heap, he picked up the dead cat. He skinned it, tanned the hide as well as he could, and made a hat. It was the first of the fur hats that we saw him wear all his life.

7

The last attempt to capture Cosimo was made by our sister Battista. On her own initiative, naturally, and undertaken without consulting anyone, in secret, the way she did everything. She went out at night with a cauldron of birdlime and a ladder, and she smeared a carob tree with the birdlime from top to bottom. It was a tree that Cosimo used to sit on every morning.

In the morning there were goldfinches stuck to the carob, beating their wings, wrens enveloped in the paste, nocturnal butterflies, leaves carried by the wind, the tail of a squirrel, and even a piece torn off Cosimo's tailcoat. Who knows if he had sat on a branch and then was able to free himself, or if instead—more likely, since I hadn't seen him wearing the tailcoat for a while—he stuck that shred there purposely to mock us. Anyway, the tree remained foully smeared with birdlime and then it dried.

We began to be convinced that Cosimo wouldn't return, even our father. Ever since my brother had begun leaping from tree to tree throughout the land of Ombrosa, the baron hadn't dared to go out in public, because he was afraid that his ducal dignity had been compromised. His face became increasingly pale and hollowed out, and I don't know how much of it was paternal anxiety and how much concern for the dynastic consequences; but the two things were now one, because Cosimo was his firstborn, the heir to the title, and if it is difficult to admit that a baron jumps through the branches like a ptarmigan, even less readily can one admit that a duke does, even a boy, and the disputed title would certainly not have found a supporting corroboration in the behavior of the heir.

Vain worries, of course, because the Ombrosotti laughed at our father's notions, and the nobles who had villas around there considered him mad. The custom of living in villas in pleasant places rather than in feudal castles was now widespread among the nobles, and as a result they tended to live as private citizens, to avoid any annoyances. Who was going to care anymore about the ancient Duchy of Ombrosa? The beauty of Ombrosa was that it was the home of all and of no one: it was bound by certain obligations to the Marquises d'Ondariva, who owned most of the lands, but had long been a free municipality, paying dues to the Republic of Genoa. We could be tranquil, between the lands that we had inherited and others that we had bought for nothing from the municipality at a moment when it was in debt. What more could one ask? There was a small society of nobles, with villas and parks and gardens extending to the sea; they all lived happily, visiting and hunting, life was cheap, they had certain of the advantages of those who are at court but without the duties, the obligations, and the expenses of having a royal family to look after, or a capital, or a politics. Our father instead had no taste for those things; he felt himself a dispossessed sovereign, and had ended by breaking off all relations with the nobles of the neighborhood (our mother, a foreigner, cannot be said ever to have had any); this also had its advantages, because by not seeing anyone we were spared many expenses and could conceal the poverty of our finances.

Not to say that we had better relations with the people of Ombrosa; you know how the Ombrosotti are, a rather mean sort, who tend to their shops; at that time lemons were starting to sell well, as the habit of sugared lemonades became widespread among the wealthy classes, and the Ombrosotti had planted lemon groves everywhere and refurbished the port, which had been ruined long ago by marauding pirates. Midway between the Republic of Genoa, possessions of the King of Sardinia, the kingdom of France, and episcopal lands, they did business with everyone and didn't give a damn about anyone, except for those dues that they paid to Genoa and that made them sweat every tax day, the motivation every year for riots against the tax collectors of the republic.

Whenever these tax riots broke out, the Baron di Rondò believed that he was on the point of being offered the ducal crown. Then he appeared in the square and presented himself to the Ombrosotti as a protector, but every time he had to rush to escape under a hail of rotten lemons. Then he said that a plot had been hatched against him: by the Jesuits, as usual. Because he had got it into his head that between him and the Jesuits there was a mortal war, and the Society thought only of plotting against him. In fact there had been some differences, because of a garden whose ownership was disputed by our family and the Society of Jesus; a quarrel had arisen, and the baron, being at the time in good favor with the bishop, had managed to have the provincial father removed from the territory of the diocese. Ever since, our father had been sure that the Society would send its agents to assassinate his life and his rights. For his part, he tried to put together a militia of the faithful to liberate the bishop, who in his opinion had fallen prisoner to the Jesuits; he gave shelter and protection to those who claimed that they were persecuted by the Jesuits, and thus he had chosen as our spiritual father that half Jansenist with his head in the clouds.

There was only one person our father trusted, and that was the *cavalier avvocato.* The baron had a weakness for his natural brother, as if for a single unfortunate son; and now I can't say whether we realized it, but surely, in the way we thought of Carrega, there must have been some jealousy that our father cared more about that fifty-year-old brother than about us boys. Besides, we weren't alone in looking at him indignantly: the *generalessa* and Battista pretended respect, but they couldn't stand him; under that submissive appearance he couldn't care less about anyone or anything, and maybe he hated all of us, even the baron, to whom he owed so much. The *cavalier avvocato* didn't say a lot; at times one might have said that he was a deaf-mute, or didn't understand the language. Who knows how he had succeeded in becoming a lawyer earlier, and if he was already confused at that time, before the Turks. Maybe he was even a person of intelligence, if he had learned from the Turks all those hydraulic calculations, the only thing he was now capable of applying himself to, and for which my father praised him exaggeratedly. I was never clear about his past, neither who his mother was nor what his relations with our grandfather had been in his youth (certainly he, too, must have been fond of him, since he had had him study to be a lawyer and had given him the title of *cavaliere*), nor how he ended up in Turkey. We didn't even know if it was really Turkey where he had lived so long, or in some barbaric state—Tunisia, Algeria, but anyway in a Muslim country, and it was said that he had become a Muslim himself. So many stories were told about him: that he had held important positions—grand dignitary of the sultan, hydraulic engineer to the diwan, or others like that—and then a palace conspiracy or jealousy between women or a gambling debt had plunged him into disgrace and he had been sold as a slave. We knew that he was found in chains, rowing among the slaves in an Ottoman galley that had been captured by the Venetians, who freed him. In Venice he lived practically as a beggar, until I don't know what else happened, a quarrel (with whom a man so shy could quarrel, heaven knows), and again he ended up in shackles. Our father ransomed him, through the good offices of the Republic of Genoa, and he returned among us, a little bald man with a black beard, bewildered, half mute (I was a child, but the scene of that evening impressed itself on me), bundled up in borrowed clothes that were too big. Our father imposed him on us as a person of authority, named him administrator, set aside for him a study that filled up with papers that were always in disorder. The *cavalier avvocato* wore a long robe and a fezlike skullcap, as many noblemen and members of the bourgeoisie were accustomed to do in their studies, except that, to tell the truth, he was almost never in his study, and he began to be seen going around dressed like that outside, in the countryside. In the end he appeared at table in those Turkish outfits, and the oddest thing was that our father, so attentive to the rules, appeared to tolerate it.

In spite of his administrative tasks, the *cavalier avvocato* almost never exchanged a word with stewards or tenant farmers or agents, given his timid character and difficulty speaking; and all the practical duties—giving orders, supervising people—fell in effect to our father. Enea Silvio Carrega kept the account books, and I don't know if our affairs went so badly because of the way he kept the accounts or if his accounts were so bad because of the way in which our affairs went. And then he made calculations and drawings for irrigation systems, and filled a big blackboard with drawings and figures and words in Turkish writing. Every so often our father shut himself in his study with him for hours (they were the *cavalier avvocato*'s longest stays there), and after a while through the closed door came the angry voice of the baron, the stormy accents of an altercation, but the voice of the *cavaliere* was almost never heard. Then the door opened; the *cavalier avvocato* came out, with his rapid little steps in the skirts of his robe, the fez straight on his head, and went through a French window and off into the park and the countryside. "Enea Silvio! Enea Silvio!" our father cried, running after him, but his half-brother was already in the middle of the vineyard or the lemon groves, and only the red fez could be seen advancing stubbornly through the leaves. Our father followed, calling him; after a while we saw them return, the baron still discussing, arms wide, and the *cavaliere* small beside him, hunched, his fists clenched in the pockets of the robe.

8

In those days Cosimo often challenged the people on the ground, challenges of marksmanship, of dexterity, partly to test his own capabilities, what he could do from up in the treetops. He challenged the urchins to quoits. They were in the area near Porta Capperi, amid the hovels of the poor and the vagabonds. From a bare, half-dead holm oak Cosimo was playing quoits when he saw a tall, slightly bent man on horseback approaching, wrapped in a black cloak. He recognized his father. The rabble dispersed; from the doorways of the hovels the women stood watching.

Baron Arminio rode up under the tree. It was a red sunset. Cosimo was in the bare branches. They looked each other in the face. It was the first time since the lunch of snails that they had been like that, face-to-face. Many days had passed, things had changed; both knew that the snails had nothing to do with it anymore, nor did the obedience of sons and the authority of fathers—that of so many logical and sensible things that could be said, all would have been out of place, and yet they had to say something.

"You're making a fine spectacle of yourself!" the father began, bitterly. "Very worthy of a gentleman!" (He had used the more formal *you,* as he did with more serious reproaches, but now that use had a sense of distance, of detachment.)

"A gentleman, Father, sir, is such in the trees as on the ground," Cosimo answered, and immediately added, "if he behaves correctly."

"A fine sentiment," the baron admitted gravely, "although a short while ago you were stealing plums from a tenant farmer."

It was true. My brother was caught out. What should he answer? He smiled, but not proudly or cynically: it was a timid smile, and he blushed.

The father smiled, too, a sad smile, and for some reason he, too, blushed. "Now you're in league with the worst bastards and beggars," he said then.

"No, Father, sir, I'm for myself, and each for himself," said Cosimo firmly.

"I invite you to come down to earth," said the baron in a peaceful, almost exhausted voice, "and resume the duties of your station."

"I don't intend to obey you, Father, sir," said Cosimo. "I'm sorry about it."

They were both uneasy, bored. Each knew what the other would say. "But your studies? And your duties as a Christian?" said the father. "You mean to grow up like a savage of the Americas?"

Cosimo was silent. They were thoughts that he hadn't yet put to himself and had no desire to. Then he said, "Just because I'm a few yards higher up, you think good teachings won't reach me?"

This, too, was a clever answer, but it was already a sort of diminishing of the scope of his gesture: a sign of weakness, therefore.

The father noticed it and pressed harder. "Rebellion is not measured in yards," he said. "Even when it seems just a few handbreadths, a journey may have no return."

Now, my brother could have given some other lofty response, maybe a Latin maxim—none come to mind now, but at the time we knew a lot by heart. Instead he had grown bored sitting there acting serious; he stuck out his tongue and cried, "But from the trees I can pee farther!"—a phrase without much meaning but which cut off the matter cleanly.

A shout arose from the rascals at Porta Capperi, as if they had heard that utterance. The Baron di Rondò's horse shied; the baron held the reins tight and wrapped himself in the cloak, as if ready to go. But he turned, pulled one arm out from under his cloak, and, pointing to the sky, which was rapidly filling with black clouds, exclaimed, "Watch out, son, there's One who can pee on all of us!" And he spurred his horse away.

The rain, long awaited in the countryside, began to fall in big scattered drops. From the hovels a stampede of boys hooded in sacks chanted, *"Ciêuve! Ciêuve! L'alga va pe êuve!"*

Cosimo disappeared, grabbing hold of the dripping leaves, which, when he touched them, showered water down on his head.

As soon as I realized that it was raining, I got worried about him. I imagined him soaking wet, holding tight to a trunk and unable to escape the slanting downpour. And I already knew that a storm would not be enough to make him come back. I ran to our mother. "It's raining—what will Cosimo do, Lady Mother?"

The *generalessa* parted the curtains and watched the rain. She was calm. "The most serious inconvenience of rain is muddy ground. Up there he's safe from it."

"But will the trees be enough to shelter him?"

"He'll withdraw into his tents."

"Which ones, Lady Mother?"

"He'll have seen to getting them ready in time."

"But don't you think it would be good to find him and give him an umbrella?"

As if the word *umbrella* had suddenly torn her away from her camp observation post and hurled her back into full maternal concern, the *generalessa* began to say, *"Ja, ganz gewiss!* And a bottle of apple syrup, warmed, wrapped in a wool sock! And an oilcloth to spread over the wood, so the dampness doesn't seep through . . . Where could he be now, poor thing . . . Let's hope you can find him . . ."

I went out into the rain loaded with packages, under an

enormous green umbrella, with another, closed, under my arm, to give to Cosimo.

I gave our whistle, but the only answer was the endless pelting of rain on the trees. It was dark; outside the garden I didn't know where to go. I walked randomly over slippery stones, soft grass, puddles, and whistled, and to make the whistle go higher I tilted the umbrella backward and the water whipped my face and washed the whistle from my lips. I wanted to go to some lands belonging to the municipality where there were a lot of tall trees, near where I thought he might have made himself a shelter, but in that darkness I got lost, and I stood there holding umbrellas and packages tight in my arms, with only the bottle of syrup wrapped in the woolen sock to warm me a little.

Then, suddenly, high up in the darkness I saw a light in the trees which couldn't be moon or stars. At my whistle I thought I heard his, in response.

"Cosimooo!"

"Biagiooo!" A voice in the rain, up at the top.

"Where are you?"

"Here! I'll come meet you, but hurry, I'm getting wet!"

We found each other. Wrapped in a blanket, he descended to the low fork of a willow to show me how to get up, by means of a complicated tangle of branches, into the beech with the tall trunk, from which that light came. I immediately gave him the umbrella and some of the packages, and we tried to climb with the umbrellas open, but it was impossible, and we got wet just the same. Finally I got to where he was leading me; I saw nothing, except a glow as if from between the flaps of a tent.

Cosimo raised one of those flaps and let me pass. In the glow of a lantern I found that I was in a kind of room, covered and closed on every side by curtains and carpets, traversed by the trunk of the beech, with a floor of boards, all resting on the large boughs. At first it seemed to me a palace, but I soon realized how unstable it was, because with two of us in there the equilibrium was dubious, and Cosimo immediately had to get busy repairing leaks and sagging places. He put out the two umbrellas I'd brought, opened, to cover two holes in the roof; but the water dripped from many other points, and we were both soaked, and as cold as if we were outside. But there was such a big pile of blankets that we could bury ourselves under them, leaving only our heads out. The lantern gave an uncertain, flickering light, and the leaves and branches projected intricate shadows on the roof and walls of that strange construction. Cosimo gulped down apple syrup, going "Ugh! Ugh!"

"It's a wonderful house," I said.

"Oh, it's still temporary," Cosimo was quick to respond. "I have to study it better."

"Did you build it all by yourself?"

"Of course! With who else? It's secret."

"Will I be able to come here?"

"No, you'd show someone else the way."

"Daddy said he won't look for you anymore."

"It has to be secret just the same."

"Because of those boys who steal? Aren't they your friends?"

"Sometimes yes, sometimes no."

"And the girl on the pony?"

"What's that to you?"

"I meant if she's your friend, if you play together."

"Sometimes yes and sometimes no."

"Why sometimes no?"

"Because I don't want to or she doesn't want to."

"And up here, her, would you let her come up here?"

Cosimo, his face dark, tried to spread a mat over a branch. "If she came here I'd let her come up," he said gravely.

"She doesn't want to?"

Cosimo lay down. "She left."

"Tell me," I said, in a whisper, "is she your girlfriend?"

"No," my brother answered, and shut himself up in a long silence.

The next day the weather was fine, and it was decided that Cosimo would resume lessons with the Abbé Fauchelafleur. It wasn't said how. A little abruptly, the baron simply invited the abbé ("Instead of staying here watching the flies, Abbé . . .") to go and find my brother, wherever he was, and have him translate some of his Virgil. Then he was afraid of having embarrassed the abbé and tried to make his task easier; he said to me, "Go tell your brother to be in the garden in half an hour for his Latin lesson." He said it in the most natural tone he could, the tone that he maintained from then on: with Cosimo in the trees everything was to continue as before.

So there was the lesson. My brother astride a branch of the elm, legs dangling, and the abbé below, sitting on a stool on the grass, repeating hexameters in chorus. I was playing nearby and for a while lost sight of them; when I returned, the abbé, too, was in the tree; with his long, thin, black-stockinged legs he tried to hoist himself onto a fork, and Cosimo helped him, holding him by the elbow. They found a comfortable position for the old man, and together they worked on a difficult passage, bent over the book. My brother seemed to be giving proof of great diligence.

Then I don't know how it happened, how the student escaped, maybe because the abbé was distracted up there and remained stupefied, looking into the void as usual—the fact is that only the black figure of the old priest was there, nesting in the branches, with the book on his knees, and he was watching the flight of a white butterfly, following it openmouthed. When the butterfly disappeared, the abbé realized that he was up in the tree and was seized by fear. He hugged the trunk and began crying, *"Au secours! Au secours!"* until people came with a ladder and gradually he calmed down and descended.

9

In other words Cosimo, despite his famous flight, lived near us almost as he had before. He was a solitary but didn't shun the people. In fact, it might be said that he cared only for the people. He went to the places where the peasants were hoeing, spreading manure, mowing the fields, and called out courteous words of greeting. They raised their heads in astonishment, and he tried to let them know right away where he was, because he had given up the habit, much indulged when we were in the trees together before, of playing peekaboo and other tricks on the people who passed below. At first the peasants, seeing him cover such distances entirely in the branches, couldn't understand, didn't know whether to take off their hats in greeting, as would be proper with a nobleman, or yell at him as if at a bratty kid. Then they got used to him and conversed with him about the work, the weather, and even showed that they appreciated his game of staying up there, neither better nor worse than many other games they saw the nobles playing.

He would be still for half hours in the tree, watching their work and asking questions about fertilizing and seeds, something it had never occurred to him to do when he walked on the ground, held back by that timidity which had never let him address a word to country people or servants. Sometimes he would indicate whether the furrow they were hoeing was straight or crooked or whether the tomatoes were already ripe in the neighbor's field; sometimes he offered to do little jobs, like going to tell the wife of a reaper that she should bring him a whetstone, or warn them that a particular garden needed to be watered. And if, going on such errands for the peasants, he saw a flight of swallows perching in a field of grain, he made a racket and waved his cap to chase them away.

In his solitary tours through the woods, human encounters were, if rarer, of a sort to impress themselves on his mind, encounters with people whom we don't normally meet. In those days a great number of itinerant poor people were camping out in the forests: charcoal burners, tinkers, glassblowers, families driven by famine far from their lands, earning their bread with insecure trades. They set up their workshops in the open and built huts of branches to sleep in. At first the fur-covered youth who passed by in the trees scared them, especially the women, who took him for a goblin spirit; but then he made friends with them, and sat for hours watching them work, and at night when they gathered around the fire he sat on a nearby branch, listening to the stories they told.

The charcoal burners, in the trampled area of ashy earth,

were the most numerous. They shouted *"Hura! Hota!"* because they were from Bergamo and their speech was incomprehensible. They were the strongest and most reserved and closely connected to one another: a corporation that was dispersed throughout the woods, with relatives and ties and quarrels. Cosimo sometimes acted as a go-between from one group to another, bringing news, carrying out commissions.

"The folk under the red oak told me to tell you that *Hanfa la Hapa Hota 'l Hoc!*"

"Tell them *Hegn Hobet Hò de Hot!*"

He kept in mind the mysterious aspirated sounds and tried to repeat them, as he tried to repeat the birdcalls that woke him in the morning.

If by now the rumor had spread that a son of the Baron di Rondò had not come down from the trees for months, our father, with people who came from abroad, still tried to keep the secret. The Counts d'Estomac came to visit, bound for France, where they had some property on the Bay of Toulon; they wanted to stay with us on the way. I don't know what sphere of interests lay beneath it: to reclaim certain goods, or confirm a see for a son who was a bishop, they needed the consent of the Baron di Rondò, and our father, as one can imagine, built on that alliance a castle of plans for his dynastic claims in Ombrosa.

There was a lunch, with so much ceremony you could have died of boredom, and the guests had with them a foppish son, a stuffed shirt in a wig. The baron introduces his children, that is, me alone, and then, "My poor daughter

Battista," he says, "lives so retired, she's very pious, I don't know if you'll see her," and here that fool introduces herself, with her nun's cap, but she's all decked out in ribbons and flounces, powder on her face, mitts. You had to understand, since the time of the young Marquis della Mela she hadn't seen a young man, apart from servants or peasants. The young Count d'Estomac bows low: she, hysterical laughter. In the brain of the baron, who had resigned himself where his daughter was concerned, new possibilities begin to whirl.

But the count betrayed indifference. He asked, "But didn't you have another, a boy, Monsieur Arminio?"

"Yes, the older," said our father. "But unfortunately he's out hunting."

He hadn't lied, because in those days Cosimo was always in the woods with a gun, lying in wait for hares and thrushes. I had gotten the gun for him, the light one that Battista used to shoot the mice, and which some time ago—neglecting her hunting—she had left hanging on a nail.

The count began to ask about the game in the neighborhood. The baron responded with generalities, because, lacking patience, as he did, and interest in the world around him, he didn't know how to hunt. I interrupted, although I was forbidden to enter into the conversations of the adults.

"And what does such a little fellow know about it?" said the count.

"I go and pick up the creatures my brother shoots, and bring them up—" I was saying, but our father cut me off.

"Who invited you into the conversation? Go play!"

We were in the garden; it was evening and still light, since it was summer. And now here came Cosimo, through the planes and the elm trees, calmly, with the cat-skin cap on his head, the gun over one shoulder, a spit over the other, and his legs in gaiters.

"Hey, hey!" said the count, rising, amused, and moving his head for a better view. "Who's there? Who's that up in the trees?"

"What's there? I don't really know . . . But maybe you thought you saw . . ." said our father, and he looked not in the direction indicated but into the eyes of the count, as if to assure himself that he was seeing clearly.

Cosimo meanwhile had arrived right above them and stopped on a fork with his legs wide.

"Ah, it's my son, yes, Cosimo, they're just boys, to give us a surprise, you see, he climbed up to the top . . ."

"He's the elder?"

"Yes, yes, of the two boys he's the older, but not by much, you know, they're still children, they play . . ."

"But he's very skillful to get up in the tree like that. And with that arsenal on his back . . ."

"Eh, they're playing . . ." And with a terrible effort of bad faith that made him red in the face: "What are you doing up there? Hey? Would you come down? Come and greet the count!"

Cosimo took off his cat-skin cap, bowed. "My respects, Sir Count."

"Ha-ha-ha!" the count laughed. "Very good, very good!

Let him stay up there, let him stay, Monsieur Arminio! Clever boy who goes through the trees!" And he laughed.

And that foolish young count could only repeat, *"C'est original, ça. C'est très original!"*

Cosimo sat there on the fork. Our father changed the subject and talked and talked, trying to distract the count. But the count every so often looked up, and my brother was always there, on that tree or another, cleaning his rifle or greasing his gaiters or putting on his heavy flannel because night was coming.

"Oh, look! He can do everything up in the treetops, the youth! Ah, how I like that! Ah, I will tell about it at court the first time I go! I'll tell my son the bishop! I'll tell my aunt the princess!"

My father was dying. Furthermore, he had another thought: he couldn't see his daughter, and the young count had also disappeared.

Cosimo had left on one of his exploratory tours; he returned out of breath. "She made him hiccup! She made him hiccup!"

The count was worried. "Oh, it's unpleasant. My son suffers a great deal from hiccups. Go, clever boy, go and see if it's over. Tell them to come back."

Cosimo leaped off, and returned more out of breath than before. "They're chasing each other. She wants to put a live lizard down his shirt to make the hiccups go away! He doesn't want her to!" And he rushed off again to see.

Thus we spent that evening in the villa, in truth not so

different from others, with Cosimo in the trees taking part as if secretly in our life, but this time there were the guests, and the news of my brother's strange behavior spread through the courts of Europe, to the shame of our father. An unjustified shame, since the Count d'Estomac had a favorable impression of our family, and so it happened that our sister Battista became engaged to the young count.

10

The olive trees, because of the way they twist, are for Cosimo comfortable and gentle paths, patient and friendly trees, with their rough bark, to pass through and to stop in, although each tree has only a few large branches and there is not a great variety of movements. In a fig, on the other hand, if you pay attention to whether it will hold your weight, there is no end of turnings; Cosimo sits under the pavilion of leaves, he sees the sun shining through their veins, the green fruit slowly swelling, he smells the latex oozing in the neck of the stems. The fig makes you its own, saturates you with its sticky liquid, with the buzzing of the wasps; after a while it seemed to Cosimo that he was becoming a fig himself, and, growing uneasy, he left. The hard service tree and the mulberry are comfortable; too bad they're rare. Similarly the walnuts, because sometimes, seeing my brother get lost in an enormous old walnut tree, as in a palace of many stories and innumerable rooms, even I—which says it all—felt a desire to imitate him, to go and live up there: so great is the strength and the certainty that that tree puts into being a tree, the insistence on being heavy and hard, expressed even in the leaves.

Cosimo would sit happily among the undulate leaves of the holm oaks (or holly oaks, as I called them, at least if they were in our park, perhaps influenced by the refined language of our father), and he loved the cracked surface of their bark; when he was lost in thought he would scrape up bits with his fingers, not from an instinct to do harm but as if to help the tree in its long labor of remaking itself. Or he would peel off the white bark of the plane trees, discovering layers of moldy old gold. He also loved rusticated trunks, like the elm's, whose knots sprout tender shoots and clumps of serrated leaves and papery samaras; but it's hard to climb in an elm, because the branches go up, slender and leafy, leaving little room for passage. In the woods he preferred beeches and oaks, because in a pine tree the dense scaffolding of branches, which aren't strong and are thickly needled, offers no space or handhold, and the chestnut, with its prickly leaves, spines, bark, and high branches, seems made purposely to keep one away.

These friendships and distinctions Cosimo recognized gradually, over time, or rather he recognized that he knew them; but already in those early days they began to be part of him, a natural instinct. Now it was the world that was different, made of narrow, curving bridges into emptiness, of knots or scales or furrows that made the bark rough, of light whose green varies according to whether the curtain of leaves is thick or thin, trembling at the first breath of air on the stems or moving like sails as the tree bends. While ours, our world, was flattened out in the background, and our figures disproportionate, and certainly we didn't understand anything about what he knew up there, he who spent the nights listening to how the wood packs with its cells the circuits inside the trunks that mark the years, and how the patches of molds spread in the north wind, and how, with a shudder, the birds sleeping in their nests tuck their heads in where the wing feathers are softer, and the caterpillar wakes, and the shrike's egg hatches. There's the moment when the silence of the countryside is distilled in the ear cavity into a fine spray of sounds, a scratching, a squeal, a rapid rustling in the grass, a plop in the water, a pattering between earth and rocks, and the cicada's screech high above all. The sounds contend with one another, hearing is able to constantly discern new ones, just as to fingers unwinding a ball of yarn every strand proves to be woven of ever finer and more insubstantial threads. Meanwhile the frogs continue their croaking, which remains in the background and doesn't change the flow of sounds, just as the light doesn't vary with the continuous winking of the stars. Yet whenever the wind rose or swept through, every sound changed and was new. Only the hint of a lowing or murmur remained, in the deepest cavity of the ear: it was the sea.

• • •

Winter came, and Cosimo made himself a fur jacket. He sewed it himself, using pieces of the hides of various beasts he had hunted: hares, foxes, marmots, and ferrets. On his head he always wore that hat made from the wild cat's skin. He also made himself trousers, of goatskin, with a leather bottom and knees. As for shoes, he finally realized that in the trees slippers were best, and he made a pair from some skin or other, maybe badger.

So he protected himself from the cold. It should be said that in those days the winters were mild, there wasn't the cold we have now, which Napoleon is said to have dislodged from Russia to follow him here. But even then spending the winter nights outside wasn't a pleasant life.

For night Cosimo had worked out a system with a goatskin sleeping bag: a goatskin with the fur on the inside, which hung from a branch. He dropped inside, disappeared completely, and slept curled up like a baby. If an unusual noise pierced the night, the fur cap emerged from the mouth of the sack, then the barrel of the gun, then he, eyes wide. (It was said that his eyes had become luminous in the dark, like cats' and owls', but I never noticed it.)

In the morning, on the other hand, when the jay sang, two fists came out of the sack, rose, and two arms extended, stretching slowly, and that stretch pulled up his yawning face, his chest, with the gun over the shoulder and the powder flask, his bowed legs (they were beginning to grow a little crooked, from the habit of always being and moving on all fours or crouching). Those legs jumped out, stretched, and so, with a shake of the back, a scratching under the fur jacket, lively and fresh as a rose, Cosimo began his day.

He went to the fountain, because he had a hanging fountain, which he had invented, or rather constructed, by giving nature a hand. There was a stream that at one point cascaded over a precipice, and nearby grew an oak with tall branches. Cosimo, with a piece of poplar bark a couple of yards long, had made a kind of gutter, which carried water from the waterfall to the branches of the oak, and so he could drink and wash. That he washed I can be sure, because I saw him myself several times; not much and not every day, but he washed; he even had soap. With the soap sometimes, when the fancy took him, he did laundry; he had a washtub carried up to the oak for the purpose. Then he spread the things to dry on ropes hung between branches.

In other words, he did everything in the trees. He had even found a way of roasting the game he hunted on a spit, without coming down. He did it like this: he lighted a pinecone with a match and threw it to the ground in a place set up as a hearth (I had prepared it, with some smooth stones), then he dropped a bundle of sticks and branches on it and regulated the flame with a shovel and tongs attached to long poles, so that he could reach the spit, which was hanging between two branches. All of this required attention, because it's easy to start a fire in the woods. Not for nothing was that hearth under the oak, near the waterfall, from which, in case of danger, he could draw all the water he wanted.

Thus, partly eating what he hunted, partly exchanging it with the peasants for fruit and vegetables, he lived pretty well, with no need for those at home to give him anything. One day we discovered that he was drinking fresh milk every morning; he had befriended a she-goat who climbed up to the fork of an olive tree, a foot or so off the ground and easy to reach, or rather, she didn't climb but went up with her hind legs, so that he, coming down to the fork with a pail, could milk her. He had the same arrangement with a hen, a fine red Paduan. He had made her a secret nest in the hollow of a trunk, and every other day he found an egg, which he drank, making two holes in it with a pin.

Another problem: taking care of his needs. At first here or there, he didn't pay attention; the world is big, he did it wherever he happened to be. Then he understood that it wasn't nice. So on the bank of the River Merdanzo he found an alder that stuck out at a most convenient and secluded point, with a fork in which one could sit comfortably. The Merdanzo was an obscure stream, hidden amid the reeds; it had a rapid current, and the neighboring towns threw their sewage in it. So the young Piovasco di Rondò lived in a civilized way, respecting the decorum of his neighbor and himself.

But a necessary human complement was missing in his life as a hunter: a dog. There was me, and I hurtled through the thickets, into the bushes, to find the thrush, the snipe, the quail that had fallen, shot in midair, or even the foxes, when, after a night of lying in wait, he stopped one with its long tail spread, just emerging from the heather. But I couldn't always escape to join him in the woods. Lessons with the abbé, studying, serving Mass, meals with our parents kept me back: the hundred duties of family life to which I submitted, because in essence the sentence that I heard constantly repeated —"One rebel in a family is enough"—wasn't unreasonable, and left its imprint on my entire life.

So Cosimo almost always went hunting alone, and to retrieve the game (when it wasn't a case of the thoughtful golden oriole, which, with stiffened wings, remained hanging on the branch) he used various kinds of fishing equipment—lines, hooks, or fishhooks—but he wasn't always successful, and sometimes a snipe would end up black with ants in the depths of a thornbush.

I've spoken so far of the tasks of a retriever. Because Cosimo at the time hunted almost solely from a blind, spending mornings or nights crouching on a branch, waiting for the thrush to perch in a treetop or a hare to appear in an open meadow. Otherwise he wandered randomly, following the song of the birds or guessing the most likely paths of furry creatures. And when he heard the barking of the bloodhounds following the hare or the fox he knew he had to stay away, because that animal wasn't for him, the solitary and casual hunter. Respectful of the rules as he was, even though from his infallible observation posts he could see and aim at the game pursued by the dogs of others, he never raised his gun. He waited until the panting hunter reached the path, ears pricked and eyes lost, and he pointed in the direction the creature had gone.

One day he saw a fox running: a red wave through the green grass, a fierce panting, whiskers bristling; it crossed the meadow and disappeared into the heather. And behind, *Wawawaaa!* the dogs.

They arrived at a gallop, surveying the ground with their noses; twice they lost the scent of the fox in their nostrils and turned on a right angle.

They were already distant when with a whimper—*Whee, whee*—one came cleaving the grass, leaping more like a fish than like a dog, a kind of dolphin that, swimming, showed a sharper muzzle and more pendulous ears than a bloodhound's. Behind, it was a fish; it seemed to swim, paddling fins or web-footed paws without legs, and was very long. It came out into the open: it was a dachshund.

No doubt he had joined the pack of bloodhounds and been left behind, young as he was—in fact still almost a puppy. The sound of the bloodhounds was now a *Bwwf* of vexation, because they had lost the trail and the compact chase was scattering into a network of noses searching a bare clearing but too impatient to find the track of the lost scent to search carefully, while the momentum was lost, and already some were taking advantage of it to pee against a rock.

So the dachshund, breathless, trotting with his nose high, unjustifiably triumphant, joined them. He whimpered slyly, still unjustifiably, *Wha-ee! Wha-ee!*

Immediately the bloodhounds growled at him, *Arrrch!*,

abandoning for a moment their hunt for the fox's scent, and pointed toward him, opening mouths made for biting: *Grrr!* Then, rapidly, they again lost interest and ran away.

Cosimo followed the dachshund, who walked around aimlessly, and the dachshund, swaying, nose distracted, saw the boy in the tree and wagged at him. Cosimo was convinced that the fox was still hiding there. The bloodhounds had scattered far away; they could be heard occasionally moving over the hills opposite with a broken and unmotivated barking, driven by the muffled voices of the hunters spurring them on. Cosimo said to the dachshund, "Go on! Go on! Look!"

The young dog began sniffing, and every so often he turned to look up at the boy. "Go on! Go on!"

Now he could no longer see the dog. He heard a crushing of bushes, then, in a burst, *Awawawaaa! Yi-ee, ya-ee, ya-ee!* He had raised the fox!

Cosimo saw the animal running in the meadow. But could he shoot a fox raised by someone else's dog? Cosimo let it go; he didn't shoot. The dachshund raised his muzzle toward him, with the look of dogs when they don't understand and don't know that they may be right not to understand, and put his nose down, following the fox.

Yi-ee, yi-ee, yi-ee! The dog forced the fox to make a whole round. Here, it was coming back. Could he shoot or could he not shoot? He didn't shoot. The dachshund looked up with a grieving eye. He had stopped barking, his tongue was hanging out, lower than his ears, and though exhausted, he kept running.

His raising of the fox had disoriented bloodhounds and hunters. An old man was running along the path with a heavy harquebus. "Hey," Cosimo said to him, "is that dachshund yours?"

"Damn you and all your relatives!" shouted the old man, who must have been in a bad mood. "Do we seem the type to hunt with dachshunds?"

"Then I'll shoot at what he raises," insisted Cosimo, who wanted to follow the rules.

"And shoot at whatever you like!" he answered, and ran off.

The dachshund raised the fox again. Cosimo fired and got it. The dachshund was his dog; he named him Ottimo Massimo.

Ottimo Massimo was no one's dog, having joined the pack of bloodhounds out of youthful enthusiasm. But where had he come from? To find out, Cosimo let the dog guide him.

The dachshund, grazing the ground, crossed hedges and ditches; then he turned to see if the boy up there could follow his path. So unusual was this route that Cosimo didn't realize right away where they were. When he realized it, his heart leaped in his chest: it was the garden of the Marquis d'Ondariva.

The villa was closed, the shutters barred; only one, in a garret, was flapping in the wind. The garden, left untended, had more than ever that aspect of an otherworldly forest.

And along the paths, now invaded by grass, and in the weed-choked flower beds Ottimo Massimo ran around happily, as if at home, chasing butterflies.

He disappeared into a bush. He returned with a ribbon in his mouth. Cosimo's heart beat harder. "What is it, Ottimo Massimo? Hey? Whose is it? Tell me!"

Ottimo Massimo wagged his tail.

"Bring it here, bring it. Ottimo Massimo!" Cosimo, descending to a low branch, took from the dog's mouth that faded scrap which had certainly been a hair ribbon of Viola's, as that dog had surely been Viola's dog, forgotten in the family's last move. In fact, now Cosimo seemed to remember him, the summer before, still a puppy, poking out of a basket on the arm of the fair-haired girl, and maybe he had just then been brought to her as a gift.

"Search, Ottimo Massimo!" And the dog hurtled amid the bamboo stalks and returned with other souvenirs: the jump rope, a torn piece of a kite, a fan.

At the top of the trunk of the tallest tree in the garden my brother carved with the tip of his sword the names *Viola* and *Cosimo,* and then, lower down, sure that it would please her even if she called him another name, he wrote: *Ottimo Massimo dachshund.*

From then on, when you saw the boy in the trees, you could be sure that if you looked in front of him, or nearby, you would see the dachshund Ottimo Massimo trotting along, belly to the ground. Cosimo had taught him the search, the stop, the retrieve—the jobs of all hunting dogs

—and there was no forest creature that they didn't hunt together. To bring him the game, Ottimo Massimo placed two paws on the trunk as high up as he could; Cosimo came down to get the hare or the partridge from his mouth and petted him. Their intimacies, their celebrations were all there. But between the ground and the branches a continuous dialogue flowed from one to the other, an intelligence, of monosyllabic barks and clicks of tongue and fingers. That necessary presence that man is for dog and dog for man never betrayed them, either one; and however different they were from all the men and dogs of the world, they could call themselves, as man and dog, happy.

II

For a long time—an entire period of his adolescence—hunting was the world for Cosimo. Also fishing, because he waited with a fishing line for eels and trout in the pools of the stream. We came to think of him as if by now he had senses and instincts different from ours, as if those skins that he had tanned for his clothing corresponded to a complete change in his nature. Of course, being in constant contact with the bark of trees, his eye fixed on the movements of feathers, fur, scales, on the range of colors which that surface of the world presents, along with the green current that circulates like the blood of another world in the veins of leaves: all these life forms as distant from the human as the stalk of a plant, the beak of a thrush, a school of fish—those borders of the wild where he had penetrated so deeply—might now have molded his mind, making him lose every semblance of man. Instead, no matter how many gifts he absorbed from his commonality with plants and his contest with animals, it was always clear to me that his place was over here; he was on our side.

• • •

But even without his willing it, certain habits became more infrequent and were lost. Such as attending the celebration of High Mass in Ombrosa. For the first months he tried to do it. Every Sunday, as we came out, the whole family in a group, in formal dress, we found him in the branches, also in some way intending formality in his dress—for example, the old tailcoat brought out again, or the three-cornered hat instead of the fur cap. We set off, he followed us through the branches, and so we advanced into the church square, stared at by the Ombrosotti (but they soon got used to it, and even our father's uneasiness diminished), all of us stiffly reserved, he jumping in the air, a strange sight, especially in winter, when the trees were bare.

We entered the cathedral and sat in our family pew; he stayed outside, perching on a holm oak beside the nave, just at the height of a big window. From our pew we could see through the glass the shadow of the branches and, in the middle, Cosimo's, with the cap on his chest and his head bowed. By an agreement my father made with the sacristan, that window was kept half open on Sundays so my brother could catch the Mass from his tree. But as time passed we stopped seeing him. The window was closed because there was a draft.

So many things that before would have been important for him were no longer. In the spring our sister became engaged.

Who would have said it, just a year earlier? Those Counts d'Estomac came with the young count, and there was a grand celebration. Every room of our house was illuminated, all the nobility of the district were present, there was dancing. Who thought anymore of Cosimo? Well, it's not true, we all thought of him. Every so often I looked out the windows to see if he would come. Our father was sad, and in that family festivity his thoughts certainly went to Cosimo, who had excluded himself from it; and the *generalessa,* who commanded the whole celebration as if she were on a parade ground, wanted only to give vent to her yearning for the absent one. Maybe even Battista, who was pirouetting, unrecognizable without her nun's clothing, in a wig that looked like marzipan and a crinoline trimmed with coral that I don't know what dressmaker had constructed for her—even she, I bet, thought of him.

And he was there, not seen—I learned later—in the shadow of the top of a plane tree, in the cold, and he saw the lighted windows, the known rooms festively decorated, the bewigged people dancing. What thoughts crossed his mind? Did he regret our life at least a little? Did he think how short was the step that separated him from a return to our world, how short and how easy? I don't know what he thought, what he wanted, then. I know only that he remained for the whole celebration, and even longer, until one by one the candles were extinguished and no window remained lighted.

• • •

Thus Cosimo's relations with the family somehow or other continued. In fact, with one member they became closer, and it can be said that only now did he get to know him: the Cavalier Avvocato Enea Silvio Carrega. Cosimo discovered that that half-addled, elusive man, of whom one never knew where he was or what he was doing, was the only member of the whole family who had a great number of occupations, and not just that, but that nothing he did was useless.

He would go out, maybe in the hottest hour of the afternoon, with the fez planted on his head, slippers flopping under the robe that hung to the ground, and disappear as if the cracks of the earth had swallowed him up, or the hedges, or the stones in the walls. Even Cosimo, who amused himself by always being on the lookout (rather, it was not that he amused himself; this was now his natural state, as if his eye embraced a horizon so wide that it included everything), at a certain point lost him. Sometimes he began running from branch to branch toward the place where the *cavaliere* had disappeared, but he never could figure out which way he had gone. There was one sign that always recurred in those places: bees flying around. Cosimo became convinced that the *cavaliere*'s presence was connected to the bees, and that to track him he had to follow their flight path. But how? Around every flowering plant there was a sporadic buzzing of bees; he must not be distracted by isolated and secondary routes but follow the invisible aerial pathway along which the thronging of bees became denser until he saw a thick cloud of them rise from behind a hedge like smoke. There were the hives, one or several, in a row on a plank, and intent on them, amid the swarm of bees, was the *cavaliere.*

Beekeeping was, in fact, one of the secret activities of our natural uncle: secret up to a point, because he himself every so often brought to the table a honeycomb dripping with honey, just pulled from the hive. But it all took place outside the radius of our properties, in places that he evidently didn't want known. This must have been a precaution, to separate the proceeds of that personal industry from the leaky bucket of the family administration; or—since certainly the man wasn't miserly, and then, what could it earn, that bit of honey and wax?—to have something that the baron his brother wouldn't stick his nose into, where he wouldn't insist on leading him by the hand; or again, not to mix the few things he loved, like beekeeping, with the many he didn't, like administration.

Anyway, the fact remained that our father would never have allowed beekeeping near the house, because the baron had an unreasonable fear of being stung, and when he happened on a bee or a wasp in the garden, he rushed absurdly along the paths, thrusting his hands into his wig as if to protect himself from the pecking of an eagle. Once the wig flew off, and the bee, startled by the sudden movement, rushed at him and stuck its stinger into the bald skull. For three days he pressed vinegar-soaked rags to his head, because he was such a man, very proud and strong in serious situations but maddened by a scratch or a pimple.

Thus Enea Silvio Carrega had split up his beekeeping operations here and there throughout the valley of Ombrosa; the landowners gave him permission to keep a hive or two or three in a piece of their fields in return for a little honey, and he was always going from place to place, bustling around the hives with gestures that made him seem to have bees' legs instead of hands, partly because sometimes, so as not to be stung, he wore black mitts. Over his face he wore a black veil, which was wrapped around the fez like a turban and at every breath stuck to his mouth and rose over it. He also had a tool that spread smoke, to keep the insects away while he rummaged in the hives. And all of it, swarming of bees, veils, cloud of smoke, seemed to Cosimo a spell that that man tried to cast in order to disappear from there, be erased, swept away, to be reborn as something other, or in another time, or another place. But he wasn't much of a magician, because he was always the same when he reappeared, maybe sucking a stung fingertip.

It was spring. One morning the air looked to Cosimo as if it had gone mad, vibrating with a sound never heard before, a buzz that grew as loud as a roar, and it was pervaded by a hail that instead of falling moved in a horizontal direction and whirled slowly, sporadically, but following a kind of denser column. It was a multitude of bees, and all around was green and flowers and sun, and Cosimo, who didn't understand what was happening, felt gripped by a consuming, fierce excitement. "The bees are escaping! Cavalier Avvocato! The bees are escaping!" he began shouting, running through the trees in search of Carrega.

"They're not escaping—they're swarming," said the voice of the *cavaliere,* and Cosimo saw him below, sprouting like a mushroom, while he made a sign to him to be quiet. Then suddenly he ran off. Where had he gone?

It was swarm season. A host of bees was following a queen out of the old hive. Cosimo looked around. Here was the *cavalier avvocato* reappearing at the kitchen door, with a pot and a pan in hand. Now he banged the pan against the pot, raising a very loud *dong! dong!,* which reverberated in the eardrums and faded in a long vibration, so irritating that it caused one to plug one's ears. Striking those copper instruments every three steps, the *cavalier avvocato* walked behind the crowd of bees. At each clang the swarm seemed to shudder, make a rapid descent, and turn around, and the buzz seemed to get softer, the flight more hesitant. Cosimo couldn't see well, but now it seemed to him that the whole swarm was converging on a point in the green and wouldn't go farther. And Carrega continued to beat the pot.

"What's happening, Cavalier Avvocato? What are you doing?" my brother asked, reaching him.

"Quick," he mumbled, "get up in the tree where the swarm stopped, but be careful not to move until I arrive!"

The bees were descending on a pomegranate. Cosimo arrived and at first saw nothing, then suddenly there was something like a big fruit, a pinecone, hanging from a branch, and it was made up of bees clinging to one another while new ones kept arriving, swelling it.

Cosimo sat at the top of the pomegranate holding his

breath. Under him hung the cluster of bees, and the bigger it got, the lighter it seemed, as if hanging by a thread, or even less, by the legs of an old queen bee, and as if made of thin cartilage, with all those beating wings that spread their diaphanous gray color over the black and yellow stripes of their abdomens.

The *cavalier avvocato* arrived skipping, with a hive in his hands. He held it out upside down under the cluster. "Go on," he said softly to Cosimo, "a slight sharp shake."

Cosimo shook the pomegranate slightly. The swarm of thousands of bees let go like a leaf, dropped into the hive, and the *cavaliere* plugged it up with a board. "Done."

Thus between Cosimo and the *cavalier avvocato* arose an understanding, a collaboration that could even be called a kind of friendship, if friendship did not seem an exaggerated term applied to two such unsociable people.

My brother and Enea Silvio met in the realm of hydraulics as well. That may seem strange, since one who is in the trees is unlikely to have much to do with wells and channels; but I've described that system of the hanging fountain that Cosimo had thought up, with a strip of poplar bark that carried water from a waterfall up to the branches of an oak. Now, even though the *cavalier avvocato* was so absent-minded, nothing that happened in the watercourses anywhere in the countryside escaped him. From above the waterfall, hidden behind a privet, he spied Cosimo pulling the conduit out from among the leaves of the oak (where he put it when he wasn't using it, with that instinct of wild creatures, which was immediately his, too, to hide everything), propping it on a fork of the oak and on the other side on some rocks on the overhang, and drinking.

Who knows what whirled in the *cavaliere*'s mind at that sight; he was gripped by one of his rare moments of euphoria. He emerged from behind the privet, clapped his hands, hopped two or three times as if he were jumping rope, sprayed water, nearly fell into the waterfall and off the precipice. And he began to explain to the boy the idea he had had. The idea was confused and the explanation very confused: the *cavalier avvocato* usually spoke in dialect, out of modesty more than out of ignorance of the language, but in these sudden bursts of excitement he went from dialect directly into Turkish, without realizing it, and couldn't be understood at all.

In brief, he had the idea of a hanging aqueduct, with a conduit supported by the branches of the trees, that would reach the opposite, uncultivated slope of the valley and irrigate it. And the refinement that Cosimo, immediately supporting his project, suggested, to use at certain points perforated trunks to provide rain for the seedbeds, sent him into raptures.

He quickly shut himself in his study, filling pages and pages with plans. Cosimo, too, got busy, because he liked everything that could be done in the trees, and it seemed to give a new importance and authority to his position up there; and in Enea Silvio Carrega he seemed to have found an unsuspected companion. They met on certain low trees; the *cavalier avvocato* climbed up on a triangular ladder, his arms loaded with rolls of drawings, and they discussed for hours the increasingly complicated developments of that aqueduct.

But it never moved into the practical phase. Enea Silvio got tired, his conversations with Cosimo became less frequent, and he never finished the designs; after a week he must have forgotten about it. Cosimo didn't regret it; he had soon realized that it was an annoying complication in his life and no more.

It was clear that in the field of hydraulics our natural uncle could have done much more. He had the passion for it, he wasn't without the particular genius necessary for that branch of study, but he was unable to accomplish anything: he got lost, and more lost, until every intention came to nothing, like poorly channeled water that flows a short distance and then is absorbed by porous ground. The reason perhaps was this: that while he could devote himself to beekeeping on his own account, almost in secret, without having to deal with anyone, erupting every so often in a gift of honey and wax that no one had asked for, these works of making channels instead required him to take account of the interests of this one and that one, submit to the opinions and orders of the baron or whoever else commissioned the work. Timid and indecisive as he was, he never opposed the will of others, but he quickly fell out of love with the work and abandoned it.

You could see him at all hours in the middle of a field, with men equipped with shovels and hoes, he with a tape measure and a rolled-up map, giving orders to dig a channel and measuring the ground with his steps, which, because they were very short, he had to lengthen exaggeratedly. He would have the men dig in one place, then in another, then break off, and he would start taking measurements again. Evening came and so the work was suspended. It was unlikely that he would decide to take it up at that point the next day. He couldn't be found for a week.

His passion for hydraulics was made up of aspirations, impulses, desires. The memory was dear to him of the beautiful, well-irrigated lands of the sultan, orchards and gardens where he must have been happy, the only truly happy time of his life; he was continually comparing the countryside of Ombrosa to those gardens of Barbary or Turkey and was driven to correct it, to try to make it match his memory; since his art was hydraulics, in that he concentrated the desire for change, but he continually clashed with a different reality and was disappointed by it.

He also practiced dowsing, unseen, because it was still a time in which strange arts could attract the prejudice against witchcraft. Once Cosimo discovered him in a field pirouetting as he held out a forked stick. That, too, must have been an attempt to repeat something he had seen others do and in which he had no training, because nothing came of it.

Understanding the character of Enea Silvio Carrega helped Cosimo in this: that he understood many things about being alone that were useful to him later in life. I would say that he always carried with him the troubled image of the *cavalier avvocato,* as a warning of what a man who separates his fate from that of others can become, and he was successful in that he never came to resemble him.

12

Sometimes Cosimo was wakened in the night by cries of "Help! Robbers! After them!"

He headed swiftly through the trees to the place where those cries were coming from. Maybe it was a farmhouse belonging to small landowners, and a family was standing outside half dressed, with their hands on their heads.

"Alas for us, alas for us, Gian dei Brughi came and carried off all the proceeds from the harvest!"

People crowded around.

"Gian dei Brughi? It was him? Did you see him?"

"It was him! It was him! He had a mask over his face, a pistol as long as this, two other masked men followed, and he was giving the orders! It was Gian dei Brughi!"

"Where is he? Where did he go?"

"Ah, yes, good for you, capture Gian dei Brughi! Who knows where he is at this hour!"

Or the one who cried out was a traveler left in the middle of the road, robbed of everything—horse, bag, cloak, and baggage. "Help! Robbery! Gian dei Brughi!"

"How did it happen? Tell us!"

"He jumped out from there, black, bearded, shotgun raised, I nearly died!"

"Quick! Let's follow him! Which direction did he go?"

"This way! No, maybe that way! He ran like the wind."

Cosimo got it in his head to see Gian dei Brughi. He ran all over the woods, following hares or birds, urging on the dachshund: "Look, look, Ottimo Massimo!" What he would have liked to flush out was the bandit in person, and not to do or say anything to him, just to look in the face a person so renowned. But he had never succeeded in meeting him, not even if he wandered around for an entire night. "It must mean that he didn't come out tonight," Cosimo said to himself; instead, in the morning, here or there in the valley was a knot of people on the threshold of a house or at a bend in the road, remarking on the latest robbery. Cosimo hurried there, and he was all ears as he listened to the stories.

"But you who are always in the woods, up in the trees," someone said once, "you've never seen Gian dei Brughi?"

Cosimo was very embarrassed. "Well . . . I don't think so . . ."

"How would he have seen him?" someone else said. "Gian dei Brughi has hiding places that no one can find, and he walks on roads that no one knows!"

"With the price he has on his head, whoever captures him will be rich for the rest of his life!"

"Yes! But those who know where he is have accounts to

settle with the law, just as he does, and if they speak up they'll go straight to the gallows, too!"

"Gian dei Brughi! Gian dei Brughi! But is it really always him committing these crimes?"

"Come on, he has so many charges against him that if he managed to prove his innocence in ten robberies, they'd've already hanged him for the eleventh."

"He's been robbing people throughout the forest along the coast!"

"In his youth he even killed one of his gang leaders!"

"He was banned even by the bandits."

"That's why he's taken refuge in our land."

"It's that we're such fine folk."

Cosimo discussed every new bit of news with the coppersmiths. Among the people encamped in the woods, there was in those days a whole pack of suspicious itinerants: coppersmiths, menders of straw chair seats, ragpickers, people who go from house to house and plan in the morning the theft they'll make in the evening. In the woods, rather than a workshop, they had a secret refuge, a hiding place for their stolen goods.

"You know, tonight Gian dei Brughi attacked a carriage!"

"Really? Well, anything's possible . . ."

"He grabbed the galloping horses by the bit and stopped them."

"Well, either it wasn't him or it wasn't horses but crickets . . ."

"What do you mean? You don't believe it was Gian dei Brughi?"

"Yes, yes, what ideas are you putting in his head? It was Gian dei Brughi, certainly!"

"What is Gian dei Brughi not capable of?"

"Ha-ha-ha!"

Listening to talk like this about Gian dei Brughi, Cosimo couldn't understand anything; he moved through the woods and went to listen to another camp of itinerants.

"Tell me, in your opinion, was that business of the carriage tonight an assault by Gian dei Brughi?"

"All assaults are made by Gian dei Brughi when they succeed. Don't you know?"

"Why when they succeed?"

"Because when they don't succeed, it means that it really was Gian dei Brughi!"

"Ha-ha! That incompetent!"

Cosimo couldn't understand. "Gian dei Brughi is an incompetent?"

The others then quickly changed their tone.

"No, no, he's a bandit who frightens everyone."

"Have you seen him?"

"Us? Who's ever seen him?"

"But you're sure he exists?"

"That's a good one! Of course he exists. And even if he didn't . . ."

"If he didn't?"

"It would be so-and-so. Ha-ha-ha!"

"But everyone says . . ."

"Of course, they have to say that: it's Gian dei Brughi who

steals and murders everywhere, that terrible bandit! We'd like to see someone doubt it!"

"Hey, you, boy, would you be bold enough to doubt it?"

In brief, Cosimo had understood that the higher up you went toward the woods, the more the fear of Gian dei Brughi that existed in the valley was transformed into a dubious and openly mocking attitude.

The curiosity to meet him passed, because he understood that Gian dei Brughi didn't matter at all to the more knowledgeable people.

One afternoon Cosimo was in a walnut tree, and he was reading. Recently a nostalgia for books had seized him: sitting all day, gun leveled, waiting for a chaffinch to show up is ultimately boring.

So he was reading *Gil Blas,* by Lesage, holding the book in one hand and the gun in the other. Ottimo Massimo, who didn't like his master to read, was circling around looking for pretexts to distract him: barking at a butterfly, for example, to see if he could get him to aim the gun.

And look, a bearded, shabby-looking man came running breathlessly down from the mountain, along the path, unarmed, and behind him were two constables, daggers drawn, shouting, "Stop him! It's Gian dei Brughi! We've run him down, finally!"

Now the bandit had gained a little distance, but if he kept going in that clumsy fashion, like one who is afraid of taking the wrong road or falling into some trap, he would soon have them on his heels again. Cosimo's walnut wouldn't support someone who wanted to climb it, but he had on the branch one of those ropes he always carried with him for helping with difficult moves. He threw one end to the ground and tied the other to the branch. The bandit saw the rope fall almost on his nose, wrung his hands in a moment of uncertainty, then grabbed the rope and climbed up rapidly, showing himself to be one of those indecisive impulsives or impulsive undecideds who seem unable to seize the right moment and yet hit it every time.

The constables arrived. The rope had already been pulled up and Gian dei Brughi was beside Cosimo among the walnut leaves. There was a crossroads. One constable went this way, one that, then they met up again and didn't know where to go. And here they ran into Ottimo Massimo, who was wagging his tail nearby.

"Hey," said one of the cops to the other, "isn't this the dog belonging to the baron's son, the one who's in the trees? If that boy's around here he'll be able to tell us something."

"I'm up here!" cried Cosimo. But he cried not from the walnut where he had been before and where the robber was hidden; he had moved quickly to a chestnut opposite, so that the cops immediately raised their heads in that direction without looking in the trees all around.

"Good day, sir," they said. "You haven't by any chance seen the bandit Gian dei Brughi running away?"

"Who it was I don't know," Cosimo answered, "but if you're looking for a little man running, he went that way toward the stream."

"A little man? He's a trunk of a man, frightening . . ."

"Well, from up here you all seem small."

"Thank you, sir!" And they headed down toward the stream.

Cosimo returned to the walnut and went back to reading *Gil Blas.* Gian dei Brughi was still hugging the trunk, pale, his hair and beard bristling red, just like heather, with dry leaves, chestnut burrs, and pine needles caught in them. He stared at Cosimo with bewilderment in his round green eyes; ugly, he was ugly.

"Did they go?" he made up his mind to ask.

"Yes, yes," said Cosimo, friendly. "Are you the bandit Gian dei Brughi?"

"How do you know me?"

"Well, like that, by reputation."

"And you're the one who never gets out of the trees?"

"Yes. How do you know?"

"Well, in my case, too, word gets around."

They looked at each other politely, like two persons of consequence who meet by chance and are pleased not to be unknown to each other.

Cosimo didn't know what else to say, and began reading again.

"What are you reading?"

"*Gil Blas,* by Lesage."

"Is it good?"

"Oh yes."

"Are you close to the end?"

"Why? Well, maybe twenty pages."

"Because I wanted to ask if you'd lend it to me when you finished." He smiled, in some embarrassment. "You know, I spend the days hidden, I never know what to do. If I had a book every so often, I mean. Once I stopped a carriage, it wasn't much, but there was a book and I took it. I carried it, hidden under my jacket; I would have given all the rest of the booty just to keep that book. At night I light the lantern, I go to read . . . it was in Latin! I didn't understand a word." He shook his head. "You see, I don't know Latin."

"Yes, well, Latin, goodness, it's hard," said Cosimo, and felt that in spite of himself he was taking a protective air. "This one is in French."

"French, Tuscan, Provençal, Castilian, I understand them all," said Gian dei Brughi. "Even a little Catalan: *Bon dia! Bona nit! Está la mar mólt alborotada.*"

In half an hour Cosimo had finished the book and lent it to Gian dei Brughi.

So began the relationship between my brother and Gian dei Brughi. As soon as Gian dei Brughi finished a book he hurried to give it back to Cosimo, took another on loan, ran off to hole up in his secret refuge, and buried himself in the book.

I got the books for Cosimo, from the library at home, and

once he had read them he gave them back to me. Now he began to keep them longer, because after he read them he handed them on to Gian dei Brughi, and often they returned with the bindings worn, with mold stains, snail trails, because who knows where the bandit stored them.

On appointed days Cosimo and Gian dei Brughi met at a certain tree, exchanged the book, and took off, because the forest was always patrolled by constables. This simple operation was very dangerous for both—for my brother as well, who would not have been able to account for his friendship with that criminal! But Gian dei Brughi was seized by such a passion for reading that he devoured novel after novel, and since he stayed hidden all day reading, in one day he would put away volumes that had taken my brother a week, and so there was no way, he wanted another, and if it wasn't the appointed day he raced through the countryside in search of Cosimo, frightening the families in the farmhouses and setting off on his tracks the entire police force of Ombrosa.

Now since Cosimo was always pressured by the bandit's requests, the books I managed to get for him weren't enough, and he had to look for other suppliers. He knew a Jewish bookseller, a certain Orbecche, who got works for him in many volumes. Cosimo would knock on his window from the branches of a locust and bring him hares, thrushes, and partridges in exchange for books.

But Gian dei Brughi had his tastes; one couldn't just give him books randomly or he came back to Cosimo to exchange them. My brother was at the age when one begins to take pleasure in more substantial readings, but he had been forced to go slowly, ever since Gian dei Brughi brought back *The Adventures of Telemachus,* warning that if he ever again gave him a book so boring he would cut down the tree beneath him.

At that point Cosimo would have liked to separate the books he wanted to read for himself in tranquility from those he got just to lend to the bandit. But no: he had at least to glance at these, too, because Gian dei Brughi became increasingly demanding and distrustful, and before taking a book wanted to hear something of the plot, and there would be trouble if he caught him out. My brother tried giving him novels of love, and the bandit showed up furiously asking if he had taken him for a silly woman. Cosimo could never guess what he would like.

In other words, with Gian dei Brughi always on his heels, reading for Cosimo, from the pastime of half an hour here and there, became his main occupation, the purpose of his whole day. And by dint of handling volumes, judging and comparing them, of having always to know more and new ones, between reading for Gian dei Brughi and the increasing need for his own reading, Cosimo developed such a passion for letters and for all human knowledge that the hours from dawn to sunset weren't enough for what he wanted to read, and he continued even in the dark by the light of a lantern.

Finally he discovered the novels of Richardson. Gian dei Brughi liked them. When he finished one, he immediately wanted another. Orbecche got a pile of volumes. The bandit had enough to read for a month. Cosimo, with peace restored, plunged into Plutarch's *Lives.*

Gian dei Brughi, meanwhile, lying on his bed, with the bristling red hair over his wrinkled brow full of dry leaves, his green eyes reddening in the effort to see, read and read, moving his jaw in the furious labor of spelling out the words, and holding up a finger wet with saliva ready to turn the page. When he read Richardson, a tendency already long latent in his soul became almost overwhelming: a desire for regular, domestic days, for family, for family feelings, for virtue, aversion for the wicked and the depraved. What surrounded him no longer interested him, or filled him with disgust. He left his hideout only to hurry to Cosimo to exchange his book, especially if it was a novel in several volumes and he was in the middle of the story. He lived like that, isolated, unaware of the storm of resentments that was brewing against him even among the inhabitants of the wood who had once been his faithful accomplices but now were tired of having an idle bandit in their way, and one who had the entire constabulary after him.

In bygone times he had been surrounded by men who had accounts to settle with the local law, maybe a small thing, habitual petty thefts, like those itinerant tinkers, or serious crimes, like his bandit companions. For every robbery or theft, these people took advantage of his authority and experience and used his name as a shield, since it was on all lips and left them in the shadows. And even those who didn't take part in the assaults enjoyed in some way their good outcome, because the woods were full of stolen goods and contraband of every kind, which had to be disposed of or resold, and all those who haunted the place found something to trade in. Unbeknown to Gian dei Brughi, the men who carried out robberies on his account relied on that terrible name to frighten their victims and get as much as possible from them: the people lived in fear; in every criminal they saw Gian dei Brughi or one of his gang and hastened to loosen the purse strings.

Those good times had lasted long; Gian dei Brughi had seen that he could live on the earnings, and little by little he'd grown stupid. He thought that things were going on as before, whereas minds had changed and his name no longer inspired any reverence.

To whom was Gian dei Brughi useful now? He was hiding out reading novels, with tears in his eyes; he wasn't pulling off robberies, he wasn't getting any goods, no one in the forest could attend to business, the constables came looking for him every day, and if an unfortunate fellow had even a slightly suspicious air they took him to the guardroom. If one adds the temptation of that price he had on his head, it seems obvious that Gian dei Brughi's days were numbered.

Two other bandits, youths who had been taken up by him and couldn't resign themselves to losing that fine gang leader, wanted to give him a chance to rehabilitate himself. They were called Ugasso and Bel-Loré and as boys had been in the band of fruit thieves. Now young men, they had become sometime bandits.

So they go and see Gian dei Brughi in his cave. He was there, lying on the straw. "Yes, what is it?" he said, without raising his eyes from the page.

"We had something to propose to you, Gian dei Brughi."

"Mmm . . . what?" And he went on reading.

"You know where the house of Costanzo the tax collector is?"

"Yes, yes . . . Eh? What? Who's the tax collector?"

Bel-Loré and Ugasso exchanged a look of annoyance. If they didn't get that damn book out from under his eyes, the bandit wouldn't understand a word. "Close the book for a moment, Gian dei Brughi. Listen to us."

Gian dei Brughi seized the book with both hands, rose to his knees, made as if to hug it to his chest, keeping it open at his place; then the desire to continue reading was too strong, and holding it tight, he raised it up so that he could stick his nose in it.

Bel-Loré had an idea. There was a spiderweb with a large spider in it, and he threw it at Gian dei Brughi, between book and nose. That wretched Gian dei Brughi had gone so soft that he was even afraid of a spider. He felt the tangle of spider legs and sticky threads and, even before he understood what it was, gave a little cry of horror, dropped the book, and began to wave his hands in front of his face, goggle-eyed and spitting.

Ugasso dove to the ground and managed to grab the book before Gian dei Brughi could put a foot on it.

"Give me back that book!" said Gian dei Brughi, trying

with one hand to free himself from spider and web and with the other to tear the book from Ugasso's hands.

"No, first listen to us!" said Ugasso, hiding the book behind his back.

"I was reading *Clarissa*. Give it back to me! I was at the climax . . ."

"Listen. We're bringing a load of wood to the taxman's house tonight. In the sack, instead of wood, there's you. When it's night, you come out of the sack—"

"And I want to finish *Clarissa*!" He had succeeded in freeing his hands from the remains of the spiderweb and was trying to struggle with the two youths.

"Listen. When night falls, you come out of the sack, armed with your pistols, you get the taxman to give you all the taxes he's collected for the week, which he keeps in a strongbox at the head of the bed—"

"Let me at least finish the chapter. Be nice . . ."

The youths thought of the times when Gian dei Brughi would point two pistols at the belly of the first who dared to contradict him. A bitter nostalgia seized them. "You take the bags of money, all right?" they insisted sadly. "You bring them to us, we give you back your book, and you'll be able to read as much as you like. All right? You're in?"

"No. It's not all right. I'm not going!"

"Oh, you won't go . . . Oh, so you won't go . . . Then watch!" And Ugasso took a page from near the end of the book ("No!" shouted Gian dei Brughi), tore it out ("No! stop!"), crumpled it up, threw it on the fire.

"Aaah! Dog! You can't do that! I won't know how it ends!" And he ran after Ugasso to grab the book.

"Then you'll go to the tax collector?"

"No, I won't go!"

Ugasso tore out two more pages.

"Stop! I haven't gotten there yet! You can't burn them!"

Ugasso had already thrown them on the fire.

"You dog! *Clarissa*! No!"

"Then you'll go?"

"I . . ."

Ugasso tore out three more pages and tossed them onto the flames.

Gian dei Brughi sat down with his face in his hands. "I'll go," he said. "But promise me that you'll wait with the book outside the tax collector's house."

The bandit was hidden in a sack, with a bundle of twigs on his head. Bel-Loré carried the sack on his back. Behind him came Ugasso with the book. Every so often, when Gian dei Brughi with a kick or a grumble indicated that he was about to repent, Ugasso let him hear the sound of a torn page, and Gian dei Brughi immediately calmed down again.

With this system the two youths, disguised as woodcutters, carried him into the house of the tax collector and left him there. They went to hide a little distance away, behind an olive tree, waiting for the hour when the robbery would be done and he would join them.

But Gian dei Brughi was in too much of a hurry; he came out before dark, and there were still too many people in the house. "Hands up!" But he was no longer the man he had been; it was as if he were watching himself from the outside, and he felt a little ridiculous. "Hands up, I said . . . Everyone in the room, against the wall . . ." No way: he didn't believe it himself anymore—he was doing it just to do it. "Are you all here?" He hadn't realized that a little girl had escaped.

Anyway, it was a job where there was not a minute to lose. But he dragged it out, the tax collector acted stupid, he couldn't find the key, Gian dei Brughi realized that they no longer took him seriously, and in his heart of hearts he was glad it had happened like that.

Finally he came out, his arms loaded with bags of gold coins. He ran almost blindly to the olive tree fixed for the meeting. "Here's everything! Give me back *Clarissa*!"

Four, seven, ten arms were flung at him, immobilizing him from shoulders to ankles. He was picked up bodily by a squad of constables and tied up like a salami. "You'll see Clarissa from behind bars!" And they carried him off to prison.

The prison was a tower on the seashore. A thicket of cluster pines grew near it. From the top of one of these cluster pines, Cosimo could get almost to the height of Gian dei Brughi's cell and see his face through the bars.

The bandit cared nothing about the interrogations and the trial; however it went, they would hang him. Rather, his thoughts were of those empty days in prison, being unable to read, and that novel abandoned in the middle. Cosimo managed to get another copy of *Clarissa* and brought it to the pine.

"How far did you get?"

"Where Clarissa escapes from the brothel."

Cosimo leafed through the pages for a bit, and then: "Ah yes, here. So," and he began to read aloud, facing the bars, which Gian dei Brughi's hands could be seen gripping.

The investigation dragged on; the bandit held out against the strappado, and it took days and days to make him confess to each of his innumerable crimes. And so every day, before and after the interrogations, he sat listening as Cosimo read to him. When *Clarissa* was finished, Cosimo, feeling he was a little sad, got the idea that Richardson, for one locked up like that, was a little depressing, and he decided to start a novel by Fielding, which with its lively action might make up a little for the bandit's lost freedom. It was during the days of the trial, and Gian dei Brughi had in mind only the adventures of Jonathan Wild.

The day of the execution arrived before the novel was finished. On the cart, Gian dei Brughi, accompanied by a friar, made his last journey as a living man. Hangings in Ombrosa took place on a tall oak in the middle of the square. The people gathered around.

When he had the noose around his neck, Gian dei Brughi heard a whistle from the trees. He looked up. There was Cosimo, with the book closed.

"Tell me how it ends," said the condemned man.

"I'm sorry to tell you, Gian," answered Cosimo, "Jonathan finally is hanged by the neck."

"Thanks. So let it be for me, too! Farewell!" And he kicked away the ladder himself, and strangled.

When the body stopped writhing, the crowd left. Cosimo stayed till night, straddling the branch from which the hanged man dangled. Every time a crow came to peck at the eyes or nose of the corpse, Cosimo waved his cap and chased it away.

13

By keeping company with the bandit, therefore, Cosimo had developed a boundless passion for reading and study, which stayed with him all his life. When you met him now he was usually sitting astride a comfortable branch, or leaning against a fork as if on a school bench, with a book open in his hand and a sheet of paper on a small board, the inkwell in a cavity in the tree, writing with a long goose quill.

Now it was he who went in search of the Abbé Fauchelafleur to give him lessons, explain Tacitus and Ovid and the heavenly bodies and the laws of chemistry, but the old priest, outside of a little grammar and a little theology, was drowning in a sea of doubts and lacunae, and to the questions of his student he spread his arms and raised his eyes to heaven.

"Monsieur l'Abbé, how many wives can one have in Persia? Monsieur l'Abbé, who is the Savoyard Vicar? Monsieur l'Abbé, can you explain to me the system of Linnaeus?"

"Alors . . . Voyons . . . Maintenant . . ." the abbé began, then he got lost and couldn't go on.

But Cosimo, who devoured books of every kind and spent

half his time reading and half hunting to pay his accounts with the bookseller Orbecche, always had some new story to tell. About Rousseau, who walked through the forests of Switzerland collecting plants; about Benjamin Franklin, who captured lightning with a kite; about the Baron de Lahontan, who lived happily among the American Indians.

Old Fauchelafleur listened to these speeches with astonished attention, I don't know whether out of real interest or only out of relief that it wasn't he who had to teach; and he assented, and responded *"Non! Dites-le moi!"* when Cosimo turned to him asking, "And do you know how it is that . . ." or with *"Tiens! Mais c'est épatant!"* when Cosimo gave him the answer, and sometimes with *"Mon Dieu!"*s that could be as much exultation in the new greatnesses of God that at that moment were revealed to him as regret for the omnipotence of evil, which under all guises inescapably dominated the world.

I was too young and Cosimo had friends only in the uneducated classes, so he satisfied his need to comment on the discoveries he was making in books by burying our old teacher in questions and explanations. The abbé, of course, had that submissive and accommodating disposition that came to him from a superior knowledge of the vanity of all things, and Cosimo took advantage of it. So the relationship of discipleship between the two was reversed: Cosimo was the teacher and Fauchelafleur the pupil. And my brother had gained such authority that he succeeded in dragging the old man, trembling, on his pilgrimages in the trees. He had him spend a whole afternoon with his thin legs dangling from the limb of a horse chestnut in the garden of the D'Ondarivas, contemplating the rare trees and the sunset reflected in the lily pond and arguing about monarchies and republics, about the just and the true in the various religions, and Chinese rites, the earthquake in Lisbon, the Leyden jar, empiricism.

I was supposed to have my Greek lesson, and the teacher couldn't be found. The whole family was alarmed; they scoured the countryside looking for him—even the fish pond was plumbed in the fear that, distracted, he had fallen in and drowned. He returned in the evening, complaining about a lumbago he had contracted from sitting for hours in such an uncomfortable position.

But it should not be forgotten that in the old Jansenist this state of passive acceptance alternated with moments of renewal of his original passion for spiritual rigor. And if while he was distracted and yielding he welcomed without resistance any new or libertine idea—for example, the equality of men before the law, or the honesty of savage peoples, or the evil influence of superstitions—a quarter of an hour later, assailed by a fit of severity and absoluteness, he became one with those ideas so lightly accepted a little before and brought to them all his need for consistency and moral strictness. Then on his lips the duties of free and equal citizens or the virtues of the man who follows natural religion became rules of a ruthless discipline, articles of a fanatical faith, outside of which he saw only a black square of corruption; all the new philosophers were too bland and superficial in their denunciation of evil, and the way of perfection, even if arduous, did not allow compromises or half measures.

Before these sudden leaps of the abbé Cosimo didn't dare to say a word, out of fear that he would censure him as inconsistent or not rigorous, and the luxuriant world that he tried to summon in his thoughts dried up before him like a marble cemetery. Luckily the abbé soon tired of these tensions of will and sat there exhausted, as if stripping the flesh off every concept to reduce it to pure essence left him at the mercy of scattered and impalpable shadows; he blinked his eyes, he gave a sigh, from a sigh he passed on to a yawn, and he reentered nirvana.

But between one state of mind and the other, he now devoted his days to following the studies undertaken by Cosimo, and he went back and forth between the trees where Cosimo was and Orbecche's shop, ordering books from booksellers in Amsterdam or Paris and picking up the new arrivals. And so he prepared his undoing. Because the rumor that at Ombrosa there was a priest who kept up with all the most wicked publications of Europe reached the ecclesiastical tribunal. One afternoon the constables appeared at our villa to inspect the abbé's cell. Among his breviaries they found the works of Bayle, still untouched, but it was just enough for them to seize him and carry him off.

It was a sad scene on that cloudy afternoon; I remember it as I watched, bewildered, from the window of my room, and I stopped studying the conjugation of the aorist, because there would not be a lesson. Old Father Fauchelafleur went down the avenue surrounded by those armed guards, and looked up at the trees, and at a certain point he darted, as if he wished to run to an elm and climb it, but his legs failed him. Cosimo was hunting in the woods that day and knew nothing about it, so they didn't say goodbye.

We could do nothing to help him. Our father shut himself in his room and wouldn't taste food because he was afraid of being poisoned by the Jesuits. The abbé spent the rest of his days between prison and monastery in continual acts of abjuration, until he died, without having understood, after an entire life dedicated to faith, what he believed in, but trying to believe firmly to the end.

Anyway, the arrest of the abbé didn't harm the progress of Cosimo's education. From that period dates his correspondence with the greatest philosophers and scientists of Europe, to whom he wrote so that they might resolve questions and objections, or even just for the pleasure of discussing with the best minds and at the same time practicing foreign languages. Too bad that his papers, which he placed in hollows in the trees known only to him, have never been discovered, and certainly must in the end have been gnawed by squirrels or grown moldy; letters written by the most famous sages of the century would have been found there.

To hold his books, Cosimo constructed, in several stages, hanging bookshelves of a sort, sheltered as well as possible from the rain and the rodents, but he was constantly changing their places according to his studies and tastes of the moment, because he considered books a little like birds and didn't want to see them still or caged; otherwise, he said, they grew sad. On the most massive of these aerial shelves he gradually lined up the volumes of the *Encyclopedia* of Diderot and D'Alembert as they arrived from a bookseller in Livorno. And if in recent times, being so absorbed in books, he had had his head a little in the clouds and had become less and less interested in the world around him, now, instead, as he read the *Encyclopedia,* certain beautiful words, like *Abeille, Arbre, Bois, Jardin,* made him rediscover all those things as if they were new. Among the books he sent for he began to include handbooks of trades and professions, for example arboriculture, and he could hardly wait to try out his new knowledge.

Cosimo had always liked to watch people working, but so far his life in the trees, his movements and his hunting, had always answered to isolated and unmotivated whims, as if he were a little bird. Now instead the need to do something useful for his neighbor possessed him. And this, too, if you looked closely, was something he had learned from the company of the bandit: the pleasure of making himself useful, of performing a task indispensable to others.

He learned the art of pruning trees and offered his services to the cultivators of orchards in winter, when the trees project irregular labyrinths of twigs and seem to desire only to be reduced to more orderly forms to cover themselves with flowers and leaves and fruit. Cosimo pruned well and asked little, so there was no small landowner or tenant farmer who didn't ask him to come by, and he could be seen, in the crystalline air of those mornings, upright, legs apart, on the low bare trees, his neck wrapped in a scarf up to the ears, raising his pruning shears and, *zac! zac!* with assured strokes, sending the small secondary branches and tips flying. He used the same skill in the gardens, with the shade and ornamental trees, equipped with a short saw, and in the forest, where he tried to replace the woodcutters' axes—which could be used only to deliver crashing blows at the foot of an ancient trunk and knock down the whole tree—with his quick hatchet, which worked just on the boughs and the tops.

In other words, he was able to make love for his arboreal element become, as happens with all true loves, a pitiless and painful love, which wounds and cuts back to enhance growth and give shape. Certainly he was always careful, in pruning and trimming the trees, to serve not only the interest of the owner of the tree but also his own, that of a traveler who has to make his paths more passable; so he worked in a way that the branches he used as a bridge between one tree and another were always saved, and gained strength from the suppression of the others. Thus by his art he helped to make nature in Ombrosa, which he had always found so benign, increasingly favorable to him, friend at once of his neighbor, of nature, and of himself. And in old age especially he enjoyed the advantages of this wise way of working, when the shape of the trees increasingly made up for his loss of strength. Then, with the advent of more unprincipled generations, with their shortsighted greed, of people who were the friend of nothing, not even of themselves, everything changed, and no Cosimo will be able to move through the trees again.

14

If the number of Cosimo's friends increased, he also made some enemies. The itinerants in the woods, in fact, after the conversion of Gian dei Brughi to good reading and his subsequent downfall, found themselves in a bad way. One night my brother was asleep in his goatskin, hanging from an ash in the woods, when he was awakened by the barking of the dachshund. He opened his eyes and there was light; it was coming from below—there was a fire right at the base of the tree, and the flames were already licking the trunk.

A fire in the woods! Who had set it? Cosimo was sure that he hadn't even lighted a match that evening. So it was a trick of those criminals! They wanted to set fire to the forest so that they could steal the wood and at the same time make the blame fall on Cosimo—not only that, but burn him alive.

At the moment Cosimo didn't think of the danger that threatened him so close by; he thought that that boundless realm of paths and refuges that were his alone might be destroyed: that was his whole fear. Ottimo Massimo ran away in order not to get burned, turning every so often to let out a desperate howl. The fire was spreading to the underbrush.

Cosimo didn't lose heart. To the ash where his refuge was at the time he had transported, as he always did, many things; among these was a small keg of orzata, to satisfy his summer thirst. He climbed up to the keg. Squirrels and bats were fleeing in alarm through the branches of the ash and birds were flying out of their nests. He grabbed the keg and was about to unscrew the plug and wet the trunk of the ash to save it from the flames when he thought that the fire was already spreading to the grass, to the dry leaves, to the brush, and would soon attack all the trees around. He decided to take a risk: "Burn the ash! If with this orzata I can wet the ground all around that the flames haven't reached yet, I'll stop the fire!" And, having removed the plug, with wavy, circular motions he directed the jet to the ground, to the outer tongues of fire, extinguishing them. So the fire in the underbrush was contained within a circle of wet grass and leaves and couldn't spread further.

From the top of the ash, Cosimo jumped onto a nearby beech. He was just in time: the burned trunk at the base crashed, in a pyre, suddenly, amid the vain squealing of the squirrels.

Would the fire be confined to that point? Already a flight of sparks and little flames was spreading; certainly the feeble barrier of wet leaves would not keep it from spreading further. "Fire! Fire!" Cosimo began to shout with all his strength. "Fi-i-ire!"

"What i-i-is it? Who's shouti-i-ing?" some voices responded. Not far away there was a charcoal kiln, and a crew of Bergamasques, friends of his, slept in a hut there.

"Fi-i-ire! Ala-a-arm!"

Soon the whole mountain resounded with cries. The charcoal burners who were scattered through the woods passed the word, in their incomprehensible dialect. Now they came running from every direction. The fire was quelled.

That first attempt at arson and attack on his life should have warned Cosimo to stay away from the woods. Instead he began to worry about how he could protect it from fire. It was the summer of a year of drought and heat. In the forests on the coast, in the direction of Provence, a huge fire burned for a week. At night its glow could be seen high on the mountain, like a vestige of sunset. The air was dry; in the heat, trees and brush were one great pile of kindling. It seemed as if the winds would spread the flames in our direction, even if some random or arson fires hadn't broken out first, joining that one to make a single blaze along the whole coast. Ombrosa lived stunned under the danger, like a fortress with a straw roof assailed by enemy firebombs. The sky did not seem safe from this charge of fire: every night dense clusters of shooting stars crossed the firmament, and we expected to see them fall on us.

In those days of general consternation, Cosimo bought up

barrels and, having filled them with water, hoisted them to the tops of the tallest trees situated in commanding places. "It may not be much, but they can be useful for something." Not content, he studied the system of streams that criss-crossed the woods, though they were half dry, and springs that produced only a trickle of water. He went to consult the *cavalier avvocato*.

"Ah yes!" Enea Silvio Carrega exclaimed, hitting his forehead with his hand. "Pools! Dams! We have to come up with some projects!" And he burst into little cries and hops of enthusiasm while myriad ideas crowded his mind.

Cosimo set him to work making calculations and plans and meanwhile got the owners of private woods, the contractors for the state woods, the woodcutters, and the charcoal burners interested. All of them together, under the direction of the *cavalier avvocato* (or rather, the *cavalier avvocato* under all of them, forced to direct them and not get distracted), and with Cosimo superintending the works from above, constructed reservoirs in such a way that at every point where a fire might break out they would know where to go with the pumps.

But it wasn't enough; a guard of firefighters had to be organized, teams that in case of alarm would immediately be able to form a chain to pass buckets of water from hand to hand and stop the fire before it spread. The result was a kind of militia that had guard duty and nighttime inspections. The men were recruited by Cosimo from among the peasants and artisans of Ombrosa. Right away, as happens in every association, an esprit de corps arose, rivalry between the teams, and they felt ready to do great things. Cosimo, too, felt a new strength and happiness: he had discovered an aptitude for bringing people together and taking the lead, an aptitude that, luckily for him, he was never tempted to abuse, and exploited only a few times in his life, always in view of achieving important results, and always winning success.

He understood this: that associations make man stronger and bring out the individual's best talents, and offer the joy, rarely felt if we remain on our own, of seeing how many honest and good and capable people there are, for whom it's worthwhile to wish for good things (whereas if we live on our own, the contrary more often happens, of seeing people's other face, the one that causes us to keep our hand on the hilt guard of our sword).

So this summer of fires was a good one: there was a common problem, and to resolve it was important to all, and each one put it ahead of his other, personal interests and was repaid by the satisfaction of finding himself in agreement with and respected by many other good people.

Later Cosimo was forced to understand that when that common problem no longer exists, associations are no longer useful as they were, and it's better to be a man alone and not a leader. But in the meantime, as a leader, he spent the nights alone in the forest, keeping watch in a tree, as he had always lived.

If he ever saw a locus of fire flare up, he had a bell set up at the top of a tree, which could be heard from a distance and would give the alarm. Fires broke out three or four times, and with this system the firefighters managed to subdue them in time and save the woods. And since arson entered into it, they discovered that those two bandits Ugasso and Bel-Loré were guilty, and had them banished from the territory of the municipality. At the end of August the storms began; the danger of fire had passed.

At that time only good things were said of my brother in Ombrosa. Those favorable rumors reached our house, too, those "But he's so clever," "But certain things he does well," in the tone of those who wish to make objective assessments of a person of a different religion or an opposing party and demonstrate that they have such an open mind they can understand even ideas very distant from their own.

The *generalessa*'s reactions to this news were brusque and cursory. "Do they have weapons?" she asked when she was told about the fire watches organized by Cosimo. "Do they practice drills?" Because she was already thinking of the formation of an armed militia that in the case of war could take part in military operations.

Our father instead listened in silence, shaking his head so that you couldn't tell if every item of news about his son was distressing to him or if, rather, he was nodding, touched by the admiration of others and waiting only to be able to hope in him again. It must have been like that, in the latter mode, because after a few days he got on his horse and went to look for him.

They met in an open space with a row of slender trees around it. The baron rode his horse up and down two or three times without looking at his son, but he had seen him. The boy, jump by jump, came from the farthest tree to those which were closer. When he was in front of his father he tipped his straw hat (which in summer replaced the wild-cat hat) and said, "Hello, Father, sir."

"Hello, son."

"Are you well?"

"As far as age and afflictions permit."

"I'm pleased to see you thriving."

"I wish to say the same of you, Cosimo. I've heard that you are exerting yourself for the common good."

"I'm concerned to safeguard the forests where I live, Father, sir."

"You know that a section of the wood belongs to us, inherited from your poor dearly departed grandmother Elisabetta?"

"Yes, Father, sir. In Belrìo. Thirty chestnuts grow there, twenty-two beeches, eight pines, and a maple. I have a copy of all the regional maps. It's precisely as a member of the family that owns the woods that I wanted to bring together all those concerned to preserve them."

"Yes," said the baron, receiving the answer favorably. But

he added, "They tell me it's an association of bakers, gardeners, and blacksmiths."

"Also, Father, sir, from all the professions, provided they are honest."

"You know that with the title of duke, you could command the vassal nobility?"

"I know that when I have more ideas than others, I give the others those ideas, if they accept them, and that is to command."

"And to command, these days, is it customary to be in the trees?" the baron had on the tip of his tongue. But what was the point of bringing up that business? He sighed, absorbed in his thoughts. Then he loosened the belt where his sword was hanging. "You're eighteen years old . . . It's time you were considered an adult. I won't live much longer . . ." And he held the sword flat with both hands. "You remember that you are the Baron di Rondò?"

"Yes, Father, sir, I remember my name."

"You would like to be worthy of the name and the title you bear?"

"I will try to be as worthy as I can of the name of man, and will be so in each of his attributes."

"Take this sword, my sword." He rose up in his stirrups, Cosimo lowered himself on the branch, and the baron managed to put it on him.

"Thank you, Father, sir. I promise you I will make good use of it."

"Farewell, my son." The baron turned his horse, gave a brief tug on the reins, rode off slowly.

For a moment Cosimo stayed still, wondering if he should have saluted him with the sword; then he reflected that his father had given it to him to serve in his defense, not to make parade-ground moves, and he kept it in the sheath.

15

Around the same time, Cosimo, frequenting the *cavalier avvocato,* noticed something strange in his behavior, or rather different from usual, whether more strange or less strange. It was as if his air of absorption came not from distraction but from a fixed, dominating thought. His garrulous moments were now more frequent, and if at one time, unsociable as he was, he never set foot in the city, now instead he was always at the port, among the groups of people or sitting on the steps with the old masters and sailors, commenting on the arrivals and departures of the ships or the offenses of the pirates.

The feluccas of the Barbary pirates still made raids off our coasts, disrupting our trade. It was a piracy of little account by now, not as in the days when running into pirates meant ending up a slave in Tunisia or Algeria or paying with one's nose and ears. Now when the Muslims managed to reach a tartan from Ombrosa, they took the cargo: barrels of cod, Dutch cheeses, bales of cotton, and so on. Sometimes ours were swifter, escaped, and fired a shot from the harquebus at the masts of the felucca, and the Barbarians responded by spitting, making crude gestures, and cursing.

In other words, it was a casual piracy, which continued because of certain credits that the pashas of those countries claimed to be owed by our merchants and ship owners, having been—in their opinion—not well served regarding some supplies, or even cheated. And so they tried to settle the account bit by bit, by means of thefts, but at the same time they continued commercial negotiations, with ongoing disputes and agreements. It was therefore not in the interest of either side to definitively snub the other, and navigation was full of uncertainties and risks, which, however, never degenerated into tragedies.

The story that I will now tell was narrated by Cosimo in many different versions: I'll keep to the one that is most richly detailed and least illogical. Even though my brother in recounting his adventures certainly added much that was invented, I, lacking other sources, always try to keep to the letter of what he said.

Thus, one time Cosimo, who, keeping a lookout for fires, had gotten in the habit of being awake at night, saw a light descending into the valley. He followed it, silent in the branches with his catlike steps, and saw Enea Silvio Carrega walking very rapidly in his fez and robe, holding a lantern.

What was the *cavalier avvocato* doing out and about at that hour—a man who usually went to bed with the chickens? Cosimo followed him. He was careful not to make any noise, although he knew that his uncle, when he walked with such animation, was as if deaf and saw only a few inches in front of his feet.

By mule tracks and shortcuts the *cavalier avvocato* reached a stretch of rocky beach along the shore and began to wave the lantern. There was no moon; on the sea nothing could be seen except the curling of foam on the nearest waves. Cosimo was in a pine a little distance from the shore, because the vegetation thinned out down there and it wasn't so easy to get everywhere on the branches. Anyway, he saw the old man in his tall fez clearly on the deserted coast, waving his lantern toward the dark sea, and out of that darkness another lantern light answered him suddenly, nearby, as if it had just been lit, and a small boat with a square sail and oars, different from the local boats, emerged swiftly and came to shore.

In the wavering light of the lanterns Cosimo saw men in turbans. Some stayed in the boat, keeping it close to the shore with shallow strokes of the oars; others got out, wearing baggy red pants, with sparkling scimitars stuck in their waistbands. Cosimo sharpened his eyes and ears. His uncle and those Berbers were talking to each other in a language that he didn't understand but often seemed to understand, and surely it was the famous lingua franca. Every so often Cosimo understood a word in our language, on which Enea Silvio was insistent, mixing it with other, incomprehensible words, and those words, ours, were names of ships, known names of tartans or brigantines that belonged to ship owners in Ombrosa and went back and forth between our port and others.

It didn't take much to understand what the *cavaliere* was saying! He was informing those pirates of the days of arrival and departure of the ships of Ombrosa, and of the cargo they carried, of the route, of the weapons they had on board. Now the old man must have reported all that he knew, because he turned and hurried off, while the pirates got back in their boat and disappeared on the dark sea. From the rapidity with which the conversation had taken place it was clear that it must be a habitual occurrence. Who knew how long the Barbary ambushes had been taking place according to our uncle's information!

Cosimo stayed in the pine, incapable of moving, of leaving the deserted beach. The wind blew, the waves eroded the rocks, the tree groaned in all its joints, and my brother's teeth chattered, not because of the chill in the air but because of the chill of that grim revelation.

That timid and mysterious old man whom we as boys had always judged untrustworthy and whom Cosimo thought he had gradually learned to appreciate and sympathize with now showed himself to be an unforgivable traitor, an ingrate who wanted to harm the land that had welcomed him as an outcast after a life of wandering. Why? Had he been driven to that point by nostalgia for those countries and those people where he must have found himself, for once in his life, happy? Or did he harbor a pitiless rancor against this land in which every mouthful must have tasted of humiliation? Cosimo was divided between an urgent impulse to report the spy's intrigues and save our merchants' cargoes and the thought of what our father would suffer because of the affection that inexplicably bound him to his natural half-brother. Already Cosimo imagined the scene: the *cavaliere* handcuffed by the police, between two flanks of Ombrosotti inveighing against him, and thus he would be led to the square, they would put the noose around his neck, hang him . . . After the funeral vigil of Gian dei Brughi, Cosimo had sworn to himself that he would never again be present at an execution, and now it was up to him to be the arbiter of a death sentence against his own relative!

All night he tortured himself with that thought, and continued all the following day, moving furiously from branch to branch, kicking, hoisting himself up by the arms, sliding down trunks, as he always did when he was in the grip of a thought. Finally he came to a decision: he would take a middle way. He would frighten the pirates and his uncle, so that they would break off their suspicious relations and there would be no need for the law to intervene. He would position himself on the pine at night, with three or four loaded guns (by now he had a whole arsenal, for the various requirements of hunting); when the *cavaliere* met the pirates he would start shooting, one gun after another, sending the bullets whistling above their heads. Hearing the gunshots, pirates and uncle would flee, each on his own. And the *cavaliere,* who certainly wasn't a bold man, suspecting that he had been recognized and sure that someone was now watching those meetings on the beach, would be wary of attempting to approach the Muslim crews again.

In fact Cosimo, with the guns aimed, waited in the pine for a couple of nights. And nothing happened. The third night, here he was, the old man in the fez stumbling as he trotted along the rocky shoreline, signaling with the lantern, and the boat approaching, the sailors in turbans.

Cosimo was ready with his finger on the trigger, but he didn't shoot. Because this time it was all different. After a brief parley, two of the pirates, disembarking, made a sign to the boat, and the others began to unload goods: barrels, chests, sacks, demijohns, handcarts piled with cheeses. There wasn't just one boat, there were many, all loaded, and a line of bearers in turbans wound along the beach, preceded by our natural uncle, who guided them with his hesitant running steps to a cave in the cliffs. There the Moors placed all those goods, certainly the booty from their recent piracies.

Why did they bring it ashore? Later it was easy to reconstruct the affair: since the Barbary felucca had to drop anchor in one of our ports (for some legitimate business, such as always existed between them and us in the midst of the thieving activities), and was thus subject to search by the customs office, the stolen goods had to be hidden in a safe place, to then be picked up again on the pirates' return. Thus the ship would also have given proof that it had nothing to do with the recent thefts and would consolidate normal commercial relations with the town.

All this background Cosimo learned clearly later. At the moment he didn't stop to ask himself questions. There was a pirate treasure hidden in a cave, the pirates had embarked on their boats and left it there: it had to be retrieved as quickly as possible. For a moment my brother thought of waking the merchants of Ombrosa who must be the legitimate owners of the goods. But right away he thought of his friends the charcoal burners, who with their families suffered from hunger in the woods. He didn't hesitate: he hurried through the branches directly to the places where, around gray clearings of beaten earth, the Bergamasques slept in crude huts.

"Hurry! Everybody come! I've discovered the pirates' treasure!"

Under the canopies and branches of the huts there was huffing, throat-clearing, cursing, and finally exclamations of wonder, questions. "Gold? Silver?"

"I couldn't see clearly," said Cosimo. "From the smell I would say there's a quantity of dried cod and pecorino cheese!"

At those words, all the woodsmen rose. Those who had guns grabbed guns, the others hatchets, spits, hoes, or shovels, but mainly they carried containers to put the goods in, even misshapen coal baskets and black sacks. A great procession set off—*Hura! Hota!*—and the women, too, went down with empty baskets on their heads, and the children wearing sacks as hoods and holding torches. Cosimo went ahead from forest pine to olive, from olive to the cluster pines of the shore.

They were about to turn onto the outcropping of the cliff beyond which the cave opened when at the top of a twisted fig appeared the white shadow of a pirate, who raised his scimitar and sounded the alarm. With a few leaps Cosimo reached a branch above him and thrust the sword into his loins, until he fell down the precipice.

In the cave there was a meeting of pirate chiefs. (Cosimo, earlier, during the back-and-forth of unloading, hadn't realized that they had stayed there.) They hear the sentinel's shout, they come out and see that they're surrounded by that horde of men and women with smoke-stained faces, hooded in sacks and armed with shovels. They raise their scimitars and rush forward to make an opening. *"Hura! Hota!" "Inshallah!"* The battle began.

The charcoal burners outnumbered the pirates, but the pirates were better armed. For what that was worth: in a fight against scimitars, of course, there is nothing better than shovels. *Ding! Ding!* And those blades from Morocco withdrew, all sawtoothed. The guns instead produced thunder and smoke and then nothing else. Some of the pirates, too (officers, evidently), had guns that were very fine to look at, all inlaid, but the flints had gotten damp in the cave and misfired. The most quick-witted of the charcoal burners hit the pirate officers in the head with their shovels and took away the guns. But because of those turbans every blow that fell on the Barbarians was deadened, as if it were hitting a cushion; it was better to kick them in the stomach, because their bellybuttons were exposed.

Since the one thing there was a good supply of was stones, the charcoal burners began to throw stones. The Moors then threw stones, too. With the stones, finally, the battle became more orderly, but since the charcoal burners were trying to enter the cave, increasingly drawn by the smell of dried cod that emanated from it, and the Barbarians were trying to flee to the launch that remained on the shore, there was no great motivation for conflict between the two sides.

At a certain point the Bergamasques made an assault that got them through the entrance of the cave. The Muslims were holding out under a hail of stones when they saw that the path to the sea was free. Why, then, were they holding out? Better to raise the sail and leave.

Reaching the launch, three pirates, all noble officers, unfurled the sail. Leaping from a pine near the shore, Cosimo hurled himself at the mast, grabbed the arm, and up there, holding tight with his knees, drew his sword. The three pirates raised their scimitars. My brother, slashing to right and to left, held all three in check. The boat, still on land, listed to one side, then the other. At that moment the moon rose and the sword given by the baron to his son flashed, along with the Muslim blades. My brother slid down the mast and plunged the sword into the chest of one pirate, who fell overboard. Swift as a lizard, he climbed back up, defending himself with two parries from the strokes of the others, then he dropped down again and pierced the second, went back up, had a brief skirmish with the third, and, sliding down again, ran him through.

The three Muslim officers were lying half in the water, half out, their beards full of seaweed. The other pirates at the mouth of the cave were stunned by the stones and blows from the shovels. Cosimo, still atop the mast, looked around, triumphant, when, springing from the cave, wild as a cat with its tail on fire, came the *cavalier avvocato,* who until then had been hiding there. He ran along the beach, head down, gave the boat a shove, separating it from the shore, jumped on, and grabbing the oars began to row as hard as possible, pulling toward the open sea.

"*Cavaliere!* What are you doing? Are you mad?" said Cosimo, holding on to the yard. "Get back to shore! Where are we going?"

But no. It was clear that Enea Silvio Carrega wanted to reach the safety of the pirate ship. Now his treason was inescapably discovered, and if he stayed on shore he would certainly end up on the gallows. So he rowed and rowed, and Cosimo, although he still held the drawn sword in his hand and the old man was unarmed and weak, didn't know what to do. In his heart he didn't want to do violence to an uncle, and besides, to get to him he would have had to climb down from the mast, and the question of whether descending to a boat was equivalent to descending to the ground or whether he had already broken his inner laws by jumping from a tree with roots to the mast of a ship was too complicated to ask himself at that moment. So he did nothing; he settled down on the yard, one leg on this side of the mast, one on the other, and went off on the waves while a light wind swelled the sail and the old man kept rowing.

He heard a bark. He started for joy. The dog Ottimo Massimo, whom he had lost sight of during the battle, was curled up in the bottom of the boat and wagging his tail as if nothing were amiss. Well then, Cosimo reflected, there wasn't anything to worry about: he was in the family, with his uncle, with his dog, he was traveling in a boat, which after so many years of life in the trees was a pleasant diversion.

The moon shone on the sea. The old man was tired now. He had difficulty rowing, and wept, and began saying, "Ah, Zaira . . . Ah, Allah, Allah, Zaira . . . Ah, Zaira, *inshallah* . . ." And so, inexplicably, he spoke in Turkish, and repeated over and over amid his tears this woman's name, which Cosimo had never heard.

"What are you saying, *cavaliere*? What's wrong? Where are we going?" he asked.

"Zaira . . . Ah, Zaira . . . Allah, Allah . . ." said the old man.

"Who is Zaira, *cavaliere*? Do you think you're going to Zaira, in this direction?"

And Enea Silvio Carrega signaled yes with his head, and spoke Turkish amid his tears, and cried that name to the moon.

About this Zaira Cosimo's mind immediately began to mull over hypotheses. Maybe the deepest secret of that elusive and mysterious man was about to be revealed. If the *cavaliere,* heading toward the pirate ship, meant to reach this Zaira, she must be a woman who was there in those Ottoman countries. Maybe his whole life had been dominated by longing for that woman; maybe she was the image of lost happiness that he pursued by raising bees or designing canals. Maybe she was a lover, a wife he had had there, in the gardens of those countries across the sea, or, more likely, a daughter, a daughter of his whom he hadn't seen as a child. In the attempt to find her he must have tried for years to establish a relationship with someone from the Turkish or Moorish ships that happened into our ports, and they must finally have given him some news. Maybe he had learned that she was a slave, and to redeem her they had proposed that he inform them about the voyages of the tartans of Ombrosa. Or it was a price he had to pay to be readmitted among them and embark for Zaira's country.

Now, with his intrigue unmasked, he was forced to flee Ombrosa, and those Berbers could no longer refuse to take him and bring him back to her. In his gasping, mumbled phrases accents of hope, of supplication, and also of fear were mixed: fear that the time still wasn't right, that some further misadventure was to separate him from the yearned-for creature.

He was no longer able to ply the oars when a shadow approached, another Barbary launch. Maybe those on the ship had heard the sound of the battle on the shore and were sending scouts.

Cosimo slid halfway down the mast so as to be hidden by the sail. The old man, on the other hand, began to shout in the lingua franca that they should take him, carry him to the ship, and he stretched out his arms. His wish was granted, in fact: two janissaries in turbans, as soon as he was in reach, grabbed him by the shoulders, lifted him up, light as he was, and pulled him into their boat. The one Cosimo was on was pushed away by the counterforce, the sail caught the wind, and so my brother, who had already imagined himself dead, escaped discovery.

As the wind carried him away, voices as of an argument reached Cosimo from the pirate launch. One word, said by the Moors, which sounded like "Marrano!," and the voice of the old man, which could be heard repeating like an idiot "Ah, Zaira!," left no doubt about the welcome the *cavaliere* had received. Certainly they held him responsible for the ambush at the cave, the loss of the booty, the death of their men; they were accusing him of having betrayed them . . . Cosimo heard a cry, a thud, then silence; to him came the memory of his father's voice, as clear as if he could hear it, crying "Enea Silvio! Enea Silvio!" as he followed his natural brother through the countryside; and he hid his face in the sail.

He climbed back up to the yard to see where the boat was going. Something was floating in the middle of the sea as if carried by a current, an object, a kind of buoy, but a buoy with a tail . . . A ray of moonlight fell on it, and he saw that it wasn't an object but a head, a head wearing a fez with a ribbon, and he recognized the upturned face of the *cavalier avvocato,* with its usual bewildered expression, open-mouthed, and the rest of him, from the beard down, was in the water and couldn't be seen. Cosimo cried, "*Cavaliere! Cavaliere!* What are you doing? Why don't you get in? Hold on to the boat! Now I'll help you climb in. *Cavaliere!*"

But the uncle didn't answer; he was floating, floating, looking up with that dazed eye that seemed to see nothing.

And Cosimo said, "Come on, Ottimo Massimo! Jump in the water! Grab the *cavaliere* by the scruff of his neck. Save him! Save him!"

The obedient dog dove in, tried to put his teeth on the old man's neck, couldn't, took him by the beard.

"By the scruff, Ottimo Massimo, I said!" Cosimo insisted, but the dog lifted the head by the beard and pushed it to the edge of the boat, and you could see that there was no longer any scruff, there was no longer any body or anything, it was only a head, the head of Enea Silvio Carrega, cut off by a stroke of the scimitar.

16

The end of the *cavalier avvocato* was first recounted by Cosimo in a very different version. When the wind carried the boat with him huddled up in the yard to shore and Ottimo Massimo followed, dragging the cut-off head, he—from the tree to which he had rapidly moved, with the help of a rope—told the people who came running at his cry a much simpler story: that is, that the *cavaliere* had been kidnapped by pirates and killed. Maybe it was a version dictated by the thought of his father, whose grief would be so great at the news of his half-brother's death and at the sight of those pitiful remains that Cosimo didn't have the heart to burden him with the revelation of the *cavaliere*'s treason. In fact, later, hearing of the depression into which the baron had fallen, he tried to construct for our natural uncle a fictitious glory, inventing a secret and shrewd struggle to defeat the pirates, to which he had supposedly been devoting himself for some time and which, discovered, had led him to his death. But it was a contradictory story, full of holes, partly because there was something else that Cosimo wanted to conceal, that is, the unloading of the pirates' booty in the cave and the intervention of the charcoal burners. And in fact, if the thing had been known, the whole population of Ombrosa would have gone into the forest to retrieve the merchandise from the Bergamasques, treating them as thieves.

After a few weeks, when he was sure that the charcoal burners had disposed of the goods, he described the attack on the cave. And those who wanted to go up and retrieve something were left empty-handed. The charcoal burners had divided everything into fair shares, the dried cod flake by flake, the sausages, the cheeses, and with what remained they had made a big banquet in the woods that lasted all day.

Our father aged greatly, and his grief at the loss of Enea Silvio had strange consequences for his character. He was gripped by a mania to insure that the works of his natural brother weren't lost. So he wanted to take care of the beekeeping himself, and prepared for it with great pomposity, although he had never before been seen near a hive. For advice he turned to Cosimo, who had learned something about it; not that he asked him questions, but he carried on a conversation about beekeeping and listened to what Cosimo said, and then he repeated it as an order to the peasants, in an irritated and condescending tone, as if these things were well known. He tried not to get too close to the hives, because of his fear of being stung, but he wanted to show that he was able to conquer that fear, and who knows what the effort cost him. In the same way he gave orders to dig certain canals, to complete a project begun by poor Enea Silvio; and if he had succeeded it would have been surprising, because the dear departed soul had never finished one.

This late passion of the baron for practical matters didn't last long, unfortunately. One day he was out there, nervous and busy with the hives and the canals; he made a sudden movement and saw a couple of bees coming toward him. He got scared, began to wave his hands, upset a beehive, and ran off with a cloud of bees behind him. Running blindly, he ended up in that canal they were trying to fill with water, and they pulled him out soaking wet.

He was put to bed. Between the fever from the bee stings and the fever from the cold he caught from getting wet, he had a bad time for a week; then he could be said to be cured. But a depression took hold of him that he wouldn't pull himself out of.

He stayed in bed and lost every attachment to life. Nothing of what he wanted to do had succeeded: no one talked anymore about the dukedom, his firstborn was still in the trees even now that he was a man, his half-brother had been murdered, his daughter was married and far away with people even more unpleasant than she was, I was still too much a boy to be close to him and his wife too brusque and authoritarian. He began to rave, to say that now the Jesuits had occupied his house and he couldn't leave his room, and as full of bitterness and obsessions as he had always lived, he died.

Cosimo, too, followed the funeral procession, going from

tree to tree, but he couldn't enter the cemetery, because the cypresses were so thick with foliage that there was no way to climb in them. He was present at the burial but on the other side of the wall, and when we all threw a handful of dirt on the coffin he threw a branch with its leaves. I thought that all of us had always been as distant from my father as Cosimo in the trees.

Now Cosimo was the Baron di Rondò. His life didn't change. It's true, he saw to the interests of our property, but always in an occasional way. When the stewards and the tenants looked for him, they never knew where to find him, and when they least wanted to be seen by him, there he was on a branch.

In order to tend to these family affairs, Cosimo now appeared more often in the city; he would linger in the big walnut in the square or in the holm oaks near the port. People paid their respects to him, called him Sir Baron, and he began to strike poses similar to an old man's, the way young men sometimes like to do, and he stayed there telling stories to a group of Ombrosotti who had settled themselves at the foot of the tree.

He continued to relate, always in different ways, the end of our natural uncle, and little by little he came to reveal the *cavaliere*'s connivance with the pirates, but to restrain the immediate indignation of the citizens he added the story of Zaira, almost as if Carrega had confided it to him before dying, and so he persuaded them even to be moved by the sad fate of the old man.

From a complete fabrication, I think, Cosimo had, through successive approximations, arrived at an almost entirely truthful version of the facts. He succeeded with that two or three times; then, since the Ombrosotti were never tired of hearing the story and there were always new listeners and they all required new details, he was induced to make additions, amplifications, hyperboles, to introduce new characters and episodes, and so the story was distorted and became more invented than in the beginning.

Now Cosimo had an audience that listened with astonishment to everything he said. He developed a taste for storytelling, and his life in the trees, and hunting, and the bandit Gian dei Brughi, and the dog Ottimo Massimo became opportunities for stories that had no end. (Many episodes of this memoir of his life are reported just as he told them at the urgings of his plebeian audience, and I say this to be forgiven if not everything I write seems true and in accord with a harmonious vision of humanity and the facts.)

For example, one of those idlers asked him, "Is it true that you've never set foot out of the trees, Sir Baron?"

And Cosimo began, "Yes. Once, by mistake, I jumped down onto the antlers of a deer. I thought I was moving onto a maple, and it was a deer that had escaped from the estate of the royal hunt and was standing there. The deer feels my weight on its antlers and flees through the woods. I can't tell you what crashing! There on top I'm getting stabbed on every side, between the sharp points of the horns, the thorns, the tree branches that hit me in the face . . . The deer was thrashing about, trying to get rid of me, I held firm . . ."

He suspended the story, and they then: "And how did you get out of it, Lordship?"

And every time he'd pull out a different finale: "The deer ran and ran, and reached the herd of deer, and seeing him with a man on his antlers, some fled, some approached, curious. I aimed the gun I always had over my shoulder and I shot every deer I saw. I killed fifty of them."

"And where were there ever fifty deer in our area?" one of those idlers asked.

"Now the breed has died out. Because those fifty were all female deer, you see? Every time my deer tried to approach a female I fired, and she fell down dead. The deer couldn't understand it, and he was desperate. Then . . . then he decided to kill himself — he ran up on a high rock and jumped down. But I grabbed on to a pine that was sticking out, and here I am!"

Or it was a battle joined between two deer with antlers, and at every clash he jumped from the antlers of one to the antlers of the other, until at a stronger butt he was catapulted into an oak.

In other words, he was gripped by that mania of storytellers who never know if the events that really happened make better stories and, in being recalled, bring with them a sea of hours passed, of detailed feelings—boredom, happiness, uncertainties, boasts, self-loathing—or those which are invented, where one works something out roughly and everything appears easy, but then the more it varies, the clearer it becomes that the teller is going back to the things he felt or knew in reality, by living.

Cosimo was still at the age when the wish to tell stories generates the wish to live, and one believes that one hasn't lived enough to tell stories. So he went off to hunt, stayed away for weeks, and then returned to the trees in the square holding by the tail weasels, badgers, and foxes, and he told the Ombrosotti new stories that, as he told them, went from being true to invented, and from invented to true.

But in all that mania there was a deeper dissatisfaction, an absence; in that search for people who would listen to him there was a different search. Cosimo still didn't know love, and without that what is any experience? What's the point of risking your life when you don't yet know the taste of life?

The girls who sold vegetables or fish passed through the square of Ombrosa, and the young ladies in carriages, and Cosimo cast quick glances from the tree and yet didn't understand why in all of them there was something he sought but it wasn't entirely in any one. At night, when the lights were on in the houses and Cosimo was alone in the branches with the yellow eyes of the owls, he came to dream of love. For the couples who met behind hedges and between the rows of vines he was full of admiration and envy, and he followed them with his gaze as they disappeared in the darkness, but if they lay down at the foot of his tree he ran away, deeply embarrassed.

Then, to overcome the natural modesty of his eyes, he lingered to observe the loves of the animals. In spring the world in the trees was a nuptial world: the squirrels made love with almost human moves and squeals, the birds beat their wings as they coupled, even the lizards ran away joined, with their tails in a knot, and the porcupines seemed to soften to make their embraces gentler. The dog Ottimo Massimo, not at all intimidated by the fact of being the only dachshund in Ombrosa, courted big sheepdog bitches, or wolfhounds, with bold ardor, relying on the natural liking he inspired. Sometimes he returned battered by bites, but a successful love was enough to make up for all the defeats.

Cosimo, like Ottimo Massimo, was the only exemplar of a species. In his daydreams he saw himself loved by beautiful girls, but how would he encounter love in the trees? In his fantasies he succeeded in not knowing where it would happen, on the ground or up where he was now: a place without place, he imagined, like a world reached by going up, not down. Maybe there was a tree so high that if he climbed it he would touch another world, the moon.

Meanwhile, this habit of chatting in the square made him feel increasingly dissatisfied with himself. And ever since a fellow coming from the nearby city of Olivabassa on market day had said, "Oh, you, too, have your Spaniard!"—and when questioned about what he meant answered, "In Olivabassa there's a whole race of Spaniards who live in the trees!"—Cosimo could have no peace until he made the journey to Olivabassa through the forest trees.

17

Olivabassa was an inland town. Cosimo got there after two days of walking, crossing dangerous stretches of thin vegetation. On the way, near the inhabited places, people who hadn't seen him before uttered cries of wonder, and some threw stones at him, so he tried to proceed as far as possible unobserved. But gradually as he approached Olivabassa he noticed that if a woodcutter or peasant or olive picker saw him, he or she showed no surprise, but, rather, the men tipped their hats in greeting, as if they knew him, and said words that were certainly not in the local dialect and which in their mouths sounded strange, like *"Señor! Buenos días, Señor!"*

It was winter, and some of the trees were bare. In Olivabassa a double row of plane trees and elms crossed the built-up area. And my brother, as he got close, saw that among the bare branches there were people, one or two or even three in each tree, sitting or standing, with a serious look. In a few jumps he reached them.

There were men in the clothes of nobles—feathered tricornes, large cloaks—and women who also appeared noble, with veils over their heads, and who were sitting on the branches in twos or threes, some embroidering, and every so often looking down into the street with a slight lateral movement of the chest and arms leaning against the branch as on a windowsill.

The men greeted him as if full of bitter understanding: *"Buenos días, Señor!"* and Cosimo bowed and tipped his hat.

Ensconced in the fork of a plane tree from which it appeared that he would never get out was an obese man who seemed to be the most authoritative among them. He had the skin of someone with liver trouble, under which the shadow of shaved whiskers and beard showed black in spite of his advanced age, and he seemed to ask a gaunt, lanky neighbor, dressed in black and also with faintly black clean-shaven cheeks, who that unknown person advancing along the row of trees was.

Cosimo thought the moment had come to introduce himself.

He arrived at the obese man's plane tree, bowed, and said, "Baron Cosimo Piovasco di Rondò, at your service."

"Rondos? Rondos?" said the obese man. *"Aragonés? Gallego?"*

"No, sir."

"Catalán?"

"No, sir. I'm from around here."

"Desterrado también?"

The lanky gentleman felt that he ought to intervene and serve as interpreter, very bombastically. "His Highness Frederico Alonso Sanchez de Guatamurra y Tobasco asks if your lordship is also an exile, since we see you climbing in these branches."

"No, sir. Or at least not an exile by someone else's decree."

"Viaja usted sobre los árboles por gusto?"

And the interpreter: "His Highness Frederico Alonso would like to ask if it's for your pleasure that your lordship follows this itinerary."

Cosimo thought for a moment, and answered, "It's because I think it suits me, although no one has imposed it on me."

"Feliz usted!" exclaimed Frederico Alonso Sanchez, sighing. *"Ay de mí, ay de mí!"*

And the one in black, explaining, increasingly bombastic: "His Highness says that your lordship should consider yourself fortunate to enjoy this freedom, which we cannot help comparing with our constraint, which, however, we endure, resigned to the will of God," and he crossed himself.

Thus, between a laconic exclamation from Prince Sanchez and a detailed version from the man in black, Cosimo managed to reconstruct the story of the colony that lived in the plane trees. They were Spanish aristocrats who had rebelled against King Carlos III for matters of disputed feudal privileges and so had been exiled with their families. Reaching Olivabassa, they had been forbidden to continue the journey: on the basis of an ancient treaty with His Catholic Majesty, those lands, in fact, could not give refuge or even be crossed by people exiled from Spain. The situation of those noble families was very difficult to resolve, but the magistrates of

Olivabassa, who didn't want to have trouble with foreign chancellors but had no reason to dislike those wealthy travelers, either, came to an accommodation: the letter of the treaty prescribed that the exiles must not "touch the ground" of that territory, so if they stayed in the trees that was sufficient and in order. So the exiles had climbed into the plane trees and the elms, with ladders provided by the town and then removed. They had been perched up there for some months, trusting in the gentle climate, in an imminent decree of amnesty from Carlos III, and in divine providence. They had a supply of Spanish ducats and bought provisions, thus bringing commerce to the city. To haul up their food, they had installed lifts. On other trees there were canopies under which they slept. In other words, they had been able to adjust well, or rather the Olivabassi had equipped them well, because they profited from it. The exiles, for their part, didn't lift a finger all day long.

It was the first time Cosimo had met other human beings who lived in the trees, and he began to ask practical questions.

"And when it rains what do you do?"

"Sacramos todo el tiempo, Señor!"

And the interpreter, who was Father Sulpicio de Guadalete, of the Society of Jesus, an exile ever since his order had been banned by Spain: "Protected by our canopies, we turn our thoughts to the Lord, thanking him for that little which suffices for us!"

"Do you ever go hunting?"

"Señor, algunas veces con el visco."

"Sometimes one of us greases a branch with birdlime for his amusement."

Cosimo was never tired of discovering how they had resolved the problems that he had faced, too.

"And washing, what do you do about washing?"

"Para lavar? Hay lavanderas!" said Don Frederico with a shrug of the shoulders.

"We give our clothes to the town laundresses," Don Sulpicio translated. "Every Monday, to be precise, we lower the basket of dirty clothes."

"No, I meant how do you wash your face and body?"

Don Frederico grunted and shrugged his shoulders, as if that problem had never presented itself.

Don Sulpicio believed that he had a duty to interpret: "According to the opinion of His Highness, these are private matters for each of us."

"And, begging your pardon, where do you take care of your needs?"

"Ollas, Señor."

And Don Sulpicio, sticking with his modest tone: "In truth we use some small jars."

Taking leave of Don Frederico, Cosimo was led off by Padre Sulpicio to visit various members of the colony in the trees where they resided. In spite of the unavoidable discomforts of their sojourn, all these hidalgos and these ladies preserved their habitual dignified attitudes. Some of the men sat astride the branches on horse saddles, a system that Cosimo found very pleasing; in so many years he had never thought of it (especially useful because of the stirrups—he noted right away—which eliminate the inconvenience of having to let one's feet dangle, something that after a while brings on a tingling sensation). Some pointed navy telescopes (one of them had the rank of admiral), which probably were useful only for looking at each other from tree to tree, for snooping and causing gossip. The women and girls all sat on embroidered cushions they had made, sewing (they were the only people in any way industrious) or caressing big cats. There were a great number of cats in those trees, and birds, the latter in cages (maybe they were victims of the birdlime), except for some free doves that came to rest on the girls' hands and were petted sadly.

In these sort of arboreal salons Cosimo was received with hospitable dignity. They offered him coffee, then immediately began to talk about the palaces they had left behind in Seville, in Granada, and about their lands and granaries and stables, and they invited him for the day when they would be restored to their privileges. Of the king who had banned them they spoke in an accent of both fanatical hatred and devout reverence, sometimes managing to separate precisely the person against whom their families were fighting and the royal title from whose authority emanated their own. Sometimes instead they quite deliberately mixed the two opposite modes of consideration in a single mental impulse; and whenever the conversation turned to the sovereign, Cosimo didn't know how to react.

Over all the gestures and conversations of the exiles hovered an aura of sadness and mourning, which corresponded in part to their nature, in part to a willful determination, as sometimes happens in those who fight for a cause whose convictions are poorly defined and try to make up for it by the grandeur of their bearing.

In the young women—who at first glance all seemed to Cosimo a little too hairy and with skin too opaque—a hint of liveliness meandered, always curbed in time. Two of them were playing badminton between plane trees. *Tic* and *tac, tic* and *tac,* then a little cry: the shuttlecock had fallen into the street. An Olivabassa kid picked it up and, to throw it back, demanded two pesetas.

On the last tree, an elm, was an old man called El Conde, shabbily dressed and without a wig. Father Sulpicio, approaching him, lowered his voice, and Cosimo imitated him. Every so often El Conde, with one arm, moved aside a branch and looked at the slope of the hill and at a plain that, sometimes green and sometimes bare, vanished into the distance.

Sulpicio murmured to Cosimo the story of a son detained in King Carlos's dungeons and tortured. Cosimo understood that while all those hidalgos were exiles, so to speak, but had every so often to recall and repeat to themselves why and how they had come to be there, only that old man truly suffered. That gesture of pushing aside the branch as if expecting to see another land appear, that gradual shifting of his gaze into the undulating distance as if he hoped never to encounter the horizon, of managing to discern a land, alas, so far away, was the first real sign of exile that Cosimo had seen. And he understood how important the presence of El Conde was for those hidalgos, as if it were what kept them together, gave them a meaning. It was he, perhaps the poorest, certainly in their land the least powerful, who told them what they were to suffer and to hope.

Returning from these visits, Cosimo saw on an alder a girl he hadn't seen before. In two jumps he was there.

She had eyes of a beautiful periwinkle color and a perfumed complexion. She was holding a bucket.

"Why when I saw everyone didn't I see you?"

"I was getting water at the well," and she smiled. Some water fell out of the bucket, which was slightly tilted. He helped her hold it.

"So you get down from the trees?"

"No. There's a twisted cherry tree that shades the well. From there we lower the buckets. Come."

They walked along a branch, climbing over the wall of a courtyard. She guided him on the walk along the cherry. Below was the well.

"You see, Baron?"

"How do you know I'm a baron?"

"I know everything," she said, smiling. "My sisters immediately told me about your visit."

"The ones playing badminton?"

"Irena and Raimunda, yes."

"The daughters of Don Frederico?"

"Yes."

"And your name?"

"Ursula."

"You're better at walking in the trees than anyone else here."

"I used to do it as a child—in Granada we had big trees on the patio."

"Would you be able to pick that rose?" A climbing rose was blooming at the top of a tree.

"A pity—no."

"All right, I will." He set off, and returned with the rose. Ursula smiled and held out her hands.

"I want to plant it myself. Tell me where."

"On my head, thank you." And she guided his hand.

"Now tell me, do you know," Cosimo asked, "how to get to that almond?"

"How?" She laughed. "I certainly don't know how to fly."

"Wait." And Cosimo threw a noose. "If you tie yourself to that rope, I'll winch you across."

"No . . . I'm scared." But she was laughing.

"It's my system. I've been traveling for years, doing it all by myself."

"Goodness!"

He transported her across. Then he followed. It was a delicate almond and not large. There they were close. Ursula was still panting and red from the flight.

"Scared?"

"No." But her heart was pounding.

"You didn't lose the rose," he said, and touched it to adjust it.

Thus, close together in the tree, with every gesture they were embracing.

"Ooh!" she said, and, he first, they kissed. So their love began, the boy happy and amazed, she happy and not at all surprised (nothing happens to girls by chance). It was the love so long awaited by Cosimo and now so unexpectedly found, and so wonderful that he couldn't understand how he could have imagined its wonder before. And the most novel thing about its beauty was its being so simple, and to the boy at that moment it seemed that it must always be so.

18

The peach trees bloomed, the almonds, the cherries. Cosimo and Ursula spent the days together in the flowering trees. Spring colored with gaiety even the grim proximity of her relatives.

In the colony of exiles my brother was immediately able to make himself useful, teaching the various ways of getting from tree to tree and encouraging those noble families to emerge from their habitual composure and practice some movements. He also set up bridges of rope, which allowed the older exiles to exchange visits. And so, in almost a year of living among the Spaniards, he endowed the colony with many tools he had invented: water reservoirs, stoves, furlined sacks to sleep in. The desire to make new inventions led him to go along with the customs of these hidalgos even when they didn't agree with the ideas of his favorite authors; thus, seeing the desire of those pious people to confess regularly, he dug out a confessional in a trunk, which the thin Don

Sulpicio could get into and, through a small window with a curtain and a grille, hear their sins.

The pure passion for technical innovations, in other words, wasn't enough to keep him from respect for the rules in force; it took ideas. Cosimo wrote to the bookseller Orbecche to send him by post to Olivabassa the volumes that had arrived in the meantime. Thus he could have Ursula read *Paul and Virginie* and *The New Heloise.*

The exiles often held meetings in a vast oak, assemblies at which they drafted letters to the sovereign. At first these were supposed to be letters of indignant protest and threat, almost ultimatums, but at a certain point one or another of them proposed milder, more respectful formulations, and the end result was a petition in which they humbly prostrated themselves at the feet of the gracious majesties, begging their forgiveness.

Then El Conde rose. They were all silent. El Conde, looking up, began to speak, in a low, vibrant voice, and he said everything that was in his heart. When he sat down again, the others were serious and silent. No one mentioned a petition anymore.

Cosimo by now was part of the community and joined in the assemblies. And there, with naive youthful fervor, he explained the ideas of the philosophers and the wrongs of sovereigns and how states could be governed according to reason and justice. But among all of them, the only ones who could pay attention to him were El Conde, who although he was old was always striving for a way to understand and react; Ursula, who had read some books; and a couple of girls who were a little brighter than the others. The rest of the colony were blockheads.

In other words, this Conde, with constant pressure, instead of always sitting and gazing at the countryside, began to want to read books. Rousseau he found a little difficult; Montesquieu, on the other hand, he liked—that was already a step. The other hidalgos nothing, although some, unbeknown to Father Sulpicio, asked Cosimo if they could borrow *The Maid* so they could read the racy pages. Thus, with El Conde mulling new ideas, the gatherings in the oak took another direction: now they talked about going to Spain to make a revolution.

Father Sulpicio didn't scent the danger at first. He wasn't very subtle by nature and, cut off from the entire hierarchy of his superiors, was no longer up to date on how minds could be poisoned. But as soon as he could reorder his ideas (or as soon as, say others, he received certain letters with episcopal seals) he began to say that the devil had sneaked into their community and they could expect a rain of lightning that would incinerate the trees and all who were in them.

One night Cosimo was wakened by a lament. He hurried with a lantern, and reaching El Conde's elm, he saw the old man bound to the trunk and the Jesuit tightening the knots.

"Stop, Father! What's this?"

"The arm of the Holy Inquisition, my son! Now it's the

turn of this wretched old man, so that he may confess his heresy and spit out the devil. Then it will be your turn!"

Cosimo drew his sword and cut the ropes. "Watch out, Father! There are other arms, which serve reason and justice!"

The Jesuit drew an unsheathed sword from under his cloak. "Baron di Rondò, your family has had a score to settle with my order for a long time!"

"My father was right!" Cosimo exclaimed, crossing swords. "The Society doesn't forgive!"

They fought, balancing on the branches. Don Sulpicio was an excellent fencer, and several times my brother found himself in a bad spot. They were on the third bout when El Conde, having recovered, began to shout. The other exiles awoke, came running, intervened between the duelers. Sulpicio immediately hid his sword and, as if nothing had happened, began to urge calm.

Passing over in silence an action so serious would have been unthinkable in any other community, but not in that one, with the desire they had to reduce to the minimum all thoughts that surfaced in their minds. So Don Frederico used his good offices and there was a kind of reconciliation between Don Sulpicio and El Conde, which left everything as it had been before.

Cosimo, certainly, had to be suspicious, and when he traveled through the trees with Ursula he was always afraid of being spied on by the Jesuit. He knew that Don Sulpicio was raising suspicions in Don Frederico so that he wouldn't let the girl go out with him. Those noble families, in truth, were brought up in very reserved habits, but there in the trees, in exile, they had stopped paying attention to many things. Cosimo seemed to them a good young man, titled, and he was able to make himself useful; no one forced him to stay there with them, and even if they understood that between him and Ursula there must be something tender, and often saw them going off through the orchards in search of flowers and fruit, they closed an eye in order not to find anything to criticize.

Now, though, with Don Sulpicio sowing ill feeling, Don Frederico could no longer pretend not to know anything. He summoned Cosimo to a meeting on his plane tree. At his side was the long black figure of Sulpicio.

"Baron, you're often seen with my *niña,* I'm told."

"She's teaching me *hablar vuestro idioma,* Highness."

"How old are you?"

"I'm about to be *diez y nueve.*"

"*Joven!* Too young! My daughter is a girl of marriageable age. *Por qué* do you go around with her?"

"Ursula is seventeen . . ."

"You are already thinking of *casarte*?"

"What?"

"She's teaching *el castellano* badly, *hombre.* I mean if you're thinking of choosing a *novia,* build yourself a house."

Sulpicio and Cosimo together made a gesture as if to put their hands out. The conversation was taking a direction that was not the one wanted by the Jesuit and even less by my brother.

"My house . . ." said Cosimo, and gestured around, at the highest branches, the clouds, "my house is everywhere, everywhere I can climb, going up . . ."

"No es esto," and Prince Frederico Alonso shook his head. "Baron, if you want to come to Granada when we return, you'll see the richest domain of the Sierra. *Mejor que aquí."*

Don Sulpicio could stay silent no longer. "But Highness, this young man is a Voltairean. He mustn't see your daughter anymore."

"Oh, *es joven, es joven,* ideas come and go, *que se case,* let them marry and it will pass, come to Granada, come."

"Muchas gracias a usted . . . I'll think about it . . ." And Cosimo, revolving his cat-skin cap in his hands, withdrew with many bows.

When he saw Ursula again he was thoughtful. "You know, Ursula, your father spoke to me. He made some speeches . . ."

Ursula was frightened. "He doesn't want us to see each other anymore?"

"It's not that . . . He'd like it, when you're no longer exiled, if I'd come with you to Granada."

"Ah yes! How wonderful!"

"Look, I love you, but I've always been in the trees, and I want to stay there."

"Oh, Cosme, we have fine trees in our land, too."

"Yes, but meanwhile, to make the journey with you I would have to get down, and once I got down . . ."

"Don't worry, Cosme. Anyway, now we're exiles and maybe we'll stay that way for our whole life."

And my brother stopped troubling himself about it.

But Ursula was wrong. Soon afterward, a letter with royal Spanish seals reached Don Frederico. The ban, by the gracious indulgence of His Catholic Majesty, was revoked. The exiled nobles could return to their homes and their possessions. Immediately there was a great swarming in the plane trees. "We're going home! We're going home! Madrid! Cádiz! Seville!"

The rumor ran through the city. The people of Olivabassa arrived with ladders. Among the exiles, some got down, to be celebrated by the people; some gathered up the baggage.

"But it's not over!" exclaimed El Conde. "The courts will hear us! And the crown!" And since at that moment none of his companions in exile appeared to want to pay attention to him, and already the ladies were worried about their no-longer-fashionable clothes, about wardrobes that would need to be refreshed, he began to make grand speeches to the population of Olivabassa: "Now let's go to Spain and you'll see! There we'll settle accounts! This young man and I will bring justice!" And he pointed to Cosimo. And Cosimo, confused, shook his head.

Don Frederico had been carried down to the ground. *"Baja, joven bizarro!"* he cried to Cosimo. "Brave youth, come down! Come with us to Granada!"

Cosimo, crouching on a branch, defended himself.

And the prince: "*Cómo no?* You'll be like my son."

"The exile is over!" said El Conde. "Finally we can undertake what we've thought about for so long! What's left to do in the trees, Baron? There's no reason for it anymore!"

Cosimo spread his arms. "I came up here before you, sirs, and I will remain after."

"You wish to retreat!" cried El Conde.

"No—resist," the baron answered.

Ursula, who was among the first to descend and with her sisters was busy filling a carriage with their baggage, rushed to the tree. "Then I'll stay with you! I'll stay with you!" And she ran up the ladder.

Four or five stopped her, tore her away, removed the ladders from the trees.

"*Adiós,* Ursula, be happy!" said Cosimo as they carried her by force into the departing carriage.

A joyous barking burst out. The dachshund Ottimo Massimo, who during the whole time his master was living in Olivabassa had displayed a snarling discontent, perhaps sharpened by continuous quarrels with the Spaniards' cats, now seemed happy again. He began to hunt, but as if in fun, the few surviving cats forgotten in the trees, who fluffed their fur and hissed at him.

Some on horseback, some in carriages, some in coaches, the exiles departed. The street emptied. My brother remained alone in the trees of Olivabassa. A few feathers were stuck to the branches, some ribbons or lace that blew in the wind, and a glove, a lace-trimmed parasol, a fan, a boot with a spur.

19

It was a summer of full moons, croaking frogs, whistling chaffinches, that summer when the baron returned and was seen again in Ombrosa. He seemed in the grip of a birdlike restlessness: he jumped from branch to branch, nosy, touchy, ineffectual.

Soon a rumor arose that a certain Checchina, beyond the valley, was his lover. Certainly the girl lived in a secluded house, with a deaf aunt, and the branch of an olive tree passed close by her window. The idlers in the square discussed whether she was or wasn't.

"I saw them, she was at the windowsill, he on the branch. He was waving his arms like a bat and she was laughing!"

"At a certain hour he jumps!"

"Certainly not. If he's sworn not to get down from the trees in his life . . ."

"Well, he made the rule, he can also make the exceptions . . ."

"Eh, if you start making exceptions . . ."

"No, no, I'm telling you—she's the one who jumps, from the window into the olive tree!"

"And how do they do it? They must be pretty uncomfortable . . ."

"I say they've never touched each other. Yes, he's courting her, or she's leading him on. But he won't come down from there . . ."

Yes, no, he, she, the windowsill, the jump, the branch—the discussions were unending. Now there was trouble with boyfriends and husbands if their lovers or wives looked up at a tree. The women, for their part, as soon as they met went *psst, psst, psst*—and who were they talking about? About him.

Checchina or not, my brother had his flirtations without ever getting down from the trees. I met him once running along the branches with a mattress over his shoulder, as naturally as when we saw him carrying over his shoulder guns, ropes, hatchets, knapsacks, flasks, powder horns.

A certain Dorotea, a loose woman, had to confess to me that she had met with him, on her own initiative, and not for profit but to get an idea.

"And what idea did you get?"

"Eh! I'm content . . ."

Another, Zobeida, told me she had dreamed of "the climbing man" (as she called him), and that dream was so knowledgeable and detailed that I think she had actually lived it.

Of course, I don't know how these affairs go, but Cosimo must have had a certain fascination for women. Ever since he had been with those Spaniards, he had attended to his person and had stopped going around bundled in fur like a bear. He wore trousers and a well-fitting tailcoat and an English-style top hat, and he shaved his beard and styled his wig. In fact, by now one could judge, from how he was dressed, whether he was going hunting or to a tryst.

The fact is that a mature noblewoman whom I won't name, here in Ombrosa (her daughters and grandchildren are still living and might be offended, but at the time it was a well-known story), always traveled in her carriage alone, with the old coachman on the box, and had herself driven along that stretch of the main road that passes through the woods. At a certain point she said to the coachman, "Giovita, the wood is teeming with mushrooms. Go on, fill that basket and then come back," and she gave him a wicker basket. The poor man, with his rheumatism, got down off the box, heaved the basket to his shoulders, left the road, and set off, making his way among the ferns in the heavy dew, going deeper and deeper in among the beeches, and leaning over to dig under every leaf to unearth a porcino or a puffball. Meanwhile the noblewoman disappeared from the carriage as if she had been transported into the sky, up through the thick leaves that overhung the road. Nothing else is known, except that those who passed by there often happened to see the carriage standing empty in the woods. Then, as mysteriously as she had disappeared, here again was the noblewoman sitting in the carriage, with a languorous gaze. Giovita returned, mud-splattered, with a few mushrooms scraped together in the basket, and they left.

Many such stories were told, especially in the houses of certain Genoese madams who held gatherings for affluent men (I, too, used to go, when I was a bachelor), and that was how a desire to visit the baron must have originated in these five ladies. In fact there's an oak that's still called the Oak of the Five Sparrows, and we old people know what it means. It was told by a certain Gè, a merchant of muscatel, and a man who can be trusted. It was a beautiful sunny day, and this Gè was hunting in the woods; he arrives at the oak and what does he see? Cosimo had taken all five up into the branches, one here and one there, and they were enjoying the warmth, all naked, with umbrellas open in order not to get sunburned, and the baron was right in the middle, reading Latin verses, I couldn't make out whether it was Ovid or Lucretius.

So many tales were told, and how much is true I don't know; at the time he was reserved and modest about those things. As an old man, on the other hand, he told stories and more stories, maybe too many, but for the most part stories that were neither in the sky nor on the earth and that not even he could make sense of. The fact is that at that time it began to be habitual, and convenient, to blame him when a girl swelled up and no one knew who it had been. A girl once recounted that she was picking olives and felt herself lifted up by two long arms, like a monkey's . . . Soon afterward she delivered twins. Ombrosa was filled with the baron's bastards, whether true or false. Now they've grown up, and some, it's true, resemble him, but it might also have been suggestion, because it was sometimes unsettling for pregnant women to see Cosimo leap suddenly from one branch to another.

Well, in general I don't believe those stories that were told to explain the births. And I don't know if he had as many women as they say, but certainly those who really had known him preferred to be silent.

And then, if he had so many women around, how to explain the moonlit nights when he roamed like a cat through the fig trees, the plums, the pomegranates around the inhabited places, in those orchards which the outermost ring of houses in Ombrosa overlooks, and moaned, and uttered sighs of a sort, or yawns, or groans, which, no matter how much he wished to control them, make them tolerable, normal expressions, came out of his throat like howls or yowls. And the people of Ombrosa, who by now knew him, caught in their sleep, weren't even frightened; they turned over under the sheets and said, "It's the baron looking for a woman. Let's hope he finds one and lets us sleep."

Sometimes an old man, one of those who suffer from insomnia and go willingly to the window if they hear a noise, would look out into the garden and see his shadow against the shadow of the fig tree's branches, projected to the ground by the moon. "You can't sleep tonight, Milord?"

"No, I've been tossing and turning and I'm still awake," said Cosimo, as if he were in bed talking, with his face sunk in the pillow, waiting only to feel his eyelids close, while instead he was hanging there like an acrobat. "I don't know what it is tonight, the heat, nerves—maybe the weather's about to change. Don't you feel it, too?"

"Eh, I do, I do. But I'm old, Milord, and you, on the other hand—your blood still flows . . ."

"Oh, yes, it flows, it certainly does . . ."

"Well, see if it flows a little farther than here, Sir Baron, because here anyway there's nothing that could give you relief, only poor families that wake at dawn and want to sleep now."

Cosimo didn't answer; he was disappearing among the leaves in other gardens. He always knew how to stay within the proper limits, and on the other hand, the Ombrosotti were always able to tolerate his strange behavior, partly because he was still the baron and partly because he was a baron different from others.

Sometimes those feral notes that came from his breast found other windows, and someone more curious to listen to them; the sign of a candle being lighted was enough, a murmur of velvety laughter, of feminine words between the light and the shadow that he couldn't grasp but surely were joking about him, or mocking him, or pretending to call him, and it was already a serious start, it was already love, for that forlorn soul who was hopping through the branches like a goldfinch.

Look, now a bolder girl appeared in the window as if to see what was up, still warm from bed, her breast uncovered, her hair loose, the smile white between strong half-parted lips, and conversations unfolded.

"Who's there? A cat?"

And he: "It's a man, a man."

"A man who meows?"

"Eh, I'm sighing."

"Why? What do you need?"

"I need what you have."

"What's that?"

"Come here and I'll tell you . . ."

People never took offense at him, or revenge, I meant, a sign—it seems to me—that he didn't constitute a great danger. Only once, mysteriously, he was wounded. The news spread one morning. The surgeon of Ombrosa had to climb up into the walnut tree where he lay moaning. He had a leg full of gunshot, small shot, for sparrows; the pellets had to be dug out one by one with a forceps. It hurt, but he soon healed. We never knew how it happened; he said the gun had gone off by accident as he was climbing over a branch.

Convalescent, immobilized on the walnut, he put new energy into his most rigorous studies. At that time he began writing a *Plan for the Establishment of an Ideal State Based in the Trees,* in which he described the imaginary Republic of Arborea, inhabited by just men. He started it as a treatise on laws and governments, but as he wrote his inclinations as an inventor of complicated stories gained the upper hand, and the result was a mixture of adventures, duels, and erotic tales, the last inserted in a chapter on marriage law. The book's epilogue should have been this: the author, having founded the perfect state in the treetops and having convinced all humanity that it should establish itself there and live happily, descended to live on the now deserted earth. It should have been, but the work remained unfinished. He sent a summary to Diderot, signing it simply "Cosimo Rondò, reader of the *Encyclopedia.*" Diderot sent him a thank-you note.

20

I can't say much about this period, because my first trip through Europe dates from then. I had turned twenty-one and could enjoy the family patrimony as I pleased, because my brother didn't need much, nor did our mother, who, poor woman, had aged greatly in recent times. My brother wanted to sign a proxy for me to have the use of the property, provided I gave him a monthly income, paid his taxes, and kept affairs in order. I had only to manage the farms, choose a wife, and already I saw before me that orderly and peaceful life that, in spite of the great upheavals of the end of the century, I've truly succeeded in living.

But before I started I allowed myself a period of travel. I was in Paris just in time to see the triumphal reception given to Voltaire, who was returning after many years for the performance of one of his tragedies. But this isn't a memoir of my life, which certainly doesn't merit writing about; I wanted only to say how throughout these travels I was struck by the fame of the climbing man of Ombrosa, in foreign countries as well. Even in an almanac I saw a figure with the caption

"L'homme sauvage d'Ombreuse (Rép. Génoise). Vit seulement sur les arbres." He was pictured as a creature all covered with fur, with a long beard and a long tail, and he was eating a locust. That figure was in the chapter on monsters, between the hermaphrodite and the siren.

In the face of fantasies like that I usually took good care not to reveal that the wild man was my brother. But I announced it loudly when, in Paris, I was invited to a reception in honor of Voltaire. The old philosopher was sitting in his chair, coddled by a group of ladies, as pleased as Punch and as prickly as a porcupine. When he learned that I came from Ombrosa, he addressed me: *"C'est chez vous, mon cher chevalier, qu'il y a ce fameux philosophe qui vit sur les arbres comme un singe?"*

And I, flattered, couldn't restrain myself from answering, *"C'est mon frère, Monsieur, le Baron de Rondeau."*

Voltaire was very surprised, maybe in part because the brother of that phenomenon appeared to be such a normal person, and began to ask me questions, like *"Mais c'est pour approcher du ciel que votre frère reste là-haut?"*

"My brother maintains," I answered, "that those who wish to look carefully at the earth should stay at the necessary distance," and Voltaire very much admired the answer.

"Jadis, c'était seulement la Nature qui créait des phénomènes vivants," he concluded. *"Maintenant c'est la Raison."* And the old sage plunged back into the chatter of his theist followers.

• • •

Soon I had to interrupt my travels and return to Ombrosa, recalled by an urgent message. Our mother's asthma had suddenly worsened and the poor woman no longer left her bed.

When I passed through the gate and looked up toward our villa, I was sure I would see him there. Cosimo had climbed up on a high branch of the mulberry, just outside our mother's window. "Cosimo!" I called, but in a faint voice. He made a sign that meant both that Mama had felt some relief and that it was still serious, and that I should go up but be quiet.

The room was in half-light. Mama, in bed with a pile of pillows that kept her shoulders raised, seemed larger than we had ever seen her. Nearby were a few servants. Battista had not yet arrived, because her husband the count, who was supposed to come with her, had been delayed by the harvest. Standing out in the shadowy room was the open window that framed Cosimo sitting on the branch of the tree.

I leaned over to kiss our mother's hand. She recognized me immediately and placed her hand on my head. "Oh, you've come, Biagio . . ." She spoke in a weak voice, when the asthma didn't compress her chest too much, but fluently and sensibly. What struck me, though, was hearing her speak without distinction to me and to Cosimo, as if he, too, were there at her bedside. And Cosimo from the tree answered her.

"Is it long since I took the medicine, Cosimo?"

"No, it's been just a few minutes, Mama, wait to take more, because it won't help now."

At a certain point she said, "Cosimo, give me a slice of orange," and I was confused. But I was even more amazed when I saw that Cosimo reached into the room through the window with a harpoon of the type used on boats and with that took a slice of orange from a side table and placed it in our mother's hand.

I noticed that for all these small things she preferred to ask him.

"Cosimo, give me the shawl."

And with the harpoon he searched among the things thrown on the chair, picked up the shawl, handed it to her. "Here, Mama."

"Thank you, son."

She always spoke as if he were a step away, but I noticed that she never asked him for things that he couldn't do from the tree. In those cases she always asked me or the women.

At night Mama couldn't sleep. Cosimo stayed in the tree to watch over her, with a lantern hanging on a branch, so that she could see him even in the dark.

Morning was the worst time for the asthma. The only remedy was to try to distract her, and Cosimo played tunes on a pipe, or imitated bird songs, or captured butterflies and then let them loose to fly around the room, or unfurled festoons of wisteria flowers.

There was a sunny day. Cosimo, with a bowl in the tree, was making soap bubbles and blowing them in through the window toward the bed of the sick woman. Mama saw those colors of the rainbow flying and filling the room and said, "Oh, what games you play!"—as when we were boys and she always disapproved of our amusements as too silly and childish. But now, perhaps for the first time, she took pleasure in a game of ours. The soap bubbles reached her face and with her breath she burst them, and smiled. A bubble settled on her lips and remained intact. We leaned over her. Cosimo dropped the bowl. She was dead.

Sooner or later happy events follow sorrowful ones; it's the law of life. A year after the death of our mother I became engaged to a girl from the local nobility. It took a lot of work to persuade my bride to come to live at Ombrosa: she was afraid of my brother. The thought that there was a man who moved amid the leaves, who spied on every move through the windows, who appeared when one least expected him, filled her with terror, partly because she had never seen Cosimo and imagined him as a kind of Indian. To remove this fear, I held a lunch outside, under the trees, to which Cosimo was invited. Cosimo ate above us, in a beech, with the plates on a small shelf, and I have to say that although he was out of practice for meals in society he behaved very well. My fiancée was somewhat soothed, realizing that apart from being in the trees he was a man just like others, but she retained an invincible distrust.

Even when, once married, we settled in the villa of Ombrosa, she avoided as much as possible not only conversation with her brother-in-law but also the sight of him, although he, poor fellow, every so often brought her bouquets of flowers or valuable skins. When children were born and began to grow up, she got it in her head that being near their uncle could have a bad influence on their upbringing. She wasn't content until we had refurbished the castle on our old estate of Rondò, long uninhabited, and took to living more up there than in Ombrosa, so that the children wouldn't have bad examples.

And Cosimo, too, began to be aware of time passing, and the sign was the dachshund Ottimo Massimo, who was getting old and had lost the desire to join the pack of bloodhounds and chase foxes or attempt absurd loves with Great Dane or mastiff bitches. He was always lying down, as if, because of the tiny distance that separated his belly from the ground when he was standing, it wasn't worth the trouble of staying upright. And stretched out there, from tail to nose, at the foot of the tree on which Cosimo sat, he raised a tired glance toward his master and almost imperceptibly wagged his tail. Cosimo was unhappy: the sense of time passing communicated to him a kind of dissatisfaction with his life, with always going up and down amid those few twigs. And nothing made him fully content anymore, not hunting or fleeting loves or books. He didn't even know what he wanted; in a frenzy he would climb rapidly up to the most tender and fragile crowns, as if seeking other trees that grew at the tops of the trees so that he could climb those, too.

One day Ottimo Massimo was restless. He seemed to scent a spring wind. He lifted his nose, sniffed, lay down again. Two or three times he got up, moved around, lay down again. Suddenly he started off. He trotted slowly now, and every so often he stopped to catch his breath. Cosimo followed him in the branches.

Ottimo Massimo took the path through the woods. He seemed to have in mind a very precise direction, because even if every so often he stopped, peed, rested, tongue hanging out, and looked at his master, he soon shook himself and started off again without hesitation. He was going into areas little frequented by Cosimo, in fact almost unknown, because it was in the direction of the hunting reserve of Duke Tolemaico. Duke Tolemaico was a feeble old man and certainly hadn't gone hunting for who knows how long, but no poacher would set foot in his preserve because the guards were numerous and always vigilant, and Cosimo, who had already had words there, preferred to stay away. Now Ottimo Massimo and Cosimo had entered Prince Tolemaico's reserve, but neither was thinking of flushing out the precious game; the dachshund trotted along following a secret call, and the baron was seized by an impatient curiosity to discover where the dog was going.

Thus the dachshund reached a point where the woods ended and there was a meadow. Two stone lions sitting on pillars bore a coat of arms. From here perhaps a park was supposed to begin, a garden, a more private part of the Tolemaico estate, but there were only those two stone lions, and beyond the meadow, an immense meadow of short green grass, the end of which could be seen only in the distance, was a background of black oaks. The sky behind had a light patina of clouds. No bird sang there.

That meadow was a sight that filled Cosimo with dismay. He had always lived in the thick vegetation of Ombrosa, sure of being able to get anywhere on his pathways, and an empty, impassable expanse, open under the sky, gave him a sensation of vertigo.

Ottimo Massimo rushed onto the meadow and, as if he were young again, ran at full speed. From the ash where he was perching, Cosimo began to whistle, to call him—"Here, come back. Ottimo Massimo! Where are you going?"—but the dog wouldn't obey, he didn't even turn; he ran on and on, over the meadow, until only a distant comma could be seen, his tail, and that, too, disappeared.

Cosimo in the ash wrung his hands. He was used to the dog's flights and absences, but now Ottimo Massimo was disappearing in this insuperable meadow, and his flight became one with the anguish Cosimo had felt a little before and charged it with an indefinite wait, an expectation of something beyond that meadow.

He was pondering these thoughts when he heard footsteps under the ash. He saw a game warden passing, hands in his pockets, whistling. To tell the truth he had a rather disheveled and distracted aspect for being one of those terrible game wardens of the preserve, yet the insignia on his uniform was that of the ducal corps, and Cosimo flattened himself against the trunk. Then the thought of the dog gained the upper hand; he addressed the game warden. "Hey, you, sergeant, have you seen a dachshund?"

The game warden looked up. "Ah, it's you! The hunter who flies with the dog that crawls! No, I haven't seen the dachshund! Did you get something good this morning?"

Cosimo had recognized one of his most zealous adversaries, and he said, "Of course not, the dog ran away and I happened to chase him here. My gun isn't loaded."

The game warden laughed. "Oh, go ahead and load it, and shoot as much as you like! Now, anyway!"

"Now what?"

"Now that the duke is dead, how would he be interested in the reserve anymore?"

"Ah, so he's dead. I didn't know."

"Dead and buried for three months. And there's a quarrel between the heirs of the first and second wives and the new little widow."

"He had a third wife?"

"Married when he was eighty, a year before he died, she a girl of twenty-one or thereabouts. I'm telling you, what madness, a bride who wasn't together with him even a day and only now begins to visit her possessions, and she doesn't like them."

"What do you mean, doesn't like them?"

"Who knows—she settles herself in a palace or in an estate, she arrives with her whole court, because she's always got a crowd of hangers-on, and after three days she finds it all ugly, all sad, and leaves. Then the other heirs emerge, throw themselves on that possession, claim the rights. And she: 'Ah, yes, and you take it!' Now she's arrived here at the hunting pavilion, but how long will she stay? I say not long."

"And where is the hunting pavilion?"

"Down there past the meadow, past the oaks."

"So my dog must have gone there . . ."

"He must have gone looking for bones. Forgive me, but it gives me the idea that Your Lordship keeps him on a strict diet!" And he burst into laughter.

Cosimo didn't answer; he looked at the impassable meadow and waited for the dog to return.

He didn't return all day. The next day Cosimo was again in the ash, gazing at the meadow as if he could no longer do without the disquiet it caused.

The dachshund reappeared toward evening, a dot in the lawn that only Cosimo's sharp eye could make out, becoming more visible as he approached. "Ottimo Massimo! Come here! Where were you?" The dog stopped, wagged his tail, looked at his master, barked, seemed to invite him to come, to follow him, but, aware of the expanse that he couldn't cross, turned back, took some hesitant steps, and then turned again. "Ottimo Massimo! Come here! Ottimo Massimo!" But the dachshund ran away, disappearing into the distance of the meadow.

Later two game wardens passed. "Still there waiting for the dog, Lordship! I saw him in the pavilion, in good hands."

"What?"

"Yes, the marquise, or rather the widow duchess—we call her marquise because she was the young marquise as a girl—greeted him as if she'd always known him. He's a dog who likes easy living, if you will allow me, Lordship. Now he's found a soft spot and there he'll stay . . ."

And the two wardens went off with a sneer.

Ottimo Massimo didn't return. Cosimo sat in the ash tree every day, gazing at the meadow as if he could read in it something that had long been consuming him inside: the very idea of distance, of the gap that can't be bridged, of the wait that can last longer than life.

21

One day Cosimo looked out from the ash tree. The sun shone brightly, and a ray crossed the meadow, which turned from pea green to emerald green. Over in the black of the oak woods some leaves moved, and a horse leaped out. In the horse's saddle was a knight, dressed in black, with a cloak—no, a skirt. It wasn't a knight, it was an amazon; she galloped at full speed and she was fair-haired.

Cosimo's heart began to pound and he was seized by the hope that that amazon would get close enough so that he could see her face clearly, and that that face would be beautiful. But besides the wait for her approach and her beauty, there was a third wait, a third branch of hope that was entwined with the other two and was the desire for that increasingly luminous beauty to answer a need to recognize a known and almost forgotten impression, a memory of which only an outline, a color, remained, and of which he would like to make all the rest reemerge, or rather find it again in something present.

And in this frame of mind he couldn't wait for her to get

close to the edge of the meadow that was near him, where the two pillars with the lions towered; but this wait began to become painful, because he had realized that the amazon wasn't cutting across the meadow in a straight line toward the lions but diagonally, so that she would soon disappear again into the woods.

He was about to lose sight of her when she turned the horse abruptly and now cut across the lawn on another diagonal, which would certainly bring her a little closer but would lead her to disappear just the same, on the opposite side of the lawn.

Meanwhile Cosimo saw with irritation that two brown horses, mounted by knights, had come out of the woods and into the meadow, but he tried to eliminate that thought immediately; he decided that those knights counted for nothing, it was sufficient to see how they banged around here and there behind her, certainly they were not to be taken seriously, and yet, he had to admit, they irritated him.

Now this time, too, the amazon, before disappearing from the meadow, turned the horse, but turned it back, away from Cosimo . . . No, now the horse turned around and was galloping this way, as if purposely to disorient the two awkward riders, who in fact were galloping into the distance and hadn't yet realized that she was heading in the opposite direction.

Now everything really was going in the right way: the amazon galloped in the sun, increasingly beautiful and increasingly responsive to Cosimo's thirst for memory, and the only alarming thing was the continual zigzag of her route, which made all her intentions unpredictable. Nor did the two horsemen understand where she was going, and, trying to follow her evolutions, they ended up covering a lot of ground in vain, but always with great goodwill and energy.

Now, in less time than Cosimo expected, the woman on horseback had reached the edge of the meadow near him, now she was passing between the two pillars surmounted by lions as if they had been put there to honor her, and she turned toward the meadow and all that was on the other side of the meadow with a broad gesture, as if of farewell, and galloped onward, passing under the ash tree, and Cosimo now had seen her clearly in face and body, erect in the saddle, the face of a proud woman and yet of a girl, the forehead happy to be above those eyes, the eyes happy to be on that face, the nose, the mouth, the chin, the neck: everything about her happy with every other thing about her, and all all all of it recalled the girl seen at the age of twelve on the swing the first day he spent in the trees: Sofonisba Viola Violante d'Ondariva.

That discovery, or rather, his having brought that discovery, unconfessed since the first instant, to the point where he could proclaim it to himself, filled Cosimo as if with a fever. He wished to cry out, so that she would look up at the ash and see him, but from his throat only the sound of a woodcock emerged, and she didn't turn.

Now the white horse galloped through the chestnut wood, and the hooves pounded the husks scattered on the ground, cracking them open and exposing the polished woody hull of the fruit. The amazon guided her horse this way and that, and now Cosimo thought she was already far away and unreachable, now, leaping from tree to tree, he saw her, to his surprise, reappear in the perspective of the trunks, and this way of moving fueled the memory that blazed in the baron's mind. He wanted to reach her with a call, a sign of his presence, but to his lips came only the whistle of the gray partridge, and she paid no attention.

The two horsemen in pursuit appeared to have even less understanding of her intentions and her route and continued to go in the wrong directions, getting caught in thornbushes or sinking into muddy swamps, while she darted off, secure and unattainable. In fact, every so often she gave the horsemen some sort of order or incitement, raising her arm with the whip or tearing off a carob pod and throwing it, as if to say they were to go there. Immediately they galloped off in that direction over fields and banks, but she had turned in another direction and wasn't looking at them anymore.

"It's her! It's her!" thought Cosimo, inflamed with hope, and he wanted to shout out her name, but from his lips came only a long sad cry, like the plover's.

Now it happened that all those comings and goings and games and tricks played on the horsemen were disposed around a line, which although it was irregular and wavy did not exclude a possible intention, and Cosimo, unable to endure the impossible enterprise of following her, said to himself, "I will go to a place where she'll come if it's her. In fact, she can be here only to go there." And, leaping along his paths, he headed toward the old abandoned park of the D'Ondarivas.

In that shade, in that scent-filled air, in that place where the leaves and the wood had other color and other substance, he felt so overcome by the memories of youth that he almost forgot the amazon, or if he didn't forget her he said to himself that it might not even be her, and anyway that wait and that hope for her were so true that it was almost as if she were there.

But he heard a noise. It was the hooves of the white horse on the gravel. The horse stopped galloping as it came through the garden, as if the amazon wanted to observe and recognize everything in detail. There was no sign of the foolish knights; she must have shaken them off.

He saw her: she was circling the pool, the little gazebo, the amphoras. She looked at the trees that had grown enormous, with hanging aerial roots, the magnolias that had become a forest. But she didn't see him, he who sought to call her with the cooing of the hoopoe, the trill of the pipit, with sounds that were lost in the dense warbling of the birds in the garden.

She had dismounted from the saddle and was walking, leading the horse behind her by the bridle. She reached the villa; she left the horse, entered the portico. She burst out, "Ortensia! Gaetano! Tarquinio! Here it needs to be whitewashed, the shutters need to be repainted, the tapestries hung! And I want the table here, there the shelf, the spinet in the middle, and the pictures all have to change places."

Cosimo realized then that the house that to his distracted gaze had seemed, as always, closed and uninhabited was now open, full of people, servants who were cleaning, arranging, airing, moving furniture, beating carpets. It was Viola who was returning, then. Viola who was settling again in Ombrosa, who was retaking possession of the villa she had left as a child! And the heart pounding with joy in Cosimo's breast was not, however, unlike a heart pounding with fear, because her return, her being so unpredictable and proud before his eyes, could mean not to have her ever again, not even in memory, not even in that secret scent of leaves and color of light through green—could mean that he would be obliged to flee her and so flee also the early memory of her as a girl.

With this alternating pounding of his heart Cosimo saw her moving among the servants, having them transport sofas, harpsichords, cupboards, and then rush out to the garden and get back on the horse, pursued by the swarm of people who still awaited orders, and now she turned to the gardeners, ordering them to restore the uncared-for flower beds and rearrange in the paths the gravel carried off by the rains and put back the wicker chairs, the swing . . .

She indicated, with broad motions, the branch from which the swing had once hung and how long the ropes should be, and its range, and as she spoke with a gesture her gaze went up to the magnolia tree in which Cosimo had once appeared to her. And in the magnolia tree, behold, she saw him again.

She was surprised. Very. That goes without saying. Of course she recovered immediately and regained her composure, in her usual way, but at the moment she was very surprised, and her eyes laughed, and her mouth, and a tooth he remembered from when she was a girl.

"You!" And then, looking for the tone of someone who is speaking of something natural but unable to hide her gratified interest, "Ah, so you've stayed here since then without ever coming down?"

Cosimo managed to transform the voice that wanted to come out like the cry of a sparrow into a "Yes, it's me. Viola, you remember?"

"Without ever, ever setting foot on the ground?"

"Never."

And she, as if she had already conceded too much: "Ah, you see that you succeeded? So then it wasn't so hard."

"I was waiting for you to come back . . ."

"Grand. Hey, you, where are you carrying that curtain! Leave everything here so I can see!" She looked at him again. Cosimo that day was dressed for hunting: hairy, with the catskin cap, with the rifle. "You look like Robinson Crusoe!"

"You've read it?" he said right away, to show that he was up to date.

Viola had already turned. "Gaetano! Ampelio! The dry leaves! It's full of dry leaves!" And to him: "In an hour, at the end of the park. Wait for me." And she hurried off to give orders, on horseback.

Cosimo flung himself into the depths: he would have liked it to be a thousand times deeper, an avalanche of leaves and branches and thorns and honeysuckle and maidenhair to sink into, plunge into, and only after being completely submerged would he begin to understand if he was happy or mad with fear.

In the big tree at the end of the park, his knees tight around a branch, he looked at the time on a large pocket watch that had belonged to his maternal grandfather, General Von Kurtewitz, and said to himself, "She won't come." Instead Donna Viola arrived almost punctually, on horseback. She stopped under the tree, without even looking up; she wasn't wearing her hat or the amazon jacket, and the lace-trimmed white blouse over the black skirt was almost nunlike. Rising in the stirrups, she held out a hand to him on the branch; he helped her; getting up on the saddle, she reached the branch, then, still without looking at him, she climbed up quickly, searched for a comfortable fork, sat. Cosimo crouched at her feet, and could begin only like this: "You've come back?"

Viola looked at him ironically. She was fair-haired, as she'd been as a child. "How do you know?" she said.

And he, not understanding the joke: "I saw you in that meadow in the duke's preserve . . ."

"The preserve is mine. I wish it would fill up with nettles! Do you know everything? About me, I mean?"

"No . . . I only now found out that you're a widow."

"Of course I'm a widow." She slapped the black skirt, explaining it, and began to speak rapidly. "You never know anything. You're up in the trees all day sticking your nose into other people's business, and then you don't know anything. I married old Tolemaico because my family forced me to, they forced me. They said I was a flirt and couldn't be without a husband. For one year I was the Duchess Tolemaico, and it was the most boring year of my life, even though I wasn't with the old man more than a week. I will never again set foot in any of their castles and ruins and rat holes, I wish they'd fill up with snakes! From now on I'm going to stay here, where I was as a child. I'll stay as long as it suits me, of course, then I'll go—I'm a widow and I can do what I like, finally. I've always done what I like, to tell the truth—I even married Tolemaico because it suited me to marry him; it's not true that they forced me to marry him, they wanted me to get married at all costs, and so I chose the most decrepit suitor in existence. 'That way I'll soon be a widow,' I said, and now in fact I am."

Cosimo was half stunned under that avalanche of news and peremptory declarations, and Viola was more distant than ever: flirt, widow, and duchess were part of an unreachable world, and all he could say was "And who were you flirting with?"

And she: "There. You're jealous. Mind, I will never let you be jealous."

Cosimo had a start, like a jealous man provoked to argue, but suddenly he thought, "What? Jealous? But why does she admit that I can be jealous of her? Why does she say, *'I will never let you'*? It's like saying she thinks that we . . ."

Then, red in the face, moved, he wanted to tell her, ask her, hear; instead it was she who asked him, abruptly, "Now you tell me, what have you done?"

"Oh, I've done things," he began to say. "I've hunted, even wild boar, but mainly foxes, rabbits, weasels, and then of course thrushes and blackbirds; then pirates, the Turkish pirates came, it was a great battle, my uncle died; and I've read a lot of books, for myself and for a friend, a bandit who was hanged; I have the whole of Diderot's *Encyclopedia* and I even wrote to him and he answered, from Paris; and I've done a lot of work, I've pruned, I saved a forest from fire—"

"And you will love me always, absolutely, above everything, and you would do anything for me?"

At this coming from her, Cosimo, stunned, said, "Yes . . ."

"You're a man who lived in the trees just for me, to learn to love me . . ."

"Yes . . . Yes . . ."

"Kiss me."

He pressed her against the trunk, kissed her. Raising his head, he was aware of her beauty as if he had never seen it before. "Goodness—how beautiful you are . . ."

"For you." And she unbuttoned the white blouse. Her breast was young, the nipples pink; Cosimo just touched it. Viola darted away through the branches as if she were flying; he climbed behind her, with that skirt in his face.

"But where are you taking me?" said Viola, as if he were leading her, not she him.

"Here," said Cosimo, and he began to guide her, and as they crossed from branch to branch he took her by the hand or by the waist and taught her the steps.

"Here." And they climbed into some olive trees that leaned out from a steep slope, and from the top of one of them the sea, which until then they had seen only in fragments amid the leaves and branches, as if it were shattered—now suddenly they discovered it calm and clear and vast as the sky. The horizon opened broad and high and the blue was taut and empty, without a sail, and the lightly sketched ripples of the waves could be counted. Only a very slight sucking, like a sigh, ran over the rocks on the shore.

With eyes half dazzled, Cosimo and Viola went back down into the dark green shade of the foliage. "Here."

On the saddle of the trunk of a walnut was a shell-like hollow, the wound from ancient work of the hatchet, and there was one of Cosimo's refuges. A boar skin was spread out, and on it was a flask, some utensils, a bowl.

Viola lay down on the boar skin. "Have you brought other women here?"

He hesitated. And Viola: "If you haven't, you're a worthless man."

"Yes. Some . . ."

He took a slap in the face, palm open. "That's how you waited for me?"

Cosimo ran his hand over his red cheek and didn't know what to say, but she seemed to have become well disposed again. "And how were they? Tell me, how were they?"

"Not like you, Viola, not like you."

"What do you know of how I am, eh, what do you know?"

She had become gentle, and Cosimo couldn't stop being surprised at these sudden turns. He came close to her. Viola was of gold and honey.

"Tell . . ."

"Tell . . ."

They knew each other. He knew her and himself, because in truth he had never known himself. And she knew him and herself, because although she had always known herself, she had never been able to acknowledge herself like that.

22

Their first pilgrimage was to that tree where, in large letters, deeply incised in the bark and already so old and disfigured that it no longer seemed the work of human hand, was written *Cosimo, Viola,* and—farther down—*Ottimo Massimo.*

"Up there? Who was it? When?"

"I. Then."

Viola was moved.

"And what does this mean?" She pointed to the words *Ottimo Massimo.*

"My dog. That is, yours. The dachshund."

"Turcaret?"

"Ottimo Massimo, that's what I named him."

"Turcaret! How I cried, when I was leaving and realized that they hadn't put him in the carriage . . . Oh, not to see you anymore didn't matter to me, but I was desperate at not having the dachshund!"

"If not for him I wouldn't have found you again! He scented in the wind that you were nearby and wouldn't rest until he found you."

"I recognized him right away, as soon as I saw him arriving at the pavilion, all out of breath. The others said, 'Where did he come from?' I bent over to look at him, the color, the spots. 'But this is Turcaret! The dachshund I had in Ombrosa as a child!'"

Cosimo laughed. She suddenly turned up her nose. "Ottimo Massimo — what an ugly name! Where do you get such ugly names?" And Cosimo's face immediately clouded.

For Ottimo Massimo, on the other hand, happiness now had no shadows. His old dog's heart, divided between two masters, was finally at peace, after striving for days and days to draw the marquise to the edges of the reserve, to the ash where Cosimo was perched. He had pulled her by the skirt, or had escaped, carrying off an object, running toward the meadow to get her to follow him, and she: "What do you want? Where are you dragging me? Turcaret! Stop it! What a naughty dog I've found!" But already the sight of the dachshund had stirred in her mind memories of childhood, nostalgia for Ombrosa. And immediately she had made preparations for the move from the ducal pavilion to return to the old villa with the exotic trees.

She had returned, Viola. For Cosimo the most wonderful period began, and for her, too, as she pounded the countryside on her white horse and, as soon as she sighted the baron between leaves and sky, rose from the saddle, climbed up slanting trunks and branches, having soon become almost as expert as he, and met him everywhere.

"Oh, Viola, I don't know anymore, I would climb, I don't know where . . ."

"To me," said Viola softly, and he was as if mad.

For her, love was a heroic exercise: pleasure was mixed with proofs of daring, with generosity and dedication and tension of all the faculties of the mind. Their world was the most intricate and twisted and impassable trees.

"There," she exclaimed, pointing to a fork high up in the branches, and together they rushed to reach it, and a contest of acrobatics began between them that ended in new embraces. They loved each other suspended over the void, supporting themselves or holding on to the branches, she throwing herself at him, almost flying.

Viola's loving obstinacy met Cosimo's, and sometimes they clashed. Cosimo shunned hesitations, softness, refined perverseness: he liked nothing that was not natural love. Republican virtues were in the air: times were brewing, severe and licentious at once. Cosimo, an insatiable lover, was a stoic, an ascetic, a puritan. Always in search of amorous happiness, he was nevertheless hostile to sensuality. He went so far as to distrust the kiss, the caress, verbal flattery, everything that obscured or claimed to replace the health of nature. It was Viola who revealed to him the fullness of it, and with her he never felt the sadness after love preached by the theologians. Indeed, he wrote a philosophical letter on that subject to Rousseau, who, perhaps distressed, didn't answer.

But Viola was also a sophisticated, capricious, spoiled

woman, all-embracing in blood and spirit. Cosimo's love filled her senses but left her imagination unsatisfied. From that arose disagreements and shadowy resentments. But they didn't last long, so various was their life and the world around.

Tired, they sought shelters hidden in the trees with the thickest foliage: hammocks that enveloped their bodies as in a folded leaf, or hanging pavilions with curtains that flew in the wind, or beds of feathers. In these apparatuses the genius of Donna Viola was revealed: the marquise had a gift for creating around herself, wherever she was, ease, luxury, and a complicated comfort—complicated to the eye, but obtained with miraculous facility, because she had to see every wish fulfilled immediately, at all costs.

On these, their aerial alcoves, the robins sat and sang, and through the curtains red admiral butterflies entered in pairs, pursuing each other. On summer afternoons, when sleep caught the two nearby lovers, a squirrel, looking for something to gnaw, entered, caressing their faces with its feathery tail or biting a big toe. Then they closed the curtains more carefully, but a family of dormice began nibbling on the roof of the pavilion and fell on them.

It was the time in which they were discovering each other, telling each other their lives, asking each other questions.

"And you felt alone?"

"I missed you."

"But only compared to the rest of the world?"

"No. Why? I always had something to do with other people: I cultivated fruit, I pruned, I studied philosophy with the abbé, I fought with the pirates. Isn't it like that for everyone?"

"Only you are like that—that's why I love you."

But the baron hadn't yet understood what it was that Viola accepted about him and what she didn't. Sometimes a little nothing, a word or a tone, was enough to cause the marquise's anger to erupt.

He, for example: "With Gian dei Brughi I read novels, with the *cavaliere* I undertook hydraulic projects . . ."

"And with me?"

"With you I make love. Like pruning, the fruit . . ."

She was silent, motionless. Right away Cosimo realized that he had unleashed her anger: her eyes suddenly became ice.

"Why, what is it? Viola, what did I say?"

She was distant as he hadn't seen or heard her, a hundred miles from him, her face marble.

"No, Viola, what is it, why, listen . . ."

Viola rose and nimbly, without need of help, began to descend from the tree.

Cosimo still couldn't understand what his mistake had been, he still was unable to think about it; maybe he preferred not to think about it, not to understand it, in order to better proclaim his innocence: "But no, you must not have understood me, Viola, listen . . ." He followed her to the lowest platform. "Viola, don't go, not like that. Viola . . ."

Now she was speaking, but to the horse, whom she had reached and untied; she climbed into the saddle and was off.

Cosimo began to despair, to jump from tree to tree. "No, Viola, tell me, Viola!"

She had galloped away. He followed her through the branches. "I beg you, Viola, I love you!" But he could no longer see her. He rushed over the unsteady branches with risky leaps. "Viola! Viola!"

When he was sure he had lost her and couldn't restrain his sobs, there she was, passing by again at a trot, without looking up.

"Look, Viola, look at what I'm doing!" And he began to bang his head against a trunk, his head bare (it was, to tell the truth, very hard).

She didn't even look at him. She was already far away.

Cosimo waited for her to return, zigzagging among the trees. "Viola! I'm desperate!" And he jumped upside down into space, headfirst, holding on to a branch with his legs and hitting head and face with his fists. Or he began breaking branches with destructive fury, and a leafy elm in a few instants was bare, stripped as if a hailstorm had passed.

He never threatened to kill himself; rather, he never threatened anything—blackmails of feeling weren't for him. What he felt like doing he did, and already as he was doing it he announced it, not before.

At a certain point Donna Viola, as unpredictably as she had become angry, abandoned her anger. Of all Cosimo's follies that apparently hadn't touched her, suddenly one would kindle in her pity and love. "No, Cosimo, dear, wait for me!" And she jumped out of the saddle and rushed to climb a trunk, and his arms, above, were ready to lift her up.

Love resumed again, with a fury equal to that of the quarrel. It was in fact the same thing, but Cosimo didn't understand it at all.

"Why do you make me suffer?"

"Because I love you."

Now it was he who got angry. "No, you don't love me! One who loves wants happiness, not suffering."

"One who loves wants only love, even at the cost of suffering."

"So you make me suffer on purpose."

"Yes, to see if you love me."

The baron's philosophy refused to go further. "Suffering is a negative state of the soul."

"Love is everything."

"Suffering should always be fought against."

"Love doesn't refuse anything."

"Some things I will never admit."

"Of course you admit them, because you love me and suffer."

Just like his despair, Cosimo's explosions of uncontainable joy were spectacular. Sometimes his happiness reached the point that he had to leave his love and go jumping and shouting and proclaiming the marvels of his lady.

"Yo quiero the most wonderful puellam de todo el mundo!"

Those idlers and old sailors who sat on the benches of Ombrosa had grown used to these rapid appearances of his. Here he could be glimpsed jumping through the holm oaks, shouting,

"Zu dir, zu dir, gundàika,
Vo cercando il mio ben,
En la isla de Jamaica,
Du soir jusqu'au matin!"

or

"Il y a un pré where the grass grows toda de oro
Take me away, take me away, che io ci moro!"

and he disappeared.

His study of classical and modern languages, although it wasn't very deep, allowed him to give in to this clamorous declaration of his feelings, and the more deeply shaken his soul was by an intense emotion, the more obscure his language became. People recall a time when, celebrating Ombrosa's patron saint, the inhabitants had gathered in the square, where the greased pole was, and the streamers and the banner. The baron appeared at the top of a plane tree and, with one of those leaps that only his acrobatic ability was capable of, jumped onto the pole, climbed to the top, shouted, *"Que viva die schöne Venus posterior!,"* slid down the soaped pole almost to the ground, stopped, climbed rapidly to the top, tore from the trophy a round rosy cheese, and, with another of his leaps, flew back up to the plane tree and fled, leaving the people of Ombrosa astonished.

Nothing made the marquise as happy as these exuberant acts, and they moved her to repay them in equally rapturous manifestations of love. The people of Ombrosa, when they saw her galloping at full speed, her face almost hidden in the horse's white mane, knew that she was racing to a meeting with the baron. Even on her horse she expressed an amorous force, but here Cosimo could no longer follow her; and although he admired her equestrian passion, it was still also for him a secret cause of jealousy and bitterness, because he saw Viola master a world vaster than his and knew that he could never have her only for himself, enclose her within the borders of his kingdom. The marquise, for her part, perhaps suffered at not being able to be both lover and amazon: she was seized at times by a vague need for her and Cosimo's love to be a love on horseback, and running through the trees was no longer enough for her; she would have liked running at a gallop on the saddle of her steed.

And in reality the horse, as a result of racing over that terrain of ascents and steep descents, had become as agile as a roebuck, and Viola now urged him at a run up certain trees, for example old olives with twisted trunks. The horse sometimes got as far as the first fork in the branches, and she got in the habit of tying him not on the ground but there in the olive. She dismounted and left him to graze on leaves and twigs.

Thus, when a gossip passing through the olive grove and raising curious eyes saw the baron and the marquise up there embracing and then went to report on it and added, "And the white horse was up there, too, at the top of a branch!" it was taken as a fantasy and not believed by anyone. Once again the secret of the lovers was safe.

23

The fact that I've just narrated proves that the people of Ombrosa, lavish as they had been with gossip about my brother's previous romantic life, confronted by this passion that ran wild one might say above their heads, maintained a respectful reserve, as if before something greater than them. Not that the behavior of the marquise wasn't reproached, but for its external features, like that breakneck galloping ("Who knows where she could be going so furiously," they said to each other, although they knew very well that she was going to a tryst with Cosimo) or that furniture that she put in the treetops. To some extent they considered it all a fashion of the nobles, one of their many eccentricities ("All in the trees now: women, men. What will they invent next?"); in other words, maybe more tolerant times were coming, but they were more hypocritical.

The baron appeared now at long intervals in the holm oaks of the square, and it was a sign that she had left. Because Viola sometimes stayed away for months, attending to her properties, which were scattered across Europe, but these departures always corresponded to moments in which their relations had suffered some jolts, and the marquise was upset with Cosimo because he didn't understand what she wished to make him understand about love. Not that Viola left offended with him: they always managed to make peace first, but in him the suspicion remained that she had decided to make that journey because she was tired of him, because he couldn't keep her, maybe she was now separating herself from him, maybe some incident of the journey or a pause for reflection would decide her not to return. So my brother lived in anxiety. On the one hand he tried to resume the life he had had before meeting her, to go back to hunting and fishing and following work on the farms, his studies, the bluster in the square, as if he had never done anything else (persisting in him was the stubborn youthful arrogance of one who won't admit he has submitted to the influence of others), and at the same time he was gratified by what that love gave him —the eagerness, the pride. On the other hand, though, he was aware that many things no longer mattered to him, that without Viola life had no flavor, that his thoughts always ran to her. The more he sought, outside the whirlwind of Viola's presence, to remaster passions and pleasures in a wise economy of the mind, the more he felt the emptiness left by her or the fever of waiting for her. In other words, his love was just as Viola wanted it, not as he claimed it was: the woman always triumphed, even if she was far away, and in the end Cosimo, in spite of himself, enjoyed it.

Suddenly the marquise would return. The season of love

in the trees began again, but also of jealousy. Where had Viola been? What had she done? Cosimo was anxious to know, but at the same time he was afraid of the way she responded to his questions, with hints, and for Cosimo every hint found a way of arousing suspicion, and though he understood that she did it to torture him, everything might really be true, and in that uncertain state of mind sometimes he masked his jealousy, sometimes he let it erupt violently, and Viola always reacted in a different and unpredictable way: sometimes it seemed that she was more than ever bound to him, sometimes that he could no longer reignite her.

What the life of the marquise was actually like during her journeys we in Ombrosa couldn't know, far as we were from the capitals and their gossip. But at that time I made my second trip to Paris, on account of certain contracts (a consignment of lemons: many nobles were also now starting to trade, and I among the first).

One evening in one of the most illustrious Paris salons I encountered Donna Viola. She was decked out in such a sumptuous hairstyle and a dress so splendid that if I didn't have difficulty in recognizing her—in fact I was startled on first seeing her—it was because she was precisely a woman not ever to be confused with anyone. She greeted me with indifference, but soon found a way of taking me aside and asking, without waiting for an answer between one question and the next, "Do you have news of your brother? Are you going back to Ombrosa soon? Wait, give him this in memory of me." And having taken from her bosom a silk handkerchief, she put it in my hand. Then immediately she let the court of admirers she led rejoin her.

"You know the marquise?" a Parisian friend asked quietly.

"Only in passing," I answered, and it was true: during her sojourns in Ombrosa, Donna Viola, infected by Cosimo's wildness, didn't care about frequenting the local nobility.

"Seldom is such beauty accompanied by such restlessness," said my friend. "Gossips have it that in Paris she goes from one lover to another, in a merry-go-round so continuous that no one can say she is his and call himself privileged. But every so often she disappears for months and months, and they say she retires to a convent, to be punished by doing penance."

I struggled to restrain my laughter, seeing that the marquise's sojourns in the trees of Ombrosa were believed by the Parisians to be periods of penitence; but that gossip also disturbed me, and I anticipated times of sadness for my brother.

To prevent ugly surprises, I wanted to alert him, and as soon as I returned to Ombrosa I went looking for him. He asked me at length about the trip, about the news from France, but I couldn't give him any political or literary news that he didn't already know.

Finally I took from my pocket Donna Viola's handkerchief. "In a salon in Paris I met a lady who knows you, and she gave me this for you, with her greetings."

He rapidly lowered the basket that hung on a string, pulled up the silk handkerchief, and brought it to his face as if to breathe in its fragrance. "Ah, you saw her? And how was she? Tell me, how was she?"

"Very beautiful and brilliant," I said slowly, "but they say that this fragrance is breathed by many nostrils . . ."

He pressed the handkerchief to his chest as if he feared that it would be torn away from him. He turned to me, red in the face. "And you didn't have a sword to stick those lies back in the throats of those who spoke them to you?"

I had to confess that it hadn't even crossed my mind.

He was silent for a moment. Then he shrugged his shoulders. "All lies. I alone know that she's mine alone." And he ran off through the branches without saying goodbye. I recognized his usual manner of rejecting anything that forced him to emerge from his world.

From then on if you saw him he was sad and impatient, jumping here and there, doing nothing. If every so often I heard him whistle in competition with the blackbirds, his call was always darker and more agitated.

The marquise arrived. As always, his jealousy pleased her: partly it excited her, partly she turned it into a game. So the beautiful days of love returned and my brother was happy.

But now the marquise never missed an occasion to accuse Cosimo of having a narrow idea of love.

"What do you mean? That I'm jealous?"

"You're right to be jealous. But you claim to submit jealousy to reason."

"Of course. That way I make it more effective."

"You reason too much. Why in the world should love be reasoned?"

"To love you more. Everything increases its power if you do it by reasoning."

"You live in the trees and you have the mentality of a lawyer with gout."

"The boldest enterprises should be experienced with the simplest heart."

He continued to spout opinions until she ran away; then he, following her, despairing, tearing his hair.

In those days an English flagship dropped anchor just outside our harbor. The admiral gave a party for the notables of Ombrosa and the officers of other ships passing through; the marquise went, and from that evening Cosimo felt again the pangs of jealousy. Two officers from two different ships fell in love with Donna Viola and were seen constantly on shore, courting the lady and trying to outdo each other in their attentions. One was a ship's lieutenant from the English flagship; the other was also a ship's lieutenant, but from the Neapolitan fleet. Having hired two chestnut mounts, the lieutenants went back and forth near the marquise's terraces, and when they met, the Neapolitan cast at the Englishman a glance that would incinerate him, while from between the half-closed eyelids of the Englishman flashed a look like the tip of a sword.

And Donna Viola? Does she, that flirt, not take to staying for hours and hours at home, coming to the window in a negligée, as if she were a new widow, just emerged from mourning? Cosimo, not having her with him in the trees, not hearing the gallop of the white horse approaching, went mad, and he took up a position (he, too) in front of that terrace, keeping an eye on her and the two ship's lieutenants.

He was planning a way of playing some trick on his rivals, which would make them return as quickly as possible to their respective ships, but seeing that Viola appeared to enjoy the courtship of both equally, he regained hope that she wished only to make fun of them both, along with him. Nevertheless, he did not relax his surveillance: at the first sign she gave of preferring one of the two, he was ready to intervene.

One morning the Englishman passes by. Viola is at the window. They smile at each other. The marquise drops a note. The officer snatches it in flight, reads it, bows, red in the face, and hurries away. A meeting! The Englishman was the lucky one! Cosimo swore not to let him reach evening peacefully.

At that moment the Neapolitan passes by. Viola throws a note to him, too. The officer reads it, brings it to his lips, and kisses it. So he considers himself the chosen? And the other, then? Against which of the two should Cosimo take action? Certainly Donna Viola had made an appointment with one of the two; as for the other, she must merely have played one of her tricks. Or did she want to make fun of both?

As for the place of the meeting, Cosimo fixed his suspicions on a summerhouse at the end of the park. Sometime earlier the marquise had had it renovated and furnished, and Cosimo was consumed by jealousy, for the time had passed when she loaded the tops of the trees with curtains and couches; now she was occupied with places where he would never enter. "I'll keep watch on the pavilion," Cosimo said to himself. "If she has arranged a meeting with one of the two lieutenants, it has to be there." And he perched in the thick foliage of a horse chestnut.

Shortly before sunset, he hears a gallop. The Neapolitan arrives. "Now I'll harass him!" thinks Cosimo and, using a blowpipe, hits him in the neck with a ball of squirrel dung. The officer starts, looks around. Cosimo leans out from the branch and as he leans out sees beyond the hedge the English lieutenant dismount from his saddle and tie his horse to a stake. "So it's him—maybe the other just happened to pass by here." And a blowpipe of squirrel dung on his nose.

"Who's there?" says the Englishman, and is about to cross the hedge, but finds himself face-to-face with his Neapolitan colleague, who, also dismounting from his horse, is likewise saying, "Who's there?"

"I beg your pardon, sir," says the Englishman, "but I must ask you to vacate this place immediately!"

"If I'm here it's by rights," says the Neapolitan. "I must invite your lordship to leave!"

"No right can prevail over mine," replies the Englishman. "I'm sorry, I can't allow you to remain."

"It's a matter of honor," says the other, "and my lineage

bears witness to it: Salvatore di San Cataldo di Santa Maria Capua Vetere, of the Navy of the Two Sicilys!"

"Sir Osbert Castlefight, third of the name!" the Englishman introduces himself. "My honor insists that you leave the field clear."

"Not before I've run you out with this sword!" And he draws it from the sheath.

"Sir, you wish to fight," says Sir Osbert, facing off.

They fight.

"It's here I wanted you, colleague, and have for a long time!" And he deals him a quarte.

And Sir Osbert, parrying: "I've been following your moves for some time, lieutenant, and I've been waiting for this!"

Equal in strength, the two ship's lieutenants were wearing themselves out in attacks and feints. They were at the peak of their ardor when—"Stop, in the name of heaven!" On the threshold of the pavilion Donna Viola had appeared.

"Marquise, this man . . ." said the two lieutenants in one voice, lowering their swords and pointing at each other.

And Donna Viola: "My dear friends! Sheathe your swords, I beg you! Is this the way to frighten a lady? I chose this pavilion as the most silent and secret place in the park, and see how just as I've fallen asleep your clash of arms wakens me!"

"But Milady," says the Englishman, "wasn't I invited here by you?"

"You were surely here to wait for me, Signora," says the Neapolitan.

A light laugh rose from Donna Viola's throat, like a beating of wings. "Ah, yes, yes, I had invited you . . . or you . . . Oh, my head is so confused . . . Well, what are you waiting for? Come in, sit down, please . . ."

"Milady, I thought it was an invitation for me alone. I am disappointed. My respects, and I ask your leave."

"I wished to say the same, Signora, and take my leave."

The marquise laughed. "My good friends . . . my good friends . . . I am so thoughtless . . . I thought I had invited Sir Osbert at one time and Don Salvatore at another. No, no, excuse me, at the same time but in different places . . . Oh, no, how can it be? Well, since you're both here, why can't we sit down and converse politely?"

The two lieutenants looked at each other, then looked at her. "Are we to understand, Marquise, that you seemed to welcome our attentions just to make fun of us both?"

"Why, my good friends? On the contrary, on the contrary . . . Your persistence could not leave me indifferent. You are both so dear . . . This is my sorrow. If I chose the elegance of Sir Osbert I should lose you, my passionate Don Salvatore, and choosing the fire of Lieutenant San Cataldo I would have to give up you, sir! Oh, why . . . why . . ."

"Why what?" asked the two officers in one voice.

And Donna Viola, lowering her head: "Why can't I belong to both at the same time?"

From the top of the horse chestnut a rustling of branches could be heard. It was Cosimo, who could no longer keep calm.

But the two ship's lieutenants were too upset to hear him. They retreated a step together. "That never, Signora."

The marquise raised her beautiful face, with her most radiant smile. "Well, I will belong to the first of you who, as proof of love, to please me in everything, will declare himself ready even to share me with his rival!"

"Signora . . ."

"Milady . . ."

The two lieutenants, bending toward Viola in a brusque bow of farewell, turned to face each other, held out their hands, shook.

"I was sure you were a gentleman, Signor Cataldo," said the Englishman.

"Nor did I doubt your honor, Mister Osberto," said the Neapolitan.

They turned their backs on the marquise and set off for their horses.

"My friends . . . Why so offended . . . Big fools . . ." said Viola, but the two officers already had their feet in the stirrups.

It was the moment that Cosimo had for some time been waiting for, anticipating the revenge he had prepared: now the two would have a rather painful surprise. Yet seeing their manly bearing in taking leave of the immodest marquise, Cosimo felt suddenly reconciled with them. Too late! The terrible mechanism of revenge could not now be removed! In the space of a second, Cosimo generously decided to warn them. "Halt there!" he shouted from the tree. "Don't sit in the saddle!"

The two officers raised their heads quickly. "*What are you doing up there?* What are you doing up there? How do you dare? *Come down!*"

Behind them Donna Viola could be heard laughing one of her fluttering laughs.

The two were perplexed. There was a third, who as it seems had witnessed the whole scene. The situation became more complex.

"In any case," they said to each other, "we two remain allies!"

"On our honor!"

"Neither of the two will agree to share Milady with anyone!"

"Never for life!"

"But if one of you should decide to agree . . ."

"In that case, allies forever! We'll agree together!"

"Right! And now onward!"

At this new dialogue, Cosimo bit a finger in rage at having tried to prevent the fulfillment of the revenge. "Let it be completed, then!" And he withdrew among the leaves. The two officers jumped into the saddle. "Now they'll scream," thought Cosimo, and it occurred to him to stop up his ears. A double shout resounded. The two lieutenants had sat on two porcupines hidden under the saddle blankets.

"Betrayal!" And they flew to the ground in an explosion of jumps and cries and whirling around, and it seemed that they would get angry with the marquise.

But Donna Viola, more furious than they were, shouted

upward, "Malicious monstrous big ape!" And she rushed toward the trunk of the horse chestnut, thus rapidly disappearing from the sight of the two officers, who thought she had been swallowed up by the earth.

Viola found herself facing Cosimo amid the branches. They looked at each other with flaming eyes, and that anger gave them a kind of purity, like archangels. It seemed they were about to tear each other to pieces, when the woman: "Oh my dearest!" she exclaimed. "Like that, that's how I want you: jealous, implacable!" Already she had thrown her arms around his neck, and they were embracing, and Cosimo no longer remembered anything.

She swayed in his arms, pulled her face away from his, as if reflecting, and then: "But the two of them, too, did you see how much they love me? They're ready to share me between them."

Cosimo seemed to rush against her, then he rose among the branches, bit leaves, beat his head against the trunk. "They are wooorms!"

Viola had left him, her face like a statue's. "You have a lot to learn from them." She turned and rapidly descended from the tree.

The two suitors, having forgotten their past disputes, had found no alternative but to start patiently looking in turn for the spines. Donna Viola interrupted them. "Quick! Get in my carriage!" They disappeared behind the pavilion. The carriage left. Cosimo, in the horse chestnut tree, hid his face in his hands.

A time of torment began for Cosimo, but also for the two former rivals. And for Viola could it possibly be called a time of joy? I think that the marquise tormented the others only because she wished to torment herself. The two noble officers were always in the way, inseparable, under Viola's windows or invited into her drawing room, or in long stays alone at the inn. She flattered both and always asked them to compete in new proofs of love, for which they declared themselves ready every time, and now they were wishing to have half of her each, and not only that, but to share her even with others, and, rolling down the slope of concessions, they couldn't stop, each one driven by the desire to thus finally succeed in moving her and getting her to keep her promises, and at the same time committed to the pact of solidarity with his rival, yet consumed by jealousy and by the hope of supplanting him, and also by the lure of the obscure degradation into which they felt themselves sinking.

At every new promise extracted from the naval officers, Viola climbed on her horse and went to tell Cosimo.

"You know that the Englishman is willing to do this and this . . . and the Neapolitan, too . . ." she cried as soon as she saw him perched gloomily in a tree.

Cosimo didn't answer.

"That is absolute love," she insisted.

"Absolute crap, all of you!" shouted Cosimo, and disappeared.

This was the cruel way they now had of loving, and they couldn't find a way out.

The English flagship weighed anchor. "You're staying, it's true?" said Viola to Sir Osbert. Sir Osbert didn't appear on board; he was declared a deserter. In solidarity and emulation, Don Salvatore also deserted.

"They have deserted!" Viola announced triumphantly to Cosimo. "For me! And you . . ."

"And I???" shouted Cosimo, with a gaze so fierce that Viola didn't say a word.

Sir Osbert and Salvatore di San Cataldo, deserters from the navies of their respective majesties, spent their days at the inn, playing dice, pale, restless, trying in turn to ruin themselves, while Viola was at the peak of discontent with herself and with all that surrounded her.

She took the horse and went into the woods. Cosimo was in an oak. She stopped below, in a meadow.

"I'm tired."

"Of them?"

"Of all of you."

"Oh."

"They've given me the greatest proofs of love—"

Cosimo spit.

"—but it's not enough for me." Cosimo looked at her. And she: "You don't think that love is absolute devotion, giving up of self . . ."

She was there in the meadow, beautiful as ever, and the coldness that slightly hardened her features and the haughty bearing of her person—it would have taken almost nothing to melt them and have her in his arms again. Cosimo could say something, anything to meet her halfway, he could say to her, "Tell me what you want me to do, I'm ready," and it would have been happiness again for him, happiness together, without shadows. Instead he said, "There can't be love unless one is oneself with all one's strength."

Viola made a gesture of opposition that was also a gesture of weariness. And yet she still could have understood him, as in fact she understood him, in fact she had on her lips the words to say, "You are as I want you," and could have immediately gone back up to him . . . She bit her lip. She said, "Be yourself alone, then."

"But then being myself has no meaning." That was what Cosimo wanted to say. Instead he said, "If you prefer those two worms . . ."

"I won't permit you to despise my friends!" she cried, and yet was thinking, "Only you matter to me, it's only for you that I do everything I do!"

"Only I can be despised . . ."

"Your way of thinking!"

"I'm one with it."

"Then farewell. I'll leave tonight. You won't see me again."

She hurried to the villa, packed her bags, left without saying a thing to the lieutenants. She kept her word. She didn't return to Ombrosa. She went to France, and historical events piled up against her wishes when she desired only to return. The Revolution broke out, then war; the marquise, at first interested in the new course of events (she was in Lafayette's entourage), then emigrated to Belgium and from there to England. In the fog of London, during the long years of the Napoleonic wars, she dreamed of the trees of Ombrosa. Then she married a lord with interests in the East India Company and settled in Calcutta. From her terrace she looked at the forests, the trees more exotic than those of the garden of her childhood, and it seemed to her that at every moment she saw Cosimo making his way among the leaves. But it was the shadow of a monkey, or a jaguar.

Sir Osbert Castlefight and Salvatore di San Cataldo remained bound together for life and for death, and took up an existence as adventurers. They were seen in the gambling houses of Venice, in Göttingen at the faculty of theology, in Petersburg at the court of Catherine II, then all trace of them was lost.

For a long time Cosimo wandered through the woods, weeping, ragged, refusing food. He wept loudly, like a newborn, and the birds that had once fled in flocks at the approach of that infallible hunter now became neighbors, on nearby treetops or flying onto his head, and the sparrows cried, the goldfinches trilled, the turtledove cooed, the thrush whistled, the chaffinch and the warbler chirped; and from their deep dens the squirrels emerged, the dormice, the field mice, and added their squeaks to the chorus, and so my brother moved amid that cloud of grief.

Then came the time of destructive violence: with every tree, he started at the top, and one leaf off, then the next, he rapidly reduced it, until it was bare as in winter, even if it didn't habitually shed its leaves. Then he went back up to the top and broke off all the twigs until he left only the large branches, and went up again, and with a pocketknife began to take off the bark, and the flayed trees exposed the white with a shivering, wounded air.

And in all that rage there was no longer resentment against Viola, but only remorse at having lost her, at not having been able to keep her bound to him, for having wounded her with an unjust and foolish pride. Because, he now understood, she had always been faithful to him, and if she brought along those other two men it was to signify that she considered only Cosimo worthy of being her sole lover, and all her dissatisfactions and tantrums were simply the insatiable yearning to make their love grow, not admitting that it could reach a peak, and he, he, he had understood nothing of this and had exasperated her to the point of losing her.

For some weeks he stayed in the woods, alone as he had never been; he no longer had even Ottimo Massimo, because Viola had taken him away. When my brother appeared again in Ombrosa, he was changed. Not even I could have any illusions: this time Cosimo really had gone mad.

24

That Cosimo was mad people had always said in Ombrosa, ever since at the age of twelve he had climbed up into the trees and refused to come down. But later, as happens, that madness of his had been accepted by everyone, and I don't mean just the fixation with living up there but the various strange aspects of his character, and no one considered him anything but an original. Then, in the full season of his love for Viola, there were the declarations in incomprehensible languages, especially the one during the feast day of the patron saint, which most judged sacrilege, interpreting his words as a heretical cry, perhaps in Carthaginian, the language of the Pelagians, or a profession of Socinianism in Polish. From then on, the rumor began to spread: "The baron has gone mad!" and the sensible added, "How can one who has always been mad go mad?"

Amid these differing opinions, Cosimo had truly become mad. If before he was dressed in skins from head to toe, now he began to adorn his head with feathers, like the natives of America, hoopoe or greenfinch feathers, in bright colors, and he wore them not only on his head but strewn on his clothes. He made himself tailcoats all covered in feathers, and imitated the habits of various birds, like the woodpecker, extracting worms and larvae from the trunks and boasting of them as of great wealth.

He also delivered praise of the birds to the people who gathered to listen to him and mock him under the trees, and from a hunter he became an advocate for the winged creatures and declared himself now a long-tailed tit, now a screech owl, now a robin redbreast, with suitable camouflages, and he made accusatory speeches against men, who couldn't recognize in the birds their true friends, and later accusatory speeches against all human society, in the form of parables. The birds also were aware of this change in his ideas and flew close to him, even if there were people listening to him below. Thus he could illustrate his speech with living examples that he pointed to on the nearby branches.

Because of this quality of his, there was a lot of talk among the hunters of Ombrosa about using him as a lure, but none ever dared to shoot the birds that alighted near him. Because the baron, even now that he was driven so far out of his senses, continued to inspire a certain awe; they made fun of him, yes, and often under his trees there was a swarm of kids and idlers who yelled insults at him, but he was also respected, and always listened to with attention.

His trees were now decorated with written pages and also posters bearing maxims of Seneca and Lord Shaftesbury, and objects: tufts of feathers, wax candles from church, sickles, crowns, busts of women, pistols, scales, tied to one another in a certain order. The people of Ombrosa spent hours trying to guess what those riddles meant—the aristocracy, the pope, virtue, war—and I think that sometimes they had no meaning but served only to sharpen people's wits and make them understand that even the most uncommon ideas could be right.

Cosimo also began to compose some writings, like *The Song of the Blackbird, The Woodpecker That Knocks, The Dialogues of the Owls,* and to distribute them publicly. In fact, it was just in this period of dementia that he learned the art of printing and began to print some sort of pamphlets or gazettes (among them *The Magpie Gazette*), which were later consolidated under the title *The Biped Monitor.* He had a bench, a frame, a press, a tray of letters, a demijohn of ink carried up into a walnut tree, and he spent days composing his pages and pulling copies. Sometimes spiders or butterflies fell in between the frame and the paper, and their impression remained printed on the page; sometimes a dormouse jumped on a page before the ink was dry and smeared it with swipes of its tail; sometimes the squirrels took a letter of the alphabet and carried it into their den, thinking that it was something to eat, as happened with the letter *Q,* which, because of that round shape with its stalk, was taken for a fruit, and Cosimo had to write certain words *cueen* and *cuality.*

All good things, but I had the impression that in that period my brother was not only completely mad but also getting a little soft in the head, which was something more serious and painful, because madness is a force of nature, for better or for worse, while softheadedness is a weakness of nature, without counterbalance.

In winter, in fact, he seemed reduced to a kind of lethargy. He was hanging from a trunk in his padded sack with only his head out, like a fledgling, and it was much if, in the warmest hours, he made a few leaps to reach the alder over the Merdanzo torrent to take care of his needs. He stayed in the sack reading idly (lighting, at dark, an oil lantern), or muttering to himself, or humming. But most of the time he was sleeping.

As for food, he had certain mysterious provisions, but he accepted dishes of minestrone and ravioli when some good soul came and brought them up on a ladder. In fact, a kind of superstition had originated among the common people that to make an offering to the baron brought good luck—a sign that he inspired either fear or affection, I believe the second. This fact that the heir of the baronial title of Rondò had begun to live on public charity seemed to me unbecoming, and above all I thought of our dear departed father, if he had known. As for me, up to that point I had nothing to reproach myself with, because my brother had always despised the family's comforts and had signed a document by virtue of which, after paying out to him a small income (most of which went for books), I had no obligation toward him. But now, seeing him incapable of obtaining food, I tried to get one of our servants, in livery and white wig, to climb up on a ladder with a quarter of a turkey and a glass of Burgundy on a tray. I thought he would refuse, for one of those mysterious reasons of principle, but he accepted immediately and willingly, and from then on, whenever we remembered, we sent a portion of our meals to him in the tree.

In other words, it was a harsh decline. Luckily, there was an invasion of wolves, and Cosimo again gave proof of his best qualities. It was a freezing winter, and snow had fallen even in our woods. Packs of wolves, driven from the Alps by hunger, descended on our shores. Some woodcutters encountered them and brought the news, terrified. The people of Ombrosa, who since the time of the fire watch had learned to unite in moments of danger, began to take turns as sentinels around the city, to keep the ravening beasts from approaching. But no one dared to go out of the inhabited area, especially at night.

"Unfortunately the baron is no longer what he used to be!" they said in Ombrosa.

That harsh winter had not been without consequences for Cosimo's health. He hung there, huddled in his goatskin like a worm in its cocoon, with his nose dripping and a dull and puffy look. There was alarm because of the wolves, and people passing below there addressed him: "Ah, Baron, once it would have been you in your trees guarding us, and now it's us guarding you."

His eyes remained half closed, as if he hadn't understood or it didn't matter. But suddenly he raised his head, sniffed, and said hoarsely, "Sheep. To drive out the wolves. They should put sheep in the trees. Tied."

People were crowding around below to hear what crazy

things he would come up with, and making fun of him. But he, huffing and clearing his throat, got up out of the sack, said, "I'll show you where," and set off through the branches.

Cosimo wanted them to bring sheep or lambs to some walnuts or oaks, in carefully chosen places between the woods and the cultivated areas, and he tied them himself to the branches, alive, bleating, but in a way so that they couldn't fall down. On each of these trees he then hid a gun loaded with bullets. He, too, dressed as a sheep: hood, jacket, trousers, all of curly sheepskin. And he sat down to wait for night outside in the trees. They all thought it was the wildest of his crazy ideas.

Instead, that night the wolves descended. Scenting the odor of the sheep, hearing the bleating, and then seeing the sheep up there, the whole pack stopped at the foot of the tree and howled, ravening jaws open, and paws planted against the trunk. And here was Cosimo, leaping through the branches, and the wolves, seeing that shape among the sheep and the man who was jumping up there like a bird, were dumbfounded, startled. Until *boom! boom!* they took two bullets right in the throat. Two, because one gun Cosimo carried with him (and reloaded every time) and another was there, ready on every tree, with the bullet in the barrel, so every time two wolves ended up lying on the cold ground. He killed a great number of them like that, and at every shot the packs retreated, disoriented, and the hunters, hurrying to where they heard the cries and the shots, did the rest.

Cosimo later told episodes of this wolf hunt in many versions, and I don't know how to say which was right. For example: "The battle was proceeding for the best when, moving toward the tree with the last sheep, I found three wolves there which had managed to climb up into the branches and were finishing her off. Half blind and dazed by the cold as I was, I arrived almost at the wolves' snouts without realizing it. The wolves, at seeing this other sheep who was walking on the branches, turned toward it, opening their jaws, which were still red with blood. My gun wasn't loaded, because after so much shooting I had no gunpowder left, and I couldn't get to the gun that was ready on that tree because the wolves were there. I was up on a smaller, somewhat delicate branch, but above me, within reach, was a stronger branch. I began to walk backward on my branch, slowly moving away from the trunk. A wolf slowly followed me. But I hung by my hands from the branch above and pretended to move my feet on that delicate branch; in reality I was holding myself suspended above it. The wolf, deceived, felt safe advancing, and the branch broke under him while I quickly hoisted myself up to the branch above. The wolf fell with a faint, doglike bark, and on the ground he broke his bones and lay there dead."

"And the two other wolves?"

"The two others were studying me, immobile. So suddenly I took off my sheepskin jacket and hood and threw them at the wolves. One of the two, seeing that white shadow of a lamb fly at him, tried to grab it with his teeth, but since he was prepared to support a great weight and that instead was an empty skin, he was thrown off and lost his balance, and he, too, ended up breaking legs and neck on the ground."

"There's still one left . . ."

"There's still one left, but since I'd thrown away my jacket my clothes were much lighter, and I had one of those sneezes that make the heavens tremble. The wolf, at that sudden new eruption, had such a start that he fell out of the tree and broke his neck, like the others."

So my brother recounted his night of battle. What's certain is that since he was already sick, the cold he got was nearly fatal. For several days he was between life and death, and was cared for at the expense of the Commune of Ombrosa, as a token of gratitude. Lying in a hammock, he was surrounded by doctors climbing up and down on ladders. The best doctors of the neighborhood were called to consult, and some prescribed enemas, some bloodletting, some mustard plasters, some fomentation. People no longer spoke of the Baron di Rondò as a madman, but all as one of the greatest minds and phenomena of the century.

This as long as he remained ill. When he recovered, things went back to the way they had been, with some saying he was wise as before, some mad as ever. The fact is that he no longer did so many strange things. He continued to print a weekly, entitled not *The Biped Monitor* but *The Reasonable Vertebrate.*

25

I don't know if a Freemasons lodge had already been established in Ombrosa at that time; I was initiated into the Masons much later, after the first Napoleonic campaign, along with a large part of the affluent bourgeoisie and minor nobility of our area, and so I don't know what my brother's early relations with the lodge were. On that subject I will cite an episode that happened around the time I'm now describing, and which various testimonies would confirm.

One day two Spaniards arrived in Ombrosa, travelers passing through. They went to the house of Bartolomeo Cavagna, pastry maker, known as a Freemason. It seems that they introduced themselves as brothers from the lodge in Madrid, and so that evening he took them to a session of the Masons of Ombrosa, who then met in the light of torches and wax tapers in a clearing in the woods. Our information about all this comes only from rumors and suppositions; what's certain is that the next day the Spaniards, as soon as they left their lodging, were followed by Cosimo di Rondò, who, unseen, watched them from the trees.

The travelers entered the courtyard of a tavern outside the gate. Cosimo lurked in a wisteria. At a table, a customer was waiting for the two; his face, shaded by a broad-brimmed black hat, couldn't be seen. Those three heads, or rather those three hats, were focused on the white square of the tablecloth, and after they had talked for a while, the hands of the unknown man began to write on a narrow piece of paper something that the two others dictated to him, and that, from the order in which he put the words down, one under the other, one would have said was a list of names.

"Good day to you, sirs!" said Cosimo. The three hats were raised, allowing three faces, eyes wide, to appear to the man in the wisteria. But one of the three, the broad-brimmed one, lowered his immediately, so that he touched the table with the tip of his nose. My brother had time to glimpse a physiognomy that didn't seem unknown to him.

"Buenos días a usted!" said the two. "But is it a custom of the place to descend from the sky like a pigeon to introduce oneself to strangers? I hope you'll come down immediately and explain it to us!"

"Those who stay up high are easily seen from every direction," said the baron, "while there are those who crawl to hide their face."

"Know that none of us are bound to show you our face, Señor, any more than we are held to show our rear."

"I know that for a certain type of person it's a point of honor to keep his face in the shadows."

"What type, please?"

"Spies, to mention one!"

The two accomplices started. The man who was leaning over remained immobile, but for the first time his voice was heard. "Or, for another, the members of secret societies," he uttered slowly.

That remark could be interpreted in various ways, Cosimo thought, and then said aloud, "That remark, sirs, could be interpreted in various ways. You say 'members of secret societies,' insinuating that I am one, or that you are, or that we both are, or that we are not, neither you nor I, but others, or because whatever the case it's a remark that can be useful for finding out what I'll say afterward."

"Cómo, cómo, cómo?" said the man in the broad-brimmed hat, disoriented, and in that disorientation, forgetting that he was supposed to keep his head down, raised it to look Cosimo in the eye. Cosimo recognized him: it was Don Sulpicio, his enemy the Jesuit in the time of Olivabassa!

"Ah! I wasn't deceived! Mask down, Reverend Father!" exclaimed the baron.

"You! I was sure!" said the Spaniard, and he took off his hat and bowed, displaying his tonsure. "Don Sulpicio de Guadalete, *superior de la Compañia de Jesús.*"

"Cosimo di Rondò, Free and Accepted Mason!"

The two other Spaniards introduced themselves with a rapid bow.

"Don Calisto!"

"Don Fulgencio!"

"Also Jesuits, you gentlemen?"

"Nosotros también!"

"But wasn't your order dissolved recently by order of the pope?"

"Not to give respite to libertines and heretics of your stamp!" said Don Sulpicio, drawing his sword.

They were Spanish Jesuits who after the dissolution of the order had taken to the countryside, seeking to form an armed militia in all the districts, to combat new ideas and theism.

Cosimo, too, drew his sword. A crowd had gathered around them.

"Be so kind as to descend, if you wish to fight *caballerosamente,*" said the Spaniard.

Farther on there was a walnut grove. It was the time of the nut harvest, and the peasants had hung some sheets between the trees to collect the nuts that they were beating down with a pole. Cosimo ran onto a walnut tree, jumped onto the sheet, and there stood upright, braking his feet, which slid on the material of that sort of large hammock.

"You climb up two handbreadths, Don Sulpicio, since I've come down more than usual!"

The Spaniard also jumped up onto the spread-out sheet. It was hard to stay upright, because the sheet kept closing up like a sack around their bodies, but the two contenders were so obstinate that they managed to cross swords.

"To the greater glory of God!"

"To the glory of the Great Architect of the Universe!"

And they slashed at each other.

"Before I plant this blade in your belly," said Cosimo, "give me news of Señorita Ursula."

"She died in a convent!"

Cosimo was distressed by the news (which, however, I think was invented on purpose), and the former Jesuit took advantage of that for a treacherous thrust. With a lunge he reached one of the corners that, tied to the branches of the trees, held up the sheet on Cosimo's side and cut it cleanly. Cosimo would certainly have fallen if he hadn't been quick to hurl himself onto Don Sulpicio's side of the sheet and hang on to an edge. As he leaped, his sword pierced the Spaniard's guard, and he ran it through his stomach. Don Sulpicio collapsed, slid down the sheet that slanted down on the side where he had cut the corner, and fell to the ground. Cosimo climbed up into the walnut tree. The two other former Jesuits lifted up the body of their dead or wounded companion (it was never clear), ran away, and were never seen again.

The people crowded around the bloody sheet. From that day my brother had the general reputation of a Freemason.

The secrecy of the society didn't permit me to learn more about it. When I joined, as I've said, I heard talk of Cosimo as of an old brother whose relations with the lodge weren't well defined, and some called him "sleeping," some a heretic who had moved on to other rites, some actually an apostate, but always with great respect for his past activity. I wouldn't even rule out that he could have been that legendary Nuthatch Mason to whom the founding of the Eastern Ombrosa Lodge is attributed, or that, in addition, the description of the first rites that were held there showed the baron's influence; suffice it to say that the initiates were blindfolded, made to climb to the top of a tree, and lowered down, hanging by ropes.

It's certain that in our area the first meetings of the Freemasons took place at night in the middle of the woods. Cosimo's presence would therefore have been more than justified, whether it was he who received from his foreign correspondents the pamphlets with the Masonic constitutions and founded the lodge here or whether it was someone else who, probably after being initiated in France or England, introduced the rites into Ombrosa as well. It's possible that Masonry had already existed for some time, unbeknown to Cosimo, and he, moving one night through the forest trees, by chance discovered in a clearing, in the light of candelabras, a meeting of men with strange garments and equipment; lingered above to listen; and then interrupted, causing confusion with some disconcerting remark, like, for example, "If you build a wall, think of what's left outside!" (a sentence I often heard him repeat), or another of his sayings, and the Masons, having recognized his high doctrine, made him a member of the lodge, with special responsibilities, who contributed to it a large number of new rites and symbols.

The fact is that the whole time my brother had to do with it, outdoor Masonry (as I'll call it, to distinguish it from the kind that later met in closed buildings) had a very rich set of rites, which involved owls, telescopes, pinecones, hydraulic pumps, mushrooms, Cartesian divers, spiders, Pythagorean tables. There was also a certain display of skulls, not only human but also craniums of cows, wolves, and eagles. Such objects and still others, including the spades, squares, and compasses of the regular Masonic liturgy, were found at that time hanging in the branches in bizarre juxtapositions and were likewise attributed to the madness of the baron. Only a few persons let it be understood that these riddles now had a more serious meaning; however, no clear separation between the signs of before and those of after could ever be traced, nor could it be ruled out that from the start they were esoteric symbols of some secret society.

Because long before Masonry, Cosimo had been connected with various trade associations or confraternities, like that of San Crispino, or the Shoemakers, or that of the Virtuous Coopers, or the Righteous Arms Makers, or the Conscientious Hatters. Since he made for himself almost all the things he needed, he knew the most varied crafts and could boast membership in many corporations, which for their part were very happy to have among them a member from a noble family, with a strange intelligence and of proved disinterest.

How the passion for a life of association that Cosimo always displayed was reconciled with his perpetual flight from civil society I've never understood, and it remains one of the larger peculiarities of his character. One might say that the more determined he was to stay hidden up in his branches, the greater the need he felt to create new relations with the human race. But although every so often he threw himself body and soul into organizing a new alliance, meticulously establishing its statutes, aims, the choice of men most suitable for each office, his companions never knew how far they could count on him, when and where they could meet him, or when, instead, he would suddenly be recaptured by his birdlike nature and not let himself be caught. Maybe, if we really want to trace these contradictory attitudes to a single impulse, we have to think that he was an enemy equally of every type of human living together in force in his times, and so he fled them all and strove stubbornly to try new ones, but none of them seemed right to him or different enough from the others; consequently his continual interludes of absolute wildness.

It was an idea of universal society that he had in mind. And every time he worked to bring people together, whether for specific goals like the fire watch or the defense against the wolves, or whether in trade confraternities like the Perfect Knife Grinders or the Enlightened Tanners—since he always arranged to have them meet in the woods, at night, around a tree, from which he preached—there was always an atmosphere of conspiracy, of a sect, of heresy, and in that atmosphere the discourse passed easily from the particular to the general, and just as easily from the simple rules of a manual trade to the plan of establishing a world republic of equals, of the free and the just.

In Masonry, therefore, Cosimo only repeated what he had

already done in the other secret or semisecret societies to which he had belonged. And when a certain Lord Liverpuck, sent by the Grand Lodge of London to visit fellow members on the Continent, happened to come to Ombrosa while my brother was master, he was so outraged by his lack of orthodoxy that he wrote to London that this d'Ombrosa must be a new Masonry of the Scottish rite, financed by the Stuarts to create propaganda against the throne of the Hanovers for the Jacobite restoration.

After that came the event I recounted, about the two Spanish travelers who introduced themselves as Masons to Bartolomeo Cavagna. Invited to a meeting at the lodge, they found everything perfectly normal; in fact they said it was just like at the East of Madrid. It was this which made Cosimo, who knew very well how much of that ritual was of his invention, suspicious, and that was why he pursued the spies and unmasked them and triumphed over his old enemy Don Sulpicio.

Anyway, I am of the opinion that those changes in the liturgy were a response to his own personal need, because after due consideration he could have taken the symbols of any of the trades except those of the mason, he who had never wanted either to construct houses of masonry or to live in them.

26

Ombrosa was also a land of vineyards. I haven't emphasized it, because, following Cosimo, I've had to stay among the forest trees. But there were vast slopes of vineyards, and in August under the foliage of the vines the Rossese grapes swelled into bunches with a dense, already wine-colored juice. Some vines grew on a trellis; I say this in part because as Cosimo got older he became so small and light and had learned the art of walking weightlessly so well that the beams of the trellises sustained him. Thus he could walk over the vineyards, and crossing like that, and with the aid of the fruit trees roundabout, and the support of the stakes called *scarasse,* he could do many jobs like pruning, in winter, when the vines are bare squiggles around an iron wire, or thin the too-thick leaves of summer, or look for insects, and in September help with the harvest.

For the harvest all the people of Ombrosa, who worked by the day, came to the vineyards, and amid the green of the vines one saw only bright-colored skirts and tasseled caps. The mule drivers loaded full baskets onto the mules and emptied them into vats; others were taken by the various collectors who came with teams of constables to check the tributes for the local nobles, for the governor of the Republic of Genoa, for the clergy and other tithes. Every year there were fights.

Questions concerning the shares of the harvest to allocate on all sides were what motivated the greater protests in the "complaint books" during the Revolution in France. In Ombrosa, too, people began to write in those notebooks, just to try, even though here it was of no real use. The idea had been one of Cosimo's, who at that time had no need to go to meetings of the lodge to discuss things with those few tippler Masons. He sat in the trees in the square, and all the people from the seacoast and the countryside gathered around to have the news explained, because he received the newspapers in the mail, and further had certain friends who wrote to him, among them the astronomer Bailly, later the *maire* of Paris, and other members of political clubs. There was something new every moment: Necker, and the tennis court, and the Bastille, and Lafayette on his white horse, and King Louis disguised as a servant. Cosimo explained and performed everything, jumping from branch to branch, and on one he played Mirabeau at the trial, and on the other Marat to the Jacobins, and on yet another King Louis at Versailles putting on the red hat to placate the old women who had come on foot from Paris.

In order to explain what the "complaint books" were, Cosimo said, "Let's try to make one." He took a school notebook and hung it from the tree with a piece of string; everyone came and marked on it the things that weren't right. They were of every kind: fishermen on the price of fish, and vinedressers on the tithes, and shepherds on the boundaries of the fields, and woodcutters in the woods belonging to the state, and then all those who had relatives in jail, and those who had been punished by the strappado for some crime, and those who were angry with the nobles on matters of women—it was unending. Cosimo thought that even if it was a "complaint book," it wasn't nice that it was so sad, and he had the idea of asking everyone to write the thing he would most like. And again each one came to have his say, this time all for the good: some wrote focaccia, some minestrone; some wanted a blonde, some two brunettes; some would have liked to sleep all day, some hunt for mushrooms all year; some wanted a carriage with four horses, some would have been content with a goat; some would have liked to see their dead mother, some meet the gods on Olympus—in short, everything good that exists in the world was written in the notebook, or rather drawn, because many didn't know how to write, or even painted in color. Cosimo, too, wrote in it: a name—Viola. The name that for years he'd been writing everywhere.

A fine notebook came out of it, and Cosimo titled it *Book of Complaints and Joys.* But when it was filled there was no assembly to send it to, so it remained there, hanging on the tree by a string, and when it rained it was left to be erased and soaked, and that sight wrung the hearts of the people of

Ombrosa because of their present poverty, and filled them with the desire to revolt.

In other words, there were also among us all the causes that led to the French Revolution. Only we weren't in France, and there was no revolution. We live in a country where causes always come true and not effects.

In Ombrosa, however, there were equally turbulent times. The Republican Army made war against the Austro-Sardinians right nearby. Massena in Collardente, Laharpe in Nervia, Mouret along the corniche, with Napoleon, who at the time was only a general in the artillery, so that he himself was responsible for the roars that sporadically reached Ombrosa on the wind.

In September people got ready for the harvest. And it seemed they were getting ready for something secret and terrible.

The furtive meetings from door to door.

"The grapes are ripe!"

"They're ripe! Ah yes!"

"I'll say ripe! They're going to pick!"

"We're all with you! Where will you be?"

"At the vineyard beyond the bridge. And you? And you?"

"At Count Pigna's."

"I at the vineyard at the mill."

"Have you seen how many constables? They're like blackbirds swooping down to peck at the clusters of grapes."

"But this year they won't peck!"

"If there are so many blackbirds, we're all hunters here!"

"But some won't show up. Some will run away."

"Why are there so many people who won't want to harvest this year?"

"In our place they wanted to put it off. But now the grapes are ripe!"

"They're ripe!"

The next day, instead, the harvest began silently. The vineyards were crowded with a chain of people along the rows, but no song arose. Some scattered calls, cries: "Are you here, too? They're ripe!" A movement of teams, something dark, maybe the sky, too, which wasn't completely overcast but a little heavy, and if a voice started a song it remained half finished, not picked up by the chorus. The mule drivers carried the baskets of grapes to the vats. Usually they first separated out the shares for the nobles, the bishops, and the governor; this year no, they seemed to have forgotten.

The collectors who had come to get the tithes were nervous; they didn't know what to do next. The more time passed and nothing happened, the more it was felt that something should happen, and the more the cops understood that they had to make a move the less they understood what to do.

Cosimo, with his catlike steps, had begun walking over the trellises. With a pair of scissors in hand, he cut a cluster here and a cluster there, in no order, offering them to the harvesters, men and women, below, to each saying something in a low voice.

The head of the constables couldn't take it anymore. He said, "Well, then, so, let's see some of these shares." He had barely spoken and had already regretted it. Through the vineyards echoed a dark sound between a roar and a hiss: it was a harvester blowing into a conch shell and spreading a sound of alarm through the valleys. From all over similar sounds responded; the vinedressers raised the conch shells like trumpets, and Cosimo did, too, from the height of a trellis.

Along the rows of vines a song spread: first broken, discordant, so that you couldn't tell what it was. Then the voices found an understanding, harmonized, gained momentum, and sang as if they were running, in flight, and the men and women standing still and half hidden along the rows, and the stakes, the vines, the clusters all appeared to run, and the grapes seemed to harvest themselves, rushing into the vats and crushing themselves, and air, clouds, and sun became must, and now the song could be understood, first the notes of the music and then some of the words, which said, *"Ça ira! Ça ira! Ça ira!"* And the youths crushed the grapes with bare red feet, *"Ça ira!"* and the girls inserted the scissors, pointed like daggers, into the thick green, cutting the twisted stems of the clusters, *"Ça ira!"* and clouds of gnats invaded the air above the piles of stalks and skins ready for the press, *"Ça ira!"* and it was then that the constables lost control, and: "Stop there! Silence! Enough of that noise! We shoot anyone who sings!" And they began to fire their guns in the air.

There was an answering thunder of rifle fire that seemed like regiments arrayed for battle on the hills. All the hunting rifles of Ombrosa exploded, and Cosimo, at the top of a tall fig, sounded the charge in the trumpetlike shell. Through all the vineyards there was a movement of people. You couldn't tell anymore what was harvest and what was fray: men grapes women shoots billhooks vine leaves poles guns baskets horses wire fists kicks of mule shins udders and everyone singing, *"Ça ira!"*

"Here are your tithes!" It ended when the constables and the collectors were chased headfirst into the vats of grapes, with their legs out, kicking. They returned without having collected anything, spattered from head to toe with grape juice, trampled skins, marc, residue, stalks entangled in guns, cartridge boxes, whiskers.

The harvest continued like a party, everyone convinced that feudal privileges had been abolished. Meanwhile we other nobles and minor nobles had barricaded ourselves in our villas, armed, ready to sell our skin dearly. (I truly didn't even stick my nose out of the entrance, mainly so that the other nobles wouldn't say that I was in agreement with that Antichrist my brother, who was reputed to be the worst instigator, Jacobin, and club member of the whole area.) But for that day, with the collectors and the troops driven out, no one was hurt.

The people were all busy preparing celebrations. They

even set up a Tree of Freedom, to follow the French fashion; only they didn't really know how to make one, and then we had so many trees that it wasn't worth putting up a fake one. So they decorated a real tree, an elm, with flowers, bunches of grapes, festoons, writings: *"Vive la Grande Nation!"* From treetop to treetop there was my brother, with the tricolor cockade on his cat-skin cap, and he delivered a lecture on Rousseau and Voltaire, of which not a word could be heard, because all the people below were dancing around and singing, *"Ça ira!"*

The joy didn't last long. Troops came in force: Genoese, to exact the tithes and guarantee the neutrality of the territory, and Austro-Sardinians, because the rumor had spread that the Jacobins of Ombrosa wanted to proclaim their annexation to the Great Universal Nation, that is, the French Republic. The rebels tried to resist, they built some barricades, they closed the gates to the city . . . But yes, something else was needed! The troops entered the city from all sides and set up blockades on every road in the countryside, and those reputed to be agitators were imprisoned, except Cosimo—because anyone who could catch him was good—and a few others with him.

The trial of the revolutionaries was held promptly, but the accused succeeded in proving that they had nothing to do with it and the real leaders were precisely those who had escaped. So they were all freed, since with the troops stationed in Ombrosa, there was no fear of other uprisings. A garrison of Austro-Sardinians also stayed, to guard against possible infiltrations by the enemy, and in command of it was our brother-in-law D'Estomac, Battista's husband, who had emigrated from France in the escort of the Count di Provenza.

So I found my sister Battista in the way again, with what pleasure I will let you imagine. She settled in my house, with her officer husband, horses, orderlies. She spent the evenings telling us about the recent executions in Paris; in fact, she had a model of a guillotine, with a real blade, and in order to explain the end of all her friends and acquired relatives she decapitated lizards, blindworms, worms, and even mice. So we passed the evenings. I envied Cosimo, who lived his days and nights on the run, hidden in some wood or other.

27

Concerning the exploits that he undertook in the woods during the war, Cosimo told so many tales, so unbelievable, that I don't feel able to confirm one version or another. I leave it to him, reporting faithfully some of his stories:

Patrols of scouts from the opposing armies ventured into the woods. Up in the branches, I strained my ears whenever I heard a step thudding among the bushes to figure out if it was Austro-Sardinian or French.

A very fair-haired young Austrian lieutenant, commanding a patrol of soldiers in perfect uniform—pigtail and ribbon, tricorne and gaiters, crossed white bands, gun and bayonet—marched them in step, two by two, trying to keep them in line on the steep paths. Ignorant of what the woods were like but certain of executing precisely the orders received, the young officer proceeded according to the routes traced on the map, continually bumping his nose against the trunks, causing the troops to slide on the smooth stones with their nailed boots or gouge their eyes on the thorns, but always conscious of the supremacy of the imperial arms.

They were magnificent soldiers. I waited for them at the pass, hidden in a pine. I had in my hand a pinecone weighing a pound and I dropped it on the head of the last in line. The soldier spread his arms, his knees buckled, and he fell among the ferns of the underbrush. No one noticed; the squad continued its march.

I caught up to them again. This time I threw a rolled-up porcupine at the neck of a corporal. The corporal bowed his head and fainted. This time the lieutenant observed the incident, sent two men to get a stretcher, and kept going.

The patrol, as if deliberately, went and got itself in trouble in the densest juniper thicket in the whole wood. And a new trap was always waiting. I had collected in a paper sack a kind of hairy blue caterpillar which made your skin swell worse than nettles if you touched it, and I rained hundreds down on them. The platoon passed by, disappeared into the thicket, reemerged scratching, hands and faces all red boils, and marched onward.

Marvelous troop and magnificent officer. Everything in the woods was so strange to him that he couldn't distinguish what was unusual, and he kept going, his forces decimated, but still proud and indomitable. I resorted then to a family of wild cats: I hurled them by the tail after spinning them in the air, which enraged them beyond all description. There was a lot of noise, especially feline, then silence and truce. The Austrians treated the wounded. The patrol, having turned white with bandages, resumed its march.

"The only thing to do here is try and make them prisoners!" I said to myself, hurrying to get ahead of them in the hope of finding a French patrol to warn of the enemy's approach. But it was a while since the French had seemed to give any sign of life on that front.

While I was crossing over some mossy places, I saw something move. I stopped, straining my ears. I could hear a kind of clattering of a stream, which became articulated into a continuous muttering, and then words could be distinguished, like *"Mais alors . . . cré-nom-de . . . foutez-moi-donc . . . tu m'emmer . . . quoi . . ."* Sharpening my eyes in the dim light, I saw that that soft vegetation was composed mainly of furry busbies and thick whiskers and beards. It was a platoon of French hussars. All their hair, saturated with dampness during the winter campaign, when spring came was flowering with molds and moss.

Lieutenant Agrippa Papillon, of Rouen, poet, volunteer in the Republican Army, commanded the outpost. Persuaded of the general goodness of nature, Lieutenant Papillon didn't want his soldiers to shake off the pine needles, the chestnut husks, the twigs, the leaves, the snails that stuck to them as they passed through the woods. And the patrol was already so fused with surrounding nature that it took my trained eye to discern it.

Among his camping soldiers, the officer-poet, with long

curly hair framing his thin face under a cocked hat, declaimed to the woods, "O forest! O night! Here I am at your mercy! Will a tender shoot of maidenhair, wrapped around the calf of these brave soldiers, thus be able to stop the destiny of France? O Valmy! How far away you are!"

I advanced. *"Pardon, citoyen."*

"What? Who's there?"

"A patriot of these woods, citizen officer."

"Ah! Here? Where is he?"

"Right under your nose, citizen officer."

"I see! What's there? A man-bird, a son of the Harpies! Might you be a mythological creature?"

"I am Citizen Rondò, the son of human beings, I assure you, both on the father's and the mother's side, citizen officer. In fact my mother was a valiant soldier in the time of the Wars of Succession."

"I understand. O times, O glory! I believe you, citizen, and I'm eager to hear the news that you seem to have come to tell me."

"An Austrian patrol is penetrating your lines!"

"What do you mean? It's the battle! It's time! O stream, gentle stream, behold, soon you will be stained with blood! Up! To arms!"

On the orders of the lieutenant-poet, the hussars gathered their weapons and belongings, but they moved in such a careless, weak way, stretching, clearing their throats, cursing, that I began to be worried about their military efficacy.

"Citizen officer, do you have a plan?"

"A plan? March on the enemy."

"Yes, but how?"

"How? In close ranks!"

"Well, if you will allow me some advice, I would keep the soldiers in place, in scattered order, letting the enemy patrol trap itself."

Lieutenant Papillon was an accommodating man and made no objections to my plan. The hussars, scattered in the woods, were difficult to distinguish from the tufts of green, and the Austrian lieutenant certainly was least apt to grasp this difference. The imperial patrol marched along the route marked on paper, with every so often a brusque "Right wheel!" or "Left wheel!" Thus they passed under the nose of the French hussars without noticing them. The hussars, silent, producing only natural noises like rustling leaves and beating wings, prepared for an encircling maneuver. From the height of the trees I signaled to them with the whistle of the quail or the cry of the owl the movements of the enemy troops and the shortcuts they should take. The Austrians, in the dark about everything, were trapped.

"Halt! In the name of liberty, fraternity, and equality, I declare you all prisoners!" they heard suddenly, shouted from a tree, and a human shadow appeared among the branches brandishing a gun with a long barrel.

"Hoorah! Vive la Nation!" And all the nearby bushes turned out to be French hussars, with Lieutenant Papillon at their head.

Dark Austro-Sardinian curses resounded, but before they

could react they had been disarmed. The Austrian lieutenant, pale but head high, handed over his sword to his enemy colleague.

I became a valuable collaborator with the Republican Army, but I preferred to do my hunting alone, making use of the forest animals, like the time I routed an Austrian column by flinging a nest of wasps at it.

My fame spread in the Austro-Sardinian camp, and was magnified to the point where it was said that the wood was teeming with armed Jacobins hidden in the treetops. The royal and imperial troops listened intently as they marched; at the slightest thud of a chestnut removed from the husk or the faintest squeal of a squirrel, they saw themselves surrounded by Jacobins and changed course. In this way, by eliciting barely perceptible noises and rustlings, I diverted the Piedmontese and Austrian columns and guided them where I wanted.

One day I led a column into some dense, thorny underbrush where I knew it would get lost. A family of wild boars was hidden in the underbrush; driven out of the mountains where the cannon thundered, the boars descended in herds to shelter in the woods lower down. The lost Austrians marched, unable to see a handbreadth in front of their noses, and suddenly a pack of hairy wild boars rose under their feet, emitting piercing grunts. Propelled snout forward, the beasts plunged between the knees of the soldiers, throwing them up in the air, and they trampled the fallen with an avalanche of pointed hooves and thrust their tusks into their bellies. The entire battalion was overcome. I was perched in the trees with my companions, and we followed them with rifle fire. Of those who returned to camp, some told of an earthquake that had suddenly shaken the thorny ground under their feet, some of a battle against a band of Jacobins who erupted from underground, because those Jacobins were none other than devils, half man and half beast, who lived in the trees or in the depths of the underbrush.

I've told you that I preferred to carry out my strikes on my own, or with those few companions of Ombrosa who had taken refuge with me in the woods after the harvest. With the French Army I tried to have as little to do as I could, because you know what armies are like: every time they move they cause disasters. But I was fond of Lieutenant Papillon's outpost, and I was not a little worried about its fate. In fact, the lack of movement on the front threatened to be fatal to the platoon commanded by the poet. Mosses and lichens were growing on the soldiers' uniforms, and sometimes even heathers and ferns; in the tops of their busbies mites made their nests, or lilies of the valley sprouted and flowered; the soldiers' boots solidified with the earth into compact clods—the whole platoon was about to put down roots. Lieutenant Agrippa Papillon's surrender to nature cast that handful of valorous men into an animal and vegetable amalgam.

They had to be awakened. But how? I had an idea and I presented myself to Lieutenant Papillon to propose it to him. The poet was declaiming to the moon.

"O moon! Round as a gun, as a cannonball, which, with the thrust of the gunpowder gone, continues its slow trajectory, rolling silently across the heavens! When you explode, moon, raising a high cloud of dust and sparks, submerging enemy armies and thrones and opening for me a breach of glory in the compact wall of the scant consideration my fellow citizens have for me! O Rouen! O moon! O fate! O National Convention! O frogs! O girls! O my life!"

And I: "*Citoyen . . .*"

Papillon, annoyed at always being interrupted, said brusquely, "Well?"

"I wanted to say, citizen officer, that there might be a system of waking your men from a now dangerous lethargy."

"Heaven willed it, citizen. I, as you see, yearn for action. And what would be that system?"

"Fleas, citizen officer."

"I'm sorry to disabuse you, citizen. The Republican Army does not have fleas. They all died of hunger from the consequences of the blockade and the high cost of living."

"I can provide them for you, citizen officer."

"I don't know if you're speaking sensibly or as a joke. Anyway, I'll make a petition to the higher commands and we'll see. Citizen, I thank you for what you do for the republican cause! O glory! O Rouen! O fleas! O moon!" And he went off raving.

I understood that I had to act on my own initiative. I got myself a good supply of fleas, and as soon as I saw a French hussar, I shot one at him from the trees with a peashooter, trying with my precise aim to get it inside his collar. Then I began to sprinkle them over the whole division, in handfuls. It was a dangerous mission, because if I'd been caught in the act my reputation as a patriot would be worthless: I would have been taken prisoner, carried to France, and guillotined as an emissary of Pitt. Instead my intervention was providential: the itching of the fleas rekindled acutely in the hussars the human and civilized need to scratch, to rub, to get rid of the fleas; they threw away the mossy garments, the knapsacks and bundles covered with mushrooms and spiderwebs; they washed, they shaved, they combed their hair; in short they regained consciousness of their individual humanity, and the sense of civilization, of deliverance from brute nature, won them back. Further, a goad to activity pricked them, a long-forgotten zeal and combativeness. The moment of the attack found them imbued with this impulse: the Armies of the Republic got the better of the enemy resistance, overwhelmed the front, and advanced to the victories of Dogo and Millesimo.

28

From Ombrosa, our sister and the émigré D'Estomac escaped just in time not to be captured by the Republican Army. The people of Ombrosa seemed to have returned to the days of the harvest. They raised the Liberty Tree, this time more in accord with the French examples, that is, a little like a greased pole. Cosimo, needless to say, climbed up it, with his Phrygian cap on his head, but he got tired immediately and left.

Around the palaces of the nobles there was some uproar, some cries: *"Aristo, aristo, to the lamppost, that's all right."* As for me, between being the brother of my brother and the fact that we had always been nobles of little account, I was left in peace; in fact, later I was even considered a patriot (thus when things changed again I had some troubles).

They set up the *municipalité,* the *maire,* all in the French style; my brother was named to the provisional council, although many did not approve, considering him insane. Those of the old regime laughed and said that it was all a madhouse.

The council meetings were held in the ancient palace of the Genoese governor. Cosimo perched on a carob tree at the height of the windows and followed the discussions. Sometimes he intervened, shouting, and gave his vote. It's well known that revolutionaries are stricter about formalities than conservatives, and they found things to complain about: that it was a system that didn't work, that it diminished the decorum of the assembly, and when in place of the oligarchic Republic of Genoa they set up the Ligurian Republic, they did not appoint my brother to the new administration.

And to say that Cosimo in that time had written and distributed a *Plan of a Constitution for a Republican City with Declaration of the Rights of Men, Women, Children, Domestic and Wild Animals, Including Birds, Fish, and Insects, and of Plants Both Forest Trees and Vegetables and Grasses.* It was a beautiful work, which could serve as a guide for all who govern; instead no one took it under consideration, and it remained a dead letter.

But Cosimo still spent most of his time in the woods, where the sappers of the French Army's Engineer Corps built a road for the transport of the artillery. With long beards that emerged from under their busbies and disappeared into their leather smocks, the sappers were different from all other soldiers. Maybe this was because behind them they trailed not that wake of disasters and ruin, like other troops, but instead the satisfaction of things that remained and the ambition to do them as well as they could. Then, they had many things to tell: they had crossed through nations, experienced sieges and battles; some of them had even seen the great things that had happened in Paris, the Bastille captured, the guillotinings;

and Cosimo spent the evenings listening to them. Putting down their hoes and shovels, they sat around a fire, smoking short pipes and raking up memories.

During the day Cosimo helped the planners mark out the road's course. No one was able to do it better than he: he knew all the places through which the road could pass with the least unevenness and the smallest loss of trees. And more than the French artillery, he always had in mind the needs of the populations of those towns without roads. There was one advantage, anyway, in the passage of all those hen-stealing soldiers: a road built at their expense.

Just as well, because by now no one could stand the occupying troops, especially since they had turned from republicans into imperials. And everyone went to the patriots to vent: "You see what your friends are doing!" And the patriots, spreading their arms and raising their eyes to the sky, responded, "Well! Soldiers! Let's hope it passes!"

Napoleon's people requisitioned pigs, cows, even goats from the stables. As for taxes and tithes, it was worse than before. Furthermore, conscription was introduced. This business of going for a soldier no one among us has ever wished to understand, and the young men who were called up took refuge in the woods.

Cosimo did what he could to alleviate these evils: he watched over the livestock in the woods when the small landowners, in fear of a raid, set them loose, or he acted as a guard for the secret transports of grain to the mill or olives to the press so that Napoleon's men wouldn't come to seize a share, or he showed the youths who had been conscripted the caves in the woods where they could hide. In short, he tried to defend the people from the abuses, but he never attacked the occupying troops, although at that time armed bands of "bearded outlaws" began to wander through the woods, making life difficult for the French. Cosimo, stubborn as he was, never wanted to contradict himself, and having been a friend of the French before, continued to think that he had to be loyal, even if so many things had changed and it was all different from what he had expected. Then it must also be kept in mind that he was starting to get old and was no longer very active on either side.

Napoleon went to Milan to be crowned and then he traveled in Italy. In every city he was welcomed with great celebrations and taken to see the curiosities and the monuments. The Ombrosotti put on the program a visit to the "patriot in the treetops," because, as often happens, while here among us no one paid attention to Cosimo, outside he was much talked of, especially abroad.

It wasn't a simple meeting. The whole thing was arranged by the municipal committee for celebrations to make a good showing. A beautiful tree was chosen; they wanted an oak, but the best positioned was a walnut, and so they decorated the walnut with some oak leaves, they put up ribbons with the French tricolor and the Lombard tricolor, some cockades, some frills. They had my brother sit up there, in holiday clothes but with the characteristic cat-skin cap and a squirrel on his shoulder.

Everything was set for ten, and a great crowd had formed in a circle, but naturally at half past eleven Napoleon still couldn't be seen, to the great annoyance of my brother, who as he got older had begun to have trouble with his bladder and every so often had to hide behind the trunk to urinate.

The emperor arrived, with his escort, their cocked hats nodding like ships. It was already midday. Napoleon, looking up through the branches at Cosimo, had the sun in his eyes. He began to speak a few phrases suited to the occasion: *"Je sais très bien que vous, citoyen . . ."* and he shielded his eyes with his hand . . . *"parmi les forêts"*—and he hopped forward so that the sun wouldn't fall right in his eyes—*"parmi les frondaisons de votre luxuriante . . ."* and he hopped the other way because Cosimo, in a bow of assent, had again exposed the sun.

Seeing Bonaparte's restlessness, Cosimo asked politely, "May I do something for you, *mon empereur*?"

"Yes, yes," said Napoleon. "Move a little more this way, please, to shelter me from the sun, there, like that, stop . . ." Then he was silent, as if assailed by a thought, and turned to the Viceroy Eugène: *"Tout cela me rappelle quelque chose—quelque chose que j'ai déjà vu . . ."*

Cosimo came to his aid. "It wasn't you, Majesty, it was Alexander the Great."

"Ah, but of course!" said Napoleon. "The meeting of Alexander and Diogenes!"

"Vous n'oubliez jamais votre Plutarque, mon empereur," said Beauharnais.

"Only then," Cosimo added, "it was Alexander who asked Diogenes what he could do for him, and Diogenes who asked him to move."

Napoleon snapped his fingers as if he had finally found the phrase he was searching for. Making sure with a glance that the dignitaries of his escort were listening to him, he said, in excellent Italian, "If I were not the Emperor Napoleon, I would have liked to be Citizen Cosimo Rondò!"

And he turned and left. The escort followed with a great clattering of spurs.

It all ended there. One might have expected that in a week the cross of the Legion of Honor would arrive for Cosimo. Instead nothing. Maybe my brother didn't care, but it would have pleased us in the family.

29

If youth vanishes quickly on the earth, just imagine in the trees, whence everything is fated to fall: leaves, fruits. Cosimo was becoming old. So many years, with all the nights spent in the cold, in the wind, in the rain, in frail shelters or none, in the open air, with never a house, a fire, warm food . . . Cosimo was now a shrunken old man, legs bowed, arms long, like a monkey, hunchbacked, bundled up in a fur cloak with a hood, like a furry friar. His face was burned by the sun, wrinkled as a chestnut, with light round eyes amid the wrinkles.

With Napoleon's army routed at the Berezina and the English squad landing at Genoa, we spent the days waiting for news of the upheavals. Cosimo wasn't seen in Ombrosa; he was perched on a pine in the woods, on the edge of the Artillery Road, where the cannons had passed on the way to Marengo, and he looked east, along the deserted track where now only shepherds with goats or mules loaded with wood met. What was he waiting for? He had seen Napoleon, he knew how the Revolution had ended; there was no more to wait for but the worst. And yet he stayed there, eyes staring, as if at any moment the imperial army were to appear at the bend, still covered with Russian icicles, and Bonaparte in the saddle, his poorly shaved chin inclined to his chest, feverish, pale . . . He would have stopped under the pine (behind him, steps would have halted in confusion, knapsacks and guns dropped on the ground, shoes removed by exhausted soldiers on the side of the road, wounded feet unbandaged), and he would have said, "You were right, Citizen Rondò. Give me the constitutions you drafted, give me your advice that neither the Directory nor the Consulate nor the Empire would listen to—let's start again from the beginning, let's raise the Liberty Tree, let's save the universal homeland!" These surely were Cosimo's dreams, his hopes.

Instead, one day three figures came trudging along the Artillery Road from the east. One, lame, was supporting himself on a crutch, another had his head in a turban of bandages; the third was the healthiest, having only a black patch over one eye. The faded rags they wore, the shreds of frogging that hung on their chests, the busbies that no longer had crowns though one had a plume, the ragged thigh-high boots seemed to have belonged to uniforms of the Napoleonic Guard. But arms they had none, or rather one brandished the empty sheath of a dagger, another held on his shoulder a rifle barrel like a stick, carrying a bundle. And they came forward singing, *"De mon pays . . . De mon pays . . . De mon pays,"* like three drunks.

"Hey, foreigners," my brother called to them, "who are you?"

"Look what sort of bird! What are you doing up there? Are you eating pine nuts?"

And another: "Who wants to give us some pine nuts? With the backlog of hunger we have, want to let us eat some pine nuts?"

"And thirst! The thirst we got eating snow!"

"We are the Third Regiment of Hussars!"

"Complete!"

"All that remain!"

"Three out of three hundred—it's not nothing!"

"For me, I survived and that's enough!"

"Ah, not yet certain, you haven't got your skin safely home yet!"

"Damn you!"

"We're the victors of Austerlitz!"

"And the screwed of Vilna! Joy!"

"Say, talking bird, tell us, where's a wine cellar in these parts?"

"We've emptied the barrels of half of Europe but we're still thirsty!"

"It's because we're riddled with bullet holes, and the wine leaks."

"You're riddled in that place!"

"A cellar that gives us credit!"

"We'll pass by and pay another time."

"Napoleon will pay."

"Prrr . . ."

"The czar can pay! He's coming behind us—give him the bills!"

Cosimo said, "There's no wine around here, but farther on there's a stream and you can quench your thirst there."

"You can drown yourself in the stream, owl!"

"If I hadn't lost my gun in the Vistula I'd already have shot and roasted you on a spit like a thrush."

"Wait, I'm going to bathe my feet in this stream, they're burning . . ."

"For me, wash my behind, too . . ."

Meanwhile all three went to the stream, took off their boots, bathed their feet, washed their face and clothes. They got some soap from Cosimo, one of those who, growing old, become clean because they're seized by that bit of self-disgust that in youth goes unnoticed; so he always had soap with him. The coolness of the water dispelled the drunkenness of the three veterans. And as the drunkenness passed, so did the cheerfulness; the melancholy of their situation repossessed them, and they sighed and moaned. But in that melancholy the clear water became a delight, and they enjoyed it, singing, *"De mon pays . . . De mon pays . . ."*

Cosimo had returned to his lookout by the side of the road. He heard galloping. A small band of light cavalry arrived, raising dust. They wore uniforms never seen before, and under the heavy busbies they showed fair bearded faces, slightly crushed, with half-closed green eyes. Cosimo greeted them with his hat. "What brings you here, horsemen?"

They stopped. "*Zdravtsvuite!* Tell us, *batiushka,* how long to get there?"

"*Zdravtsvuite,* soldiers," said Cosimo, who had learned a little of all languages, even Russian. "*Kuda vam?* To get where?"

"To get where this road gets . . ."

"Eh, this road to get there gets to many places. Where are you going?"

"*V Parizh.*"

"Well, for Paris there are more convenient—"

"*Nyet, nie Parizh. Vo Frantsiyu, za Napoleonom. Kuda vediot eta doroga?*"

"Eh, in many places: Olivabassa, Sassocorto, Trappa . . ."

"*Kak?* Aliviabassa? *Nyet, nyet.*"

"Well, if you want you can also go to Marseilles . . ."

"*V Marsel . . . da, da, Marsel . . . Frantsiya . . .*"

"And what are you going to do in France?"

"Napoleon came to make war on our czar, and now our czar is chasing Napoleon."

"And where do you come from?"

"*Iz Charkova. Iz Kieva. Iz Rostova.*"

"So you've seen some fine places! And do you like it better here among us or in Russia?"

"Nice places, ugly places, we like Russia."

A gallop, a cloud of dust, and a horse stopped, mounted by an officer who shouted to the Cossacks, "*Von! Marš! Kto vam pozvolil ostanovitsiya?*"

"*Do svidaniya, batiushka!*" they said to Cosimo.

"*Nam pora . . .*" And they spurred their horses.

The officer had remained at the foot of the pine. He was tall, slender, with a noble, sad expression; he raised his bare head toward the sky veined with clouds.

"Bonjour, monsieur," he said to Cosimo. *"Vous connaissez notre langue?"*

"Da, gospodin ofitsèr," my brother answered, *"mais pas mieux que vous le français, quand-même."*

"Êtes-vous un habitant de ce pays? Êtiez-vous ici pendant qu'il y avait Napoléon?"

"Oui, monsieur l'officier."

"Comment ça allait-il?"

"Vous savez, monsieur, les armées font toujours des dégâts, quelles que soient les idées qu'elles apportent."

"Oui, nous aussi nous faisons beaucoup de dégâts . . . mais nous n'apportons pas d'idées . . ."

He was melancholy and troubled, and yet he was a victor. Cosimo felt sympathetic and wished to console him. *"Vous avez vaincu!"*

"Oui. Nous avons bien combattu. Très bien. Mais peut-être . . ."

A burst of shouting could be heard, a thudding sound, a clash of weapons. *"Kto tam?"* said the officer. The Cossacks returned, dragging some half-naked bodies along the ground, and in their hands they were holding something, in the left hand (the right was grasping the broad curved sword, unsheathed and, yes, dripping blood), and this something was the bearded heads of those three drunken hussars. *"Frantsuzy! Napoleons!* All killed!"

The young officer, with a curt order, had them taken

away. He turned his head. He spoke again to Cosimo. *"Vous voyez . . . La guerre . . . Il y a plusieurs années que je fais le mieux que je puis une chose affreuse: la guerre . . . et tout cela pour des idéals que je ne saurais presque expliquer moi-même . . ."*

"I, too," said Cosimo. "I've lived for many years for ideals that I wouldn't know how to explain even to myself, *mais je fais une chose tout à fait bonne: vis dans les arbres."*

The officer turned from melancholy to nervous. *"Alors,"* he said, *"je dois m'en aller."* He gave a military salute. *"Adieu, monsieur . . . Quel est votre nom?"*

"Le Baron Cosmo de Rondeau," Cosimo shouted after him, for he had already left. *"Proshchaite, gospodin . . . Et le vôtre?"*

"Je suis le Prince Andrei . . ." And the horse's gallop carried off his surname.

30

Now I don't know what this nineteenth century, which began so badly and continues worse, has in store. The shadow of the Restoration weighs on Europe: all the innovators—whether Jacobins or Bonapartists—defeated; absolutism and Jesuits hold the field again; the ideals of youth, the Enlightenment, the hopes of our eighteenth century all ashes.

I confide my thoughts to this notebook, nor would I otherwise be able to express them: I've always been a moderate man, without grand impulses or cravings, father of a family, with a noble lineage, enlightened in ideas, obedient to laws. The excesses of politics have never shaken me too strongly, and I hope that it continues like that. But what sadness within!

It was different before: there was my brother. I said to myself, "There's him, he'll take care of it," and I attended to living. For me the sign that things had changed wasn't the arrival of the Austro-Russians or the annexation of Piedmont or the new taxes or whatever, but that when I opened the window I no longer saw him balancing up there. Now that he isn't there, it seems to me that I should think of so many things

—philosophy, politics, history. I follow the newspapers, I read books, I rack my brains, but the things that he wanted to say aren't there, it's something else that he meant, something that embraced everything, and he couldn't say it in words but only by living as he lived. Only by being as ruthlessly himself as he was until his death could he give something to all men.

I remember when he got sick. We realized it because he took his bed to the big walnut tree in the middle of the square. Before, with the instinct of a wild animal, he had always kept hidden the places where he slept. Now he felt the need to be always in sight of others. It wrung my heart: I had always thought that he wouldn't like to die alone, and that was perhaps already a sign. We sent a doctor, up on a ladder; when he came down, he frowned and shrugged, arms spread.

I went up the ladder. "Cosimo," I began, "you're over sixty-five—how can you continue to stay up there? What you wanted to say you've said, we've understood, you had great strength of mind, you did it, now you can come down. Even those who've spent their whole life at sea, at a certain age they disembark."

Of course not. He said no with his hand. He hardly spoke anymore. He got up every so often, wrapped in a blanket up to his head, and sat on a branch to enjoy a little sun. He went no farther. There was an old woman of the people, a saintly woman (maybe an old lover of his), who went to clean and bring him hot food. We kept the ladder leaning against the trunk because there was always a need to go up to help him, and also because we hoped that he would at any moment decide to come down. (Others hoped; I knew what he was like.) There was always a circle of people around in the square who kept him company, discussing among themselves and sometimes addressing a remark to him, although they knew he had no desire to speak.

He got worse. We hoisted a mattress into the tree and managed to balance it; he lay down willingly. We felt some remorse in not having thought of it earlier. To tell the truth, he didn't at all reject comforts; although he was in the trees, he had always tried to live as comfortably as he could. Then we hastened to give him other comforts: some matting to protect him from the air, a canopy, a brazier. He improved a little, and we brought him an armchair, securing it between two branches; he began to spend the days there, wrapped in his blankets.

But one morning we didn't see him either in the bed or in the chair; we looked up, fearful. He had climbed to the top of the tree and was astride a very high branch, wearing only a shirt.

"What are you doing up there?"

He didn't answer. He was half rigid. He seemed to be up at the top by a miracle. We prepared a big sheet of the type used for gathering olives, and we were twenty holding it, stretched, because we expected that he would fall.

Meanwhile a doctor went up; it was a difficult ascent, two ladders had to be tied together. He came down and said, "Let the priest go."

We had already agreed that a certain Don Pericle would

try, a friend of his, a constitutional priest at the time of the French who had enrolled in the lodge before it was forbidden to the clergy and who had been recently readmitted to his offices at the bishopric, after many travails. He went up with his vestments and the ciborium, and behind him the server. He stayed up there a while—they seemed to be plotting—then he came down.

"Did he take the sacraments, then, Don Pericle?"

"No, no, but he says it's all right, for him it's all right." We couldn't get out any more.

The men who were holding the sheet were tired. Cosimo was up there and wasn't moving. A wind came up, from the southwest; the top of the tree swayed; we were ready. Then in the sky appeared a hot-air balloon.

Some English balloonists were making experiments with flight in a hot-air balloon along the coast. It was a beautiful balloon, decorated with fringes and flounces and bows, with a wicker basket hanging from it, and inside two officers with gold epaulettes and pointed cocked hats looked through a telescope at the countryside below. They aimed the telescope at the square, observing the man in the tree, the stretched sheet, the crowd, strange aspects of the world. Cosimo, too, had raised his head, and looked attentively at the balloon.

When, look, the hot-air balloon was seized by a gust of the southwest wind; it began to run in the wind, spinning like a top and heading toward the sea. The balloonists, without losing heart, were working to reduce—I think—the pressure of the balloon and at the same time rolled down the anchor, seeking to hook it onto some support. The anchor flew silver in the sky, hanging on a long rope, and obliquely following the course of the balloon it passed over the square, nearly at the height of the top of the walnut, so that we were afraid it would hit Cosimo. But we couldn't suppose what in an instant our eyes would see.

The dying Cosimo, at the moment when the rope of the anchor passed by him, made one of those leaps that were usual with him in his youth, grabbed the rope, with his feet on the anchor and his body huddled, and so we saw him fly away, dragged in the wind, barely braking the course of the balloon, and disappear in the direction of the sea . . .

The hot-air balloon crossed the gulf and succeeded in landing later on the other side. Attached to the rope was only the anchor. The balloonists, too involved in trying to stay on course, hadn't noticed anything.

It was supposed that the dying old man had disappeared while he was flying over the middle of the gulf.

So Cosimo disappeared, and didn't even give us the satisfaction of seeing him return to earth dead. In the family tomb there is a stele that recalls him with the words "Cosimo Piovasco di Rondò. He lived in the trees. He always loved the earth. He ascended into the sky."

Every so often as I write I break off and go to the window. The sky is empty, and to us old people of Ombrosa, habituated to living under those green domes, it hurts the eyes to look at it. One would say that the trees didn't bear up after my brother left, or that men were seized by the fury of the ax. Then, the vegetation has changed: no more the holm oaks, the elms, the oaks; now Africa, Australia, the Americas, the Indies extend branches and roots here. The ancient trees have retreated upward: on top of the hills the olives, and in the mountain woods pines and chestnuts; down on the coast it's an Australia red with eucalyptus, elephantine with ficus, enormous and solitary garden plants, and all the rest is palms, with their disheveled tufts, inhospitable desert trees.

Ombrosa is no longer there. Looking at the empty sky, I wonder if it really existed. That ornamentation of branches and leaves, forks, lobes, feathers, minute and without end, and the sky appearing only in irregular flashes and cutouts, maybe existed only because my brother passed there with the light step of a long-tailed tit, was an embroidery, made on nothing, that resembles this thread of ink, as I've let it run for pages and pages, full of erasures, of references, of nervous blots, of stains, of gaps, that at times crumbles into large pale grains, at times thickens into tiny marks resembling dotlike seeds, now twists on itself, now forks, now links knots of sentences with edges of leaves or clouds, and then stumbles, and then resumes twisting, and runs and runs and unrolls and wraps a last senseless cluster of words ideas dreams and is finished.

(1957)

About the Author

ITALO CALVINO's superb storytelling gifts earned him international renown and a reputation as "one of the world's best fabulists" (*New York Times Book Review*). He is the author of numerous works of fiction, as well as essays, criticism, and literary anthologies. Born in Cuba in 1923, Calvino was raised in Italy, where he lived most of his life. At the time of his death, in Siena in 1985, he was the most translated contemporary Italian writer.